DEAD
STEVEN WINSHEL
EAST

DEAD
STEVEN WINSHEL
EAST

Dead East

By Steve Winshel

Copyright 2012 by Steve Winshel

Cover and Interior by Heather Kern at popshopstudio.com

Paperback ISBN: 978-0-9915167-4-2

E-book ISBN: 978-0-9849812-1-2

ALSO BY
STEVEN WINSHEL

Murder in Mind

Catalyst

A Twisted Path

B rilliantly white walls surrounded a dozen children playing in the courtyard. Quiet men hand-scrubbed them each evening. Now they reflected the late afternoon sun, echoing the slap of a hard rubber ball each time it banged against a wall and into the hands of a little girl playing in one corner. A puff of dirt swirled and then resettled with each bounce. Two teen boys kicked a worn soccer ball at the other end of the courtyard, navigating between the legs of the swarm of children. Voices called to one another to come play a jumping game, or to wrangle over who would get to eat the first cookie when they went home. The sounds ricocheted off the walls and were like notes from a choir. Beyond the wide north wall was the school building, not much larger than the courtyard. On the other side, the south wall separated the children from the packed dirt road that split Sharzi into two tiny villages. The road ran straight for a hundred yards before resuming its winding path for another quarter mile and then emerging into desert that appeared like a mirage and went to infinity. Looking up into the glare of the sun, one saw the tops of three-story buildings and escarpments made of hand-molded clay and ancient cement.

Over the cacophony of the youngsters playing and mothers chattering as they entered the courtyard to pick up their charges and walk them home for the afternoon meal, no one heard the rumble of approaching vehicles.

The lead Humvee came around the bend at the beginning of the stretch of road. The grinding of an engine fighting too much sand and not enough oil caught the attention of a woman in full Burkha about to step into the school entrance. Only her eyes were visible, but they conveyed fear and contempt with clarity. An armored car following a few feet behind the Humvee cleared the curve and both vehicles began to cover the fifty yards of straightaway to the school.

From an open window above and next to the school a large, rough stone arced over the balcony. It lazily tumbled, seeming to waft like a leaf, picking up speed as it descended to the empty road. The space beneath it filled with the front of the Humvee just as the stone seemed ready to fall harmlessly to the dirt. The loud crack startled the driver as the glass in front of him shattered into a thousand spidery strands. Breaks squealed and metal strained against inertia to bring the driver and soldier next to him slamming forward, the vehicle sharply turning to the right and ramming into a low wall in front of a home on the main street. The armored car cut left to avoid hitting the side of the Humvee, now blocking most of the street. All movement stopped and for several heartbeats, the only sound was of cursing and motors running. The woman entering the school froze; the children and other parents inside the courtyard and those scattered throughout the small structure were still unaware of the tableau just yards from them.

Jarvis stepped out from the passenger's side of the armored car, M-16 angled down but balanced in his arm to quickly raise and point in any direction. He moved to the Humvee, using it as a shield while looking inside. He took in the rock, the windshield, and the empty street.

"Rock from up there." He spoke to the two men in the Humvee, but loudly enough for the sergeant in the driver's seat of the armored vehicle behind him and the two soldiers in the back seat to hear. He pointed to the open balcony to his left with the muzzle of his rifle.

"God dammit!" The Humvee driver pushed open his door and stomped into the center of the road.

"Stay near your vehicle until we secure the area!" Jarvis barked.

"Shit, Jarvis, it's just some god damned kid." The Humvee driver wore his helmet askew and had a plastic water bottle in one hand. He started around the front to pull out the rock that was embedded in the windshield.

"I said get back…" Jarvis' next words were cut off by a single shot from behind and to his right, the side of the street opposite the school. The bullet tore out the driver's throat. A geyser of blood shot upward before the dead man could crumple to the ground. His knees hit the dirt the same time a burst of automatic fire began to strafe the Humvee from the same direction as the rifle shot. Jarvis was already rolling on the ground, backwards to the relative safety of the armored vehicle.

"Down, down, down!" He returned fire in the direction of the burst that was tearing up the side of the Humvee, cutting through the metal doors. Jarvis could hear the dying groans of the soldier on the passenger side. He looked across the street, where the rock had come from, the trigger for the ambush. New gunfire would come from there any second. The enemy did not disappoint. Just as Jarvis rolled under the armored car, half a dozen shots struck the side of the vehicle above him. Unlike the Humvee, they did not penetrate.

Shouts from inside the armored vehicle. Instructions to one another, and the sergeant's voice over it all.

"Jarvis! Get in, get in!"

Under the armored car, the still-running motor almost drowned out all sound. Jarvis dragged himself in a half-circle against the rough dirt road to look at the spot where the first shots had come, killing the Humvee driver. No one was visible. He spun back to see the other side of the street, banging his helmet against the oil pan on the undercarriage. Sweat poured onto his face. A burst of automatic gunfire from the direction of the school raked the driver's door just above Jarvis' head. He ducked and waited for it to stop.

The Humvee blocked any forward progress for the armored car. They'd have to move it or back away. Neither option was promising. Jarvis heard the door on the other side of the armored vehicle open. Automatic fire spat out, this time coming from one of his guys. Jarvis could see the boots of the soldier. Muddy, torn, brown canvas. Legs of camouflage pants covered in dirt. Their passenger, Brin, had spent three weeks alone, hidden in the desert, half-buried in berms, moving slowly from rock to crevice. Stopping for hours, sometimes for an entire day. Chameleon, patient and inexorable. He'd scouted, alone, gathering information. Sometimes taking a single shot, set up days in advance. Jarvis' team had picked him up this morning to bring him back to civilization for a couple days.

A staccato of gunfire came from the open window opposite the school, raining down on the armored car. They were caught in a crossfire. Brin had stopped shooting and Jarvis could hear the two soldiers still in the armored vehicle yelling instructions.

"RPG!" Brin shouted and Jarvis whipped around to see where the blast would come from. But Brin wasn't warning of incoming fire. He was arming Jarvis. A three-foot long metal tube slid under the armored car and hit Jarvis in the side. He rolled over and grabbed the heavy gun that shot a grenade up to a hundred yards with deadly accuracy. In one movement he flipped up the safety and pulled the scope to his eye. The space under the car was just enough for him to squeeze the grenade launcher onto his shoulder if he pressed down on the dirt road with his chest and strained his neck. The angle was hard and he had to expose himself to the open air to point it up enough to get the balcony in his sights. It was far enough to the left of the school that there was little danger of collateral damage. He pulled the trigger just as another round of automatic fire hit the roof of the armored car.

The kick from the launcher slammed his head into the floor runner on the driver's side. The sound of the retort hadn't reached his ears before the grenade hit the open balcony and the explosion created a volcano of white rock and plaster. Shouts of wounded men speaking Farsi rose over the ruckus. Less than two minutes had passed since the US Army vehicles had come around the bend. The scene inside the school was furiously calm, as parents raced to cover their children and keep them from going outside to see the action. A few bits of rock from the shattered balcony fell onto the courtyard, but no one was injured.

Jarvis waited, holding his breath. Nothing. The next burst of gunfire would come from the opposite side of the street again, where Brin was. He began to turn around, opened his mouth to tell Brin to get in the armored car and they would turn around, get the hell out. Before he could get the words out, he heard Brin shout again.

"RPG!" Jarvis was confused for a moment, looking at the weapon still in his hand, the extra grenade attached to the underside. Then he understood. The tone was different in Brin's voice. RPG, but this time it was incoming.

Jarvis scrambled out from under the armored car, back towards the side of the street with the balcony he'd just fired on. The risk of being shot was lower than being blown up. He pulled himself up and turned to open the door of the armored car to get the other two soldiers out. His sergeant waved him off, opening the door himself and pulling at the soldier behind him.

"Go, go, go!" the driver screamed.

Jarvis ran across the street and dove for a low wall beneath what remained of the balcony he'd destroyed. On the other side of the armored car, Brin ran in the opposite direction, toward the muzzle of the grenade launcher, his gun firing. Jarvis held his helmet down with one hand and peered over the wall. He saw the two soldiers getting out of the armored vehicle, Brin running hunched over, gun blazing, and above them all in the sky, coming over the low buildings on the outskirts of the village, a US helicopter equipped with small, deadly missiles.

Almost in slow motion, Jarvis saw the grenade spit out of the launcher across the street and head toward the armored car. The explosion was almost instantaneous. Jarvis locked eyes with his sergeant, or thought he did, as the vehicle burst into flames and the two soldiers coming out the driver's side were shredded. Burning pieces of car and flesh rained down on the street. Jarvis felt a spray, not sure if it was fuel or blood. He pulled his head down and immediately there was a second explosion, next to him on the same side of the street. The wall of the courtyard erupted, the concussive force throwing Jarvis three feet back. Large chunks of rock and plaster fell into the space that moments ago had been filled with children playing and shouting.

Jarvis was uninjured. He leapt up and saw the helicopter closing in, large caliber machine guns strafing the building across the street where Brin had been running. Brin lay splayed on the street, in one piece, moaning. The helicopter passed over the street and hovered 150 feet above the school, guns at the ready. Jarvis waved to the helicopter and looked back to Brin.

Two men in Afghan garb, wearing scarves covering their faces, were on either side of him. Another held an automatic rifle at the ready. The two soldiers in the helicopter were not looking that way. The men in the street dragged Brin toward the building where the grenade had been launched. Jarvis jumped up but the Afghan man with the gun sprayed bullets in his direction and Jarvis could not return fire, dropping to the ground instead. The helicopter turned toward the street and the soldier strapped against the open door returned fire at the Afghan who'd pinned down Jarvis. The man in the street was cut in half, but Brin was already gone.

Jarvis pulled at the radio on his belt.

"One man alive, they've got him in the building below you. Hold fire!"

The helicopter would land only to pick up the wounded, careful not to risk losing more men or equipment to the Taliban or Al-Qaeda or whoever hated the Americans at the moment. The voice of the pilot came over the radio and Jarvis could see the man's mouth moving a hundred feet up in the air at the same time.

"Another ground patrol is on the way. 17 minutes out."

Jarvis looked across the street, then above where the balcony had

been. No movement. Moans and cries of anguish came from the rubble
to his left, from what was left of the wall of the school's courtyard and
the people buried beneath or cut down by flying fragments of rock. Eerie
silence filled the space between the shouts for help. In the distance, a siren
slowly emerged. The village was small, but after generations of war they
were prepared for death and violence. An ambulance would be there in
moments. The warren of homes and shops across the street where Brin
had disappeared stretched back further than he could see. Brin might
be in the building from where the grenade had been fired. Or he could
be two hundred yards deep in the maze of narrow walkways and angled
doors that were less navigable by a stranger than a Greek labyrinth. Four
men were dead already. Jarvis had fought in the first Gulf War. He'd seen
what happened to captured US soldiers. He would not let a fifth die today.
Jarvis took a deep breath and ran, zig-zag, across the street toward the open
doorway. No one shot at him.

He reached the door where Brin had been taken and put his back against
the adobe wall next to it. The accumulated heat from the day transferred from
the wall to his shoulders. Jarvis quickly poked his head around to the open
doorway and pulled back, less to get a look and more to create a target and
see if anyone took a shot. Silence. He spun through the door, M-16 pointed
forward and sweeping the room. It was empty, except for spent shells on the
floor. There were few windows and the transition from bright sunlight to the
shaded interior made everything seem shadowy and dangerous. It was. Jarvis
saw the one opening to his left and ran quickly across the room. This time
he didn't bother to sneak a look. He passed through what may have been an
abandoned shop and then out a back door into an alley. A movement to his
right and he whipped around, finger on the trigger. A child stood in a doorway
twenty feet down, large brown eyes not judging the soldier. Jarvis held the gun
tightly. He'd seen children approach US Army vehicles, hands out begging for
scraps of food, grenades hidden beneath their ragged clothes. The boy held his
stare, then raised a hand. He pointed in the other direction. Solemn, silent.
Jarvis turned and ran that way.

The sound of the ambulance was getting louder and the thump of the helicopter was persistent, but both became muted as he followed the winding path of the alley away from the street. He passed under a colonnade and instead of shouldering along a narrow walkway he was suddenly in an open space, dozens of people milling about. They were talking, some still engaged in commerce and ignoring the explosions they'd heard from the street a hundred yards away. Inured to bedlam, their lives continued. Others huddled and pointed at the sky where the helicopter was visible but distant and smoke drifted in several directions. Fewer people than Jarvis would have expected stopped to look at the armed soldier bursting into the bazaar.

Jarvis looked around, taking in every group, trying to read body language and intent. No sign of the men who had taken Brin just moments earlier. Jarvis suddenly felt alone, vulnerable. Not everyone in the country hated the Americans, but none embraced another invader. The smart thing to do would be to wait for the squad that was ten minutes away. Jarvis ran across the open space, deeper into the crowd. He looked at each corner of the bazaar, trying to read every face, interpret the dust swirling at every entryway or door. Nothing spoke to him. He looked up, searching the second floor of the building encircling the plaza. As he turned around, the panicked shouts of dozens of voices rang out just as a searing pain hit his right shoulder. The sound of the rifle shot followed. Jarvis spun from the force and almost dropped his gun. Instinct shifted it to his left hand and as he completed his turn he dropped into a crouch and raised the rifle. It was set to semi-automatic and the first two shots hit brick and window but the next four struck the gunman on the balcony. Jarvis looked down and caught the eye of one of the people whose heads he had just fired over, inches separating them from the bullets that found their mark. Blood poured from his right shoulder and he took a quick glance before running across the courtyard to the building where the shot had come from. There was an exit wound – the bullet had passed through.

Jarvis skirted the hunched men and women who tried to take cover from the impending firefight. No more bullets flew. He rushed through the open doorway, gun arcing back and forth. He expected half a dozen men, a grenade launcher, perhaps a tank. Nothing. Stairs to his left led to the man he'd shot. No one came racing down to shoot at him. One foot on the bottom step, Jarvis stopped. Except for the cries from the courtyard, there was silence. No footsteps running above him. No shouts of warning or cries of courage. But not complete silence. There was a buzzing noise. A hum. Jarvis looked around the room. It was a living room, someone's home. Carpet, a couple chairs. One painting on a wall. A small closet covered by a long blanket. And a heavy door at the back of the room. The humming came from behind the blanket.

Jarvis crossed the room and pushed aside the blanket. On the floor sat a squat, shiny new machine, buzzing like a beehive. A generator. In the back of the tiny closet, a hole had been drilled and a power cord ran from the generator into the gap. The cord angled down, not up. There was a basement.

Jarvis backed out of the small space and looked at the heavy door to his left. He gently tried the latch. It gave easily, quietly. Wincing from the pain, he kept the rifle in his left hand and forced his right to slowly pull back the door. Steps led down into the dark, turning to one side just before the light gave way to shadow. Jarvis stepped in and carefully pulled the door almost shut behind him. In the silence, he could begin to make out voices. They were urgent, angry, but controlled. Jarvis took a few steps down, gun pointing forward. With each step the voices got louder. Just before the turn in the stone stairway, he could make out a few words. They were in Arabic and he strained to remember any of his six weeks of language training a dozen years earlier before his first deployment in the Gulf.

There was a loud clicking noise and the murky shadow ahead of him was instantly illuminated as though a bright light had been lit. Jarvis pulled back instinctively but he was still out of sight. His eyes adjusted once again and Jarvis moved forward to the edge of the light and crouched on the stair just before the bend where he would be able to see into whatever was below – and they would see him. A few words now emerged out of the stream of increasingly agitated language. One voice rose above the others, defiant and confident. Jarvis made out a phrase he'd learned and heard many times: God is great. And he recognized a few others that were less encouraging: American pig, which sounded almost eloquent in Farsi. Invader, killer, children – these were words he'd heard thrown at him not just in the classroom but occasionally in the street. The tone of the speaker's voice became more emotional, strident, like a rising crescendo reaching for a final note. Jarvis poked his head around the corner and pulled it back almost before his eyes could focus. It took him a moment to interpret the image that burned onto his eyes like a horrible photograph. On the opposite wall a large gray sheet hung like in a photographer's studio. A bright light shone against the image in front of the tarp – a man in traditional Afghan garb holding a medium sized sabre. He was looking toward the light, which blinded him from seeing Jarvis' brief peering around the corner. But he wasn't looking into the light – he was looking at a camera on a tripod, a ridiculously small video camera. And the camera was taking in the scene, of the man holding the sabre in one hand and a tightly bound but conscious Brin in the other. Four other men, their backs to the staircase, operated the camera and lights, shouting encouragement to their comrade. Over the din, Jarvis heard one voice that he did not have to interpret.

"Fuck you, asshole." Brin.

The Afghan man's voice continued to rise and Jarvis could feel the fury, the exultant victory the man felt. The cheers of the others were those of a mob watching the guillotine in 18th century France. They were calling for death, for vengeance, for a good old-fashioned beheading. Jarvis flicked the setting to single shot on his rifle. He took a deep breath, slowing his racing heart and ignoring the light-headedness that tried to embrace his brain from blood loss. He stood and turned the corner, aiming more from memory than the sight of what was before him. As he pulled the trigger the first time, he took in the movement of the man's arm as it began to pull across Brin's throat. It would take several strokes, more of a sawing motion, to complete the act. But the first slide of the blade would sever Brin's carotid artery and seal his fate before the horror of the beheading could be complete. Jarvis' shot found its mark with almost comical accuracy. The man's forehead seemed to cave in slightly. The momentum of the movement of the sword across Brin's throat was inevitable and unstoppable, but the backward force from the shot lessened the pressure. Blood seeped but did not gush.

Hoping more than assuming his shot had been accurate, Jarvis flicked the gun into semi-automatic. The other men in the room were stunned for only an instant and turned toward the stairs. Each held a gun. Jarvis strafed the men hitting three almost instantly. Two died before they could point their weapons at Jarvis but the third was mortally wounded and bent on killing Jarvis as his final act. Jarvis pulled the trigger again and the man's torso ripped open and his gun flew out of his hand. Jarvis turned to the one man he had not hit and saw the muzzle of a Russian rifle flash. The wall next to him splintered and the next sound was of the Afghan's weapon being switched to automatic. Jarvis pulled his own trigger and nothing happened – he'd spent his final rounds. He dropped the M-16 and reached for his sidearm but it was too late. The Afghan raised his gun and uttered a final expletive. He pulled the trigger as Jarvis raised his gun, knowing it would not matter but unwilling to give up. The spray of bullets, though, missed Jarvis wide to the left as the man flew forward in an explosive rush as though hit by a truck. Brin, launching himself like a torpedo, bleeding, bound, and beaten, landed on top of the Afghan. He began to bang his head against the man who struggled and tried to turn to push Brin off. The American smashed his forehead against the man's neck and ear, then against his nose and mouth as his former captor squirmed around to face him. The gun was still in the Afghani's hand and he brought it up to shoot Brin whose arms were uselessly tied to his side. One shot rang out and the man laid still. Brin looked up into the barrel of Jarvis' service revolver. Still on top of the dead Afghan, Brin smiled.

"Hey, thanks, man. Tried to stay calm, but guess I sorta lost my head."

Jarvis' heart raced and he began to feel faint. He smiled, or thought he did, and as he crumpled to the ground and almost onto Brin, he heard shouts – American voices – and feet running across the floor above. The voices got louder and as he passed out he looked down again and the grin of the bleeding soldier grew larger and broader until it filled his vision like the Cheshire cat.

Jarvis sat loosely in the driver's seat, the radio filling the car with low sounds of a KCRW late-night talk show. The topic was troop withdrawals from one of the countries where America was at war. He fiddled with the controls on the steering wheel and took it down to a murmur. Nothing was open at 2:15 a.m. so the flashlight beam playing back and forth in the alley ahead and to his left screamed for attention. The main street where he'd parked more than seven hours ago was deserted. The strip mall abutting the alley contained a Quizno's, a check cashing place, a liquor store masquerading as a convenience market, and a small pharmacy. It was the last that held Jarvis' attention.

The door of the BMW was virtually silent as it opened and Jarvis slid out. No oncoming traffic threatened and he stepped quickly and quietly to the curb. The eighteen-inch section of pine 2-by-four was almost invisible as he held it to his side. He reached the alley just as the beam from the flashlight widened, signaling its owner was nearing the mouth and about to reach the sidewalk. Jarvis paused for a moment and a dark shadow emerged from the alley and turned to its right, away from Jarvis and toward the banged up mini Toyota truck a hundred feet up the street. Jarvis resumed his walk, just a few steps behind the figure, unnoticed. Five steps and Jarvis was immediately behind. Hooded sweatshirt, baggy pants, and a large green Hefty bag slung over the figure's shoulder. Without breaking stride, Jarvis swung the makeshift club up with a turn of his hips. The force caught the burglar precisely as aimed, almost dislocating his shoulder and forcing the bag to drop. A grunt flew from the man's mouth and before his body could hit the brick wall, Jarvis hit him again – not as hard, just a stunning jolt, on the side of the head. The man bounced off the wall and was on the ground, too confused to know whether to grab his shoulder or his ear where a lump was already forming.

Jarvis made the decision for him, grabbing his collar and dragging the man backwards in the direction they'd both just come. Still no one in sight. The captive moaned and then started to complain as the discomfort of being slid along a cement sidewalk pierced his shock and surprise.

"Who the…what the hell are you doin', man? Get the hell offa me!"

He struggled as if getting away from Jarvis were an option. Jarvis shifted his grip and gave him a tap on the other ear with the club and the complaining was replaced by a yelp of pain.

They reached the car and Jarvis opened the back door, half picking up the man and shoving him in.

"Don't bleed on the seat." He shut the door and used the remote entry key to lock the doors. Without looking back, he returned to the spot where the trash bag had fallen. Its contents had started to spill out. He spun the bag with one hand while holding it in the air with the other, then tossed it over his shoulder like a knapsack and headed back to the car. Unlocking with a press of the key, he opened the front passenger door and tossed the bag on the seat. The protestations from the guy in the back were starting to become more coherent and easily drowned out the radio. Jarvis closed the passenger door and opened the back door. The guy scrambled further back into the seat, but still mouthed off.

"I'm gonna kill you, man, you know who you're messin' with?" The threat was softened by the guy's back pressing up against the opposite door as if that would spring it open.

Jarvis pulled a plastic handcuff from his back pocket and dragged the man closer to him by the ankle.

"Yeah, I know who I'm messing with." He jerked the guy's hands together and looped one end of the plastic through the locking mechanism on the other. Cheap, short-term, effective.

"Goddammit, this is kidnapping you prick! You better…" He stopped when Jarvis showed him the piece of 2-by-4.

In a pocket in the back seat, a roll of duct tape created a circular impression. Jarvis pulled it out and the man's eyes grew wide. He pulled off an eight-inch strip and tore a few millimeters with his teeth and ripped the rest. Jarvis grabbed the guy by the hair and pulled him close, pressing the duct tape over his mouth and sliding his hand back and forth to make sure there was a tight seal. Any objections were muffled.

The guy's eyes widened further, comically, as he looked down and noticed the plastic on the floor and dark towel on the seat. Jarvis followed his look and shook his head.

"Nope, you're doing all the bleeding you're going to do. That's just to keep it clean." He waited. "Unless you keep squirming." The man settled down.

Jarvis shut the door and climbed in the driver's seat. With the press of a button, the engine started. He looked both ways before pulling into the empty street and didn't turn around as he spoke to the space in front of him.

"Let's go have a chat with your father."

CHAPTER THREE

Jarvis pulled into the driveway on a tree-lined street in Brentwood. The house was dark, mimicking all the others. Motion-activated floodlights flicked on as he stopped at the front door halfway around the circular drive. Jarvis cut the engine and pressed a button on his phone. The ringing reverberated over the car's speakers. Half a dozen times before a groggy male voice replaced the ringing.

"What? Yes, hello? Who is this?"

"It's Jarvis. I'm out front." The sound of sheets rustling came over the line, then an incoherent woman's voice mumbling something.

"Nothing, shhh, dear. Go back to sleep," in a whisper.

Jarvis disconnected just as the young man in the back started to moan in emotional agony. Jarvis ignored him and waited. The front door opened as a hallway light clicked on behind the figure. Robe open, large belly protruding, the man was almost as wide as he was tall. Olive skin absorbed the light from the outside lamps. He gestured quickly, angrily, furtively toward the car. Jarvis got out and opened the back door, pulling his passenger out with a handful of shirt. The only sounds the previously obstreperous young man made was a snort that hovered between contempt and fear.

One hand on his charge, the other carrying the twisted bag filled with pharmaceuticals, Jarvis dragged both to the front door. The father opened it wide and ushered them in. The look on his face was of fury waiting to be unleashed. His mouth trembled and he was unable to speak. He pointed to the living room off to the right, enveloped in darkness. The size of the house from the outside promised rooms further back from which sounds would not escape. Jarvis pushed the son in that direction but did not follow. The son was breathing heavily now, dried blood on his face. Shame and indignation battled; the former won. The father looked ready to explode and in the momentary silence that balanced the three men, he gave in to his rage and slapped his son hard and solidly across the face. The retort was like a shot and the son was surprised and broken.

Jarvis watched without reaction. "Here. It's mostly narcotics. Some meth makings." He tossed the bag onto the floor between the father and son. "Don't rough him up too much. He wasn't born an asshole."

It was the father's turn to register indignation. Jarvis ignored it. "I used about $3500 of the retainer. I'll send you a bill for the balance."

Jarvis left through the front door, his walk to the car triggering the outside floodlights again. He heard the urgent, hushed tirade begin as the door closed off the sounds from the house. With his back to his client, his mind was on home and an hour of sleep before starting again.

CHAPTER FOUR

The open window sent a cooling breeze through the room. Ocean sounds buffeted the darkness. Jarvis flipped on the bedside lamp, a low-watt bulb giving just enough light to read by and leaving the rest of the bedroom shrouded in black. He propped a pillow against the headboard and picked up the leather journal. Lying on his back, he opened to the page about a quarter from the end, held by an old laundry ticket he'd used for years as a bookmark. He didn't need to look at the clock to know it was within a couple minutes of 3:15 a.m., his internal circadian keeping eternal synch with the hour. The last entry was the previous night's, identified only by time, not day or year. He scribbled *3:15 a.m.* below it and began to chew on the end of the pen. Events of the day and evening ran through his mind, some parts at high speed like the fast-forward button on the DVD player, others almost comically slow. He scratched out a few lines, hesitating only occasionally.

The hand of the father
Falls heavily on the shoulder of the son.
It is a burden, a gift, a curse.
And it is there long after he is gone.

Jarvis closed the book without reading what he'd written. Tossing it onto the nightstand along with the pen, he killed the light and rolled onto his stomach. A flickering image of his father, decades old, flitted across the palette of his closed eyes before he fell into an immediate, deep sleep.

The clock showed 4:18 a.m. when Jarvis quickly, steadily emerged to consciousness. A few rays of pre-dawn light bent around the house and snuck into the bedroom. Refreshed, fully alert, he rolled out of bed and headed to the garage. Ten minutes later he was hitting the heavy bag and sweating freely, cobwebs gone, another full day ahead. After forty-five minutes of punching, his breathing heavy and rasping, he stopped just as the cell phone perched on one of the shelves lining the garage vibrated violently. Wiping his hands against the only dry spot on his sweatpants, he picked it up. He recognized the digits as those commonly used in movies where they never gave a real phone number– 555.555.5555. Only one person he knew punched that into their cell so it displayed when they made a call. Someone who cracked open a new cell phone burner every week and reached out to Jarvis sometimes just as often, and sometimes not for six months or longer. Brin.

Jarvis answered. "Hey."

The voice that responded wasn't Brin. And there were sirens in the background.

CHAPTER FIVE

"Who is this?"

Jarvis ignored the question. "You've got three seconds tell me who you are and then you're going to hear a click."

There was a two-second silence, and the man's voice continued. "This is Detective Lance Rayford, LAPD. You want to explain why you're the only number programmed into a disposable phone I found on a guy slumped in a booth at Nate and Al's, no ID, not a spec of paper, and fingerprints no one's ever recorded?"

Jarvis' heart jumped into his throat. He croaked out his question. "How'd he die?"

The cop snorted over the line. "He ain't dead, not yet. Just close. And I'll ask one more time: who is this?"

"Detective, I'll assume the man is in an ambulance or at a hospital and you're still at the scene. Tell me where he is and I'll meet you there."

Silence on the line again. Waiting.

"My name is Jarvis. The man is a friend of mine." Only the sound of a fading siren came over the connection.

This time the cop sighed, knowingly. "Okay, Jarvis, meet me at Cedars Sinai in an hour. And plan on being a lot more talkative." The line went dead before Jarvis could kill it himself.

The cold shower lasted no more than two minutes and Jarvis was in the car, hair damp and hand gripping the steering wheel harder than he wanted to. The NPR news played quietly over the speakers as he raced along an almost empty Sunset Boulevard toward the hospital.

CHAPTER SIX

J arvis pulled up to the valet outside the emergency room at the Beverly Hills hospital. He snatched the ticket from the guy in a red vest. It was late and the Sunday night troublemakers had already been stitched up and sent home. Jarvis walked across the linoleum and only had to wait a few seconds for one of the nurses to ask him what he needed.

"Guy came in half an hour ago, followed by a cop – probably plain clothes, probably pissed, definitely waiting for me." He gave her a smile that was half as effective as it would have been if it weren't Brin behind the double doors. She didn't need to check her admission chart. Instead she nodded and walked back into the unseen warren of curtains and private healthcare. Less than a minute passed and the detective Jarvis had spoken to came through the automatic doors. There was a weary look on his still-young face and Jarvis could tell the cop may have been on the job no more than a decade but he'd seen a lot.

Rayford pulled a notebook out of his jacket pocket and looked Jarvis over once, thoroughly. He didn't shake hands or introduce himself.

"Your pal's in pretty bad shape. What's the nature of your relationship?" He pulled up a couple feet from Jarvis, pen poised over paper.

"He's a friend. Long time. What happened to him?"

Rayford weighed going tit-for-tat or demanding this witness just answer his questions. He read something in Jarvis that told him which way to go.

"Not sure yet. Breathing is shallow, he seems comatose, but no outward signs of violence, not a heart attack, not a stroke. They're running tests."

Jarvis nodded and waited.

"Your friend doesn't carry a lot of stuff with him. Like a wallet or ID. How about a name?"

Jarvis hesitated and Rayford formed a look of disappointment. "Brin. Jerome Brin, but I've never heard anyone use his first name." Rayford wrote it down. "You won't find much, no records, at least not for the past few years." Jarvis paused. "Not since he got out of the Rangers."

Rayford looked up from his notebook and fixed Jarvis with a deeper stare this time. "How 'bout we go back and you say hello." He signaled the nurse and the doors opened.

Jarvis followed the detective past a couple of gurneys, mostly empty but one with a very old, seemingly dead man who nonetheless breathed noisily through his mouth. At the end of the corridor they turned left and went into a small room filled with equipment. One doctor bent over the bed in the middle and Jarvis could see only the hand of the man lying on the blue sheet, but he recognized it instantly. Slender palms, fingers tapered, covered with calluses. Jarvis sensed the room had been buzzing with activity only moments ago. The doctor turned his head and looked back and forth between the two men standing in the door.

"He's stable, but not good. Some kind of poison. Not just bad gefilte fish." He deadpanned the line and Jarvis would have laughed if had hadn't wanted to break the doctor's jaw. "We're running some tests, but I can't tell you what we can do or how he'll be until I know what's going on."

Rayford jotted down a few notes then watched Jarvis walk over to the bed. Jarvis looked at Brin's face. It was paler than the last time he'd seen him. And thinner than ten years earlier when he'd almost been decapitated. It had been five months since they'd spoken. That day Brin had shown up on a stakeout just as the surveillance target figured out he was being watched…and was coming around the back of his house toward Jarvis carrying a shotgun. The target spent the next three months in a hospital bed like the one Brin was in now.

Jarvis turned from the bed, back toward Rayford. "I'm a PI. You going to help or get in my way?"

CHAPTER SEVEN

The two men sat across from one another in an empty hospital cafeteria. The soft sound of institutional breakfasts being prepared seeped from the kitchen. Rayford's notebook sat open on the Formica surface, the cover damp from the earlier swipe of a wet cloth. He twirled his pen across his fingers like it was a baton in the hands of a cheerleader.

"I get that you're pissed. I get that you wanna go find whoever did this. But you're not gonna get there any faster being the Lone Ranger." Rayford didn't get his own unintended pun right away, then remembered what little he now knew about Brin. "You know what I mean."

Jarvis drained the last half-inch of bad coffee and looked the detective hard in the eye, not unsympathetically. "I don't know much about Brin's life except when I see him, which isn't often. He just shows up. What he does the rest of the time, I don't know – but I'll find out. He wasn't the kind of guy to circumvent trouble."

Rayford's brow went up. "Circumvent trouble?"

Jarvis laughed and stood. "That trait could piss some people off. I've got your number. If I come across anything that'll help, I'll call."

Rayford stood, too. "We don't need a vigilante. If you interfere with my investigation…" It was a threat, but Jarvis read behind it to the offer of mutual help. He nodded and walked out of the cafeteria and through the hospital to the parking lot. It was late morning and the inside of his car was already hot. He didn't turn over the engine, just sat with the door and windows closed, absorbing the heat. He watched an ambulance pull up and an old sedan limp in behind, a grim-faced woman behind the wheel. A couple of doctors crossed the lot toward the entrance. Jarvis closed his eyes and leaned back, the hot leather satisfyingly burning his neck.

After Brin had provided unexpected back-up a few months earlier, they'd had a brief chat. Waiting for the ambulance to arrive and wondering if it would get there before the guy expired, they'd nodded at one another.

"How ya been?" Jarvis folded his arms.

Brin stood like a soldier while Jarvis leaned against the hood of his car. "Pretty good, pretty good." He kept swiveling his head, in case there were a sniper or approaching armored tank in the tree-lined neighborhood.

Jarvis pulled out a pack of gum and offered it to Brin. Brin took one without breaking his vigilant scanning of the surrounding area and split-level homes. A shadow passing overhead caught his attention and he displayed slight disappointment that it was a large black crow and not an unmanned drone armed with sidewinder missiles.

The moaning of the man on the ground caught no one's attention. The faint hum of a siren became audible and threatened to turn into a wail within moments.

"You know we're even now, right? No more of this commando Ninja shit." Jarvis unwrapped a piece of gum and put the pack back in his pocket.

Brin had already pocketed his. "Yup, totally even." Jarvis smiled around his gum. It was the same conversation they'd had for almost a decade.

"Wanna have dinner? We'll get some girls and you can cook at your place." Jarvis had never been to Brin's place. He wasn't entirely sure that Brin's "place" wasn't a bed of leaves in a well-hidden spot ten miles out in the Angeles Forest. He had a way of reaching Brin if need be, and it didn't quite involve beaming an image of bat wings onto a cloud in the night sky. There was a phone number that no doubt was a dozen steps removed from Brin but had a voicemail he could check. Jarvis had been meaning to introduce him to the wonders of the Internet.

Brin's smile was only in his voice. "Sure. I'll send out an invite."

Jarvis looked away, following the flight of the crow as it hunted for an open trashcan. Jarvis counted to ten and turned back. The empty space where Brin had been gave Jarvis a clear view of the man writhing on the ground. As the ambulance pulled up, the crow spotted a broken trash bag half a block away, the bird's attention drawn to the spot by a figure quickly jumping over a fence and disappearing into a wooded area.

Sitting in his car now outside the hospital, the memory made Jarvis smile. The car seat had cooled and he turned over the engine with the punch of a button. He needed to find out why Brin had been eating at the deli in Beverly Hills. He might have liked pastrami, but he wouldn't have chosen to catch an early breakfast with a bunch of early-rising old Jewish men at Nate and Al's at 5:00 a.m. on a Sunday unless it was related to something he was working on. And since that was the only lead, with no residence or papers or cell phone records, Jarvis headed down Doheny toward the restaurant.

CHAPTER EIGHT

Before interrogating the wait staff, customers, and anyone within a six-block radius of the restaurant, Jarvis decided to see if Brin had left a car full of clues parked near the deli. Nate and Al's sat in the middle of Beverly Drive in Beverly Hills, buffered by Tiffany's, Van Cleefs, Harry Winston, and other shops that didn't offer pastrami sandwiches for about ten bucks. A ten would barely cover the tip for the valet at the jewelry and clothing stores. Brin might have parachuted in from a low-altitude single-engine plane piloted by a former Iraq war Air Force buddy, or surreptitiously jumped on the back of a delivery truck twenty miles away and ridden the undercarriage to Beverly Hills. But he probably drove.

If Brin had driven, he wouldn't have parked at a meter just in case he was poisoned or otherwise delayed and a ticket was issued. He didn't like to draw attention or provide any proof of his existence that could be traced back to him. More likely any vehicle he used was at least a few blocks away, and maybe as much as a mile. It would need to be innocuous, but with ready access and egress. Jarvis tried to think as Brin would have, then added a couple layers of paranoia. He pulled into an empty spot in front of a fire hydrant half a block from Nate and Al's and ignored the cop writing tickets on the expired meter a few cars down. Plenty of street parking, if you could get it. No lot for the deli, but a pretty big one at the Gelsons across the street. It was underground and there was no guard taking tickets. On the other hand, the grocery store closed at 10. Jarvis kept scanning.

There were public garages on this block, and at least three more within easy walking distance. All required you to take a ticket on the way in. Three or four blocks north, the residential part of Beverly Hills began—mansions and all the rest. Wide, empty streets. And permit parking only. Jarvis put his car into drive and planned on circling the block in an every widening pattern. He got to the corner of Beverly Drive and Santa Monica Bld, staying in the right lane so he could make the turn, when he saw a small ramp to his left going through a gated entrance. He cut across two lanes and was rewarded with the middle finger of the guy who'd been texting and about to drive his Lexus through the red light. Jarvis waved and smiled, irritating the guy more.

Jarvis did not need to take a ticket to go up the small ramp and into the cramped parking lot that contained about fifty spaces. This was one of those hidden gems. It gave refuge to drivers weary of circling the blocks and not wanting to enter one of the gargantuan public lots. This one was open to anyone and was used by both shoppers and employees because the meters were good for up to 24 hours. One long aisle to drive down, two rows of cars, one on either side. This lot hadn't been converted yet from coins to credit card. Brin would have loved it – no chance of being traced. Paranoia at its very best.

Jarvis played meter maid and rolled slowly past the cars, swiveling his head from side to side. A red Maserati had a flashing screen on the meter, but that wasn't Brin's style. Down ten more spots was a Prius with a ticket already on the window. The owner would be pissed – in Santa Monica, owners of the holier-than-though car didn't have to feed meters. In Beverly Hills, though, no one avoided their civic duty. Then he found it. Second to last spot on the right. Five year old Ford pick-up. Nothing special, no marks or stickers or permits. Just a truck, with a parking ticket stuck under the wiper blade on the driver's side. Jarvis stopped directly behind it, eliciting a brief but irritated horn blast from the woman behind him. He waved her around and got out of his car after she'd passed and glared at him.

Jarvis circled the truck, peering into the untinted driver's window, then pressing between the front bumper and metal posts of the fence it almost touched. There were no visible bits of paper, maps, empty coffee cups inside. He got to the passenger side and peered in, not bothering to try the door handle. Back around the bed of the truck, which was spic-and-span clean. The truck looked new even though it was at least five years old. Brin hadn't boosted it or bought it recently. He must've owned and used this truck for a while and there had to be a clue. Jarvis looked around and saw no security cops, no shoppers, no homeless. He went back to the passenger side and made a sharp jab with his elbow on the smaller pane on the front of the main side window. It created a spidery web of cracked glass, but remained in place. He pulled out his wallet and took an AmEx card and his gas credit card from the fold and held them together. Wedging them against the rubber trim next to the shattered pane, he used his palm as a hammer and with a couple of hard shots the makeshift wedge moved half an inch in. He twisted and pulled at the same time, opening enough space to put two fingers in. Wriggling down another half inch, he gave a sharp tug and the pane peeled away like the skin of a fish. No alarm rang out. He reached through the hole and flipped the lock.

The truck was clean, as if a forensic team had picked it over and removed every scrap of paper. Every fiber of material that could be used to trace the owner or anyone who'd ever been in the car. Probably because that's what Brin had done.

Jarvis opened the glove compartment and flipped through the half-decade old manual. No registration, or sunglasses, or burnt out tail light bulbs. No map leading him to Brin's lair. Certainly no clues about who had poisoned him. Jarvis swung over to the driver's side and sat behind the wheel. He flipped down the visor, half expecting a note to fall out. That was where soldiers kept pictures and letters and anything personal when they were driving around the desert in a Humvee ten years earlier. The back of the visor was as clean as the rest of the truck. Jarvis sighed and put his hands on the steering wheel. He tried to be Brin, think about what he'd seen driving here. Jarvis looked in the side mirror to see if anyone was watching him toss the vehicle. Only an empty row of cars. He turned to the passenger side and looked at the oversized rectangular mirror that would have shown if anyone had been pulling up alongside Brin waving a gun, a common occurrence in Afghanistan. Jarvis laughed as he read the writing on the side mirror, that objects appeared closer than they actually were. In Afghanistan they'd written on the bottom of them: Objects in mirror may be trying to kill your ass.

The writing, seen from across the front seat and through the window, looked worn. Jarvis squinted, then slid over to the passenger side. He couldn't lower the window without the key in the ignition, but he could read through the perfectly clean glass. The writing had been altered. From a few feet away, it read exactly as it should. But up close, some of the letters were made up of other letters. The O in Objects was actually several smaller letters forming a circle. Jarvis opened the door and got out, leaning in close to the mirror. He had to skim all the letters comprising the O to find a starting point where it made sense. And then it did. Brin had left him a message – just in case.

Jarvis pulled a small notebook out of his back pocket and pen from the front of his jacket. He wrote in a straight line. All the letters comprising the O. He squinted at the next few letters, but they were solid. Then the C, also made up of small squiggles that resolved to letters as he focused on them. The S and then on to the next word. The N from In and the M from Mirror. Only letters that were continuous, with no question about where the path of smaller letters would go, had been altered.

No more after that. Jarvis looked at the letters he'd written down and the message they conveyed. It was an address. His address, of his home in Malibu. And a string of digits. The digits looked like a telephone number, or a code. And then Jarvis recognized them – coordinates. Jarvis laughed out loud at Brin's brazen hiding place for whatever it was he wanted his friend to find. He took out his car key and scraped away the letters on the mirror. Jarvis closed the passenger door and tried to picture where on his property the coordinates pointed and how hard it would be to find whatever it was Brin had left. He pulled out of the lot, leaving the truck behind him to be towed and discarded since. Brin wouldn't reuse a compromised vehicle when he recovered. When, not if. Jarvis drove toward the beach.

CHAPTER NINE

J arvis tried to remember the last time he'd seen Brin at his home on the beach. It'd been years. But that didn't mean he hadn't been there. Sneaking into enemy territory undetected was Brin's specialty. The BMW sped along Sunset Boulevard and blazed north on Pacific Coast Highway until it reached the small community of modest homes and condos that contrasted with the beach mansions that made Malibu famous. Jarvis wound around a sandy road off the main street and pulled into his carport. From the glove compartment he took a blocky piece of electronics that looked to be one part oversized scuba watch and one part iPad.

GPS devices sold in stores weren't allowed by law to be accurate by more than ten feet. The military didn't want regular Joes able to pinpoint their location on a map too closely. His GPS was a little more accurate –within inches. He flipped it on and entered the coordinates from the notebook. A map instantly appeared along with a directional arrow. Jarvis got out of the car, eyes intent on the arrow. It flowed forward, like the lights on an airport landing strip. He followed the direction it pointed but had to stop when he encountered the wall a dozen feet to the left of his front door. He keyed open the door and went into the hallway, holding the GPS in one hand and angling it in the direction of the arrow. It was turning green.

He took a few steps towards the living room and as his body turned, the arrow reoriented to his right. It directed him to the kitchen and as he walked, the arrow began to move more quickly and the color shifted from yellow to light green. By the time he passed the kitchen table, the green was darker and the flickering more insistent. The arrow pointed a little to his left and he almost bumped into the refrigerator. The arrow was now an insistent deep green and seemed to want to leap off the screen. Jarvis held the GPS closer to the fridge and the arrow turned into a large green dot, which spun frantically and launched a loud beeping. He put the GPS on the counter and opened the fridge, expecting to find a gift-wrapped clue. Instead, he only saw a poorly wrapped half-eaten chicken and his last beer. He began to rifle through the random contents, looking for something that didn't belong or had been disturbed. The luncheon meats looked fine. If Brin had hidden something here it wouldn't be in a perishable item. Inside a panel, or behind a motor deep in the guts of the refrigerator. Jarvis felt the inside walls of the fridge for anything that might have some give or look like it had been opened and replaced. There was nothing.

He stood and closed the door. Leaning back on the counter in the center of the kitchen, he looked at the metallic surface. Getting down on one knee he checked the floor to see if there were scratch marks where the heavy appliance had been pulled out so someone could remove a metal plate or unhinge a door. It was clean. Not so clean that it looked like someone had recently wiped it. Jarvis reached under and felt for any anomalies. He was disappointed to find nothing. Checking the fridge reminded him he hadn't eaten since the night before. He opened the door of the freezer section above the regular refrigerator and pulled out one of the half dozen pints of Ben & Jerry's. Before he closed the door and reached for a spoon, he noticed the heavy blanket of frost surrounding most of the freezer, reducing its capacity because of his neglect. Jarvis put the ice cream down on the counter and took a heavy knife off the rack next to the stove. He began to chip away at the two inches of ice pack.

A spray of ice flew into his face and then a couple of chunks came away. There was something at the bottom, a slip of paper or plastic. Jarvis scraped away as much of the accumulated ice as he needed then clawed at the corner of rectangular scrap with his fingers. It was laminated, a couple inches high and four or five wide. It peeled off like the glass on Brin's car, resisting but giving. He closed the freezer, ignoring the melting shards that puddled on the floor. The piece of laminated paper was frosted and streaked. Jarvis wiped it against his shirt, held it between two hands to warm it and turn the fragments of ice to water. It took just a few seconds. Now he could read the writing. Handwritten, clean block letters. A few lines of text and at the bottom, a string of meaningless letters and numbers. Jarvis held the message close to make out the small writing.

Silent sky, quiet desert, nothing breathing but one man,
Laying alone, unseen, unknown, unconnected.
Waiting. Time stopped, but not the world,
Which passed slowly by, not knowing, not seeing, not caring.
Until his finger slowly squeezed, barely moving, just far enough.
And a bullet streaked through the unbroken canvas that painted their lives,
Tearing a hole, ripping through flesh, starting a torrent of blood. Ending a life,
Starting another wait. Ambivalence.

The last word was underlined.

Jarvis recognized the bad poem. It was his. He walked quickly to his bedroom and pulled out the composition notebook. He looked at the first entry, dated almost a year ago. It wasn't in this book. He went to the closet and pulled out a small box. It was filled with the same kind of notebook, black and white covers neatly arranged in two stacks. Jarvis took a handful out and began to check the dates printed on the front. He quickly found the one he wanted, from three years earlier. Flipping through the pages, he found the entry. Written in his own hand, much sloppier than what Brin had printed and laminated, was the same poem.

Every night, before closing his eyes and falling into deep dream sleep for the single hour that was all he needed, all he ever got, Jarvis jotted down a few lines of something. Maybe a poem, or an idea for a movie-of-the-week. A novel or a short story. When he was feeling adventurous it might be the lyrics to a song. It was just a way to release his mind, to exercise a part of his brain that seemed to accumulate thoughts during the day but never had expression. It was never to be read by someone else, any more than the quiet confessions to a psychiatrist should ever be shared outside the sanctity of the therapist's couch. Brin had been here, reading from this book.

At the bottom of this fragment of poem Jarvis had scratched out in the middle of the night years earlier, one inspired by memories of Brin who had visited that week three years ago, was a line in Brin's same handwriting. It was a website address.

Jarvis went to the iPad lying carelessly on some clothes atop his dresser and flicked the screen on. He typed in the address and the screen quickly filled with a black background. In the center were two white boxes, one labeled Username and the other Password. Across the top of the page was just one line: Secure storage. There were no links, nothing that said what the site did or how to sign up or who ran it. It was clearly for people who already knew what it was. Jarvis had thought Brin too paranoid to be on the grid, to use websites or anything online. But this must have been a very, very secure environment. He stared at the empty spaces that waited for him to type something. Brin had made it very difficult for anyone to find the clues – the truck mirror, a private journal only he and Jarvis knew about with an entry that would only have been meaningful to the two of them, and an ultra-secure website. He wouldn't have made it hard to get in if he'd trusted how difficult he'd made finding the clues. Jarvis looked at the slip of laminated paper still in his hand and slowly typed in the string of digits and randomly capitalized and lower-case letters interspersed. That had to be the password. He pondered the username for a moment and then it was obvious. He typed in Ambivalence. It was one of the few times he'd done anything that resembled titling one of his bits of writing before drifting into brief slumber.

There was no button to indicate logging in or going to the next step so he just hit the Return button. Nothing happened for a moment, and then the screen switched to a white background and in the center was an icon of a folder. Nothing special, the same icon used by every computer operating system in the world – yellow folder with a small tab. It sat alone, no markings, no label, no explanation of where it came from or what it held. Jarvis clicked twice on it by tapping the screen. It opened instantly. Jarvis stood and stared at a list of documents. They had dates, but no names. The first one was created almost seven years ago. This was Brin's history. And Jarvis understood instantly it was how his friend was going to help him find whoever had put him near death.

CHAPTER TEN

Jarvis clicked a document dated a couple months ago. It opened on a page with half a dozen lines of notes. Brin was as meticulous in his electronic record-keeping as he was in stalking a target. Despite the fact the words were standard fonts appearing on a computer screen, they seemed to carry his concise, tight handwriting. Jarvis read short, functional sentences: where Brin had been, who he had seen, why he'd been following them. As he scrolled through the half dozen pages, he began to formulate a picture of the life Brin had been leading. There was no mention of where he lived, or shopped, or what he ate. It was all business. But from his description of tailing a motorcycle through city streets, to staking out a restaurant downtown for three straight nights, to being paid in tobacco and raw steaks by a client, Jarvis imagined his friend moving through life. Zig-zagging, never in one place too long, but always with the same theme. He was like Jarvis, helping people in tough spots, only he didn't have a license or live in a place with an address. Or get paid in American currency.

Jarvis closed the document and opened another. Same rhythm. He read quickly through the half dozen pages covering a week, then opened another. Nothing interesting, nothing relevant. Another, and another. Finally he clicked on the document dated one week earlier. This was a long entry, written all on the same day. Brin was following someone, a young man. There was no mention of why he was pursuing him. There was a log of the man's daily activities. Home, work, gym. How fast he drove, what route he took. If Jarvis didn't know better he'd think this was prep work for an assassination. But something was different. Brin made reference to his tours in the Middle East. The young man reminded him of soldiers he'd seen or killed. Brin was cautious but fascinated by his quarry. The final entry on the last page made Jarvis shiver. It was just two words: Made contact.

He went back and re-read the entire document, word for word, looking for clues. He moved to the bed and jotted down notes on a white legal pad. Opened the document dated just prior to the last one and searched for any other tidbits. After half an hour he had one page of writing. There was a story there, but it didn't jump out at him. Not yet. What he had was a location, a description of a young man, some odd behavior by Brin and the man he followed, and a poisoning. Good thing he was a detective. Jarvis rubbed his eyes and looked out the bedroom window to the ocean. It was mid-day and the waves were too gentle for the real surfers. Just a few kids wading in the breakers. He went into the kitchen and made the breakfast he'd skipped when the call had come from the cop Rayford. He absently downed the eggs, cheese, onions and capers and stood at the sink drinking strong black tea while he washed the frying pan. His mind was playing out the last couple days, but from Brin's perspective. Something had to have been off for him to be the victim instead of the hunter. Something had distracted him, or convinced him to let down his guard. Jarvis went to the hall closet and took out the Glock he used for serious business. It cut into his hip when he drove, but he ignored the twinge as he headed out onto PCH and toward the suburbs of the San Fernando Valley where Brin had started to follow his target.

Jarvis got halfway up the 405 freeway to Mulholland when his phone rang. He ignored the California law and put the cell against his ear.

"Yeah."

Rayford skipped the pleasantries. "Find anything?"

"Nothing," Jarvis lied. The bimmer picked up speed as the road steepened and other cars were slowed by gravity. "You?"

The detective sighed audibly despite the lousy signal. "I suppose. Some old woman at the grocery store tipped over and now she's in a coma." He paused. "Kinda like your friend."

Jarvis cut across three lanes of traffic and was on the Getty Center off ramp before the yelling from the other cars had died down. "Where are you?"

"The Ralph's at Pico and Century City."

He didn't have to ask where it was or why a major crimes detective had been called in for a slip-and-fall in the produce section. Brin's condition was no accident and the cops had their eyes peeled. They'd been right to do so. Jarvis was in the parking lot in ten minutes, clocking an average speed of 83 mph and instigating a lot of raised middle fingers.

Rayford must have gotten to the scene within minutes of the woman collapsing and called Jarvis as he was walking in the door because Jarvis passed the gurney being wheeled out by paramedics. The old lady must've been in her 70s but looked as if she hadn't missed a meal in any of those years. There was a smear of something yellow and sticky on her face and it bubbled slightly with her shallow breaths. She looked like she'd fallen asleep while eating a bowl of scalloped potatoes and fallen face-first into it. She also looked like she probably wouldn't be waking up soon. Jarvis followed the line of gawkers to the spot where a couple of uniformed cops were putting up a barrier of yellow tape, brighter than the smears of food on the woman's face. They wrapped it around a stand with loaves of fresh bread and then across twenty feet of linoleum to hook on a stand holding bottles of wine, eventually creating a hexagon around an area that included a row of hot-food trays protected by a massive sneeze guard, a cheese sample stand, and a rotating display of sunglasses. Jarvis could see a mess on the floor near the ready-to-eat stand. Scalloped potatoes, heavy on the cheese. He'd guessed right.

A guy wearing a white button-up shirt and sporting an ID card clipped to the pocket was obviously the store manager. He was gesticulating to Rayford, who didn't bother pretending to write down the tirade. As Jarvis got closer he picked up the gist. Sales were being lost, customers leaving, flow to the aisles disrupted. Rayford kept a dead look on his face and waited for the manager to take a breath.

"Would you like me to shut the place down for a week while we do a full investigation?"

The manager's mouth opened and then stopped. He wasn't dumb, just limited.

Rayford turned to Jarvis and ducked under the freshly-wrapped tape to meet him near an open olive bar with a much smaller sneeze guard.

"I'm guessing she didn't slip on the potatoes and break a hip?"

Rayford wasn't in the mood for repartee. "Pupils dilated, breathing shallow, and pulse thready. Looks a lot like your buddy Brin and she didn't have a stroke either." He looked around at the crowd. "The woman's a regular, roams around the store leaning on a cart like it's a walker. Puts a few things in the basket, but mostly grazes."

He looked through a few pages on his notebook. "Half a dozen people saw her fall, like a sack of potatoes, then convulse a little. No one wanted to do mouth-to-mouth. We tracked her path through the store. Some grapes in produce, free sample of pizza down aisle four, couple of cheese squares over there," he pointed with the notebook, "and then the main course at the hot food bar."

The cart the woman had been pushing was still there, angled into the long trough of food. Main dishes, vegetables, desserts, all separated into metal bins and all with some variation of coagulation covering them. A plastic container with half a spoonful of three or four undistinguishable foodstuffs rested in the front of her cart. A spoon was on the floor next to the cart.

"She'd been working her way down the line, smorgasbord style."

A tech arrived from behind them. He had half a dozen plastic evidence bags containing grapes, cheese cubes, and something that might have been bits of microwaved pizza.

"Brin wouldn't have hung around if he'd been feeling like crap. Whatever it is works fast. Probably in the hot food."

Rayford nodded. "Probably, but can't take any chances. We'll have to shut down the place until we've run tests." He said it loudly enough for the manager to hear and the reaction was an audible, unintelligible choking sound. Rayford gave a barely perceptible shake of the head to Jarvis – they'd only need to confiscate the areas the woman had used as a movable feast.

"You know the shit storm this is going to cause?"

This time Rayford closed his eyes and shook his head. "Serial poisoner? Yeah, a lot of paperwork."

Jarvis laughed and pointed to the floor. "Stay away from the scalloped potatoes. I'll give you a ring later to hear what you found."

"Really? Sure you don't just want me to send you a copy of the report?"

Jarvis turned to head back out. "Don't worry, it'll be a trade. I should know something by then."

He pushed past the gathering crowd and headed to the parking lot to resume his trip to a house in the San Fernando Valley.

CHAPTER ELEVEN

In the late fall, twenty degrees can separate the air in Beverly Hills from the ambient temperature of the flatlands of Tarzana along Ventura Boulevard. Jarvis watched the gauge climb into the seventies and then low eighties as he waited for lights to turn green and cars to slowly accelerate for half a block until another red forced the line to a full halt again. Turning north on Reseda Boulevard and passing half a dozen strip malls that were progressively less cared for, eventually bordering on dilapidated, he came to the side street named in Brin's ledger. Magnolia Avenue had neither magnolias nor the grandeur of an avenue. He rolled past trees that seemed kin to the strip malls a couple blocks away and noted the increasing prevalence of chain link fences, dearth of actual grass, and greater density of pickup trucks. 19438 was better kept than the others, but only because there were no Beware of Dog signs or chipped paint adorning sagging external walls. He slowed but did not stop then made a U-turn a couple blocks further on and came back. Stopping in front of what was either an abandoned one-bedroom home or the residence of someone who had died weeks ago and not yet been discovered, Jarvis pulled over and looked more carefully at the house Brin had targeted.

There was no garage so the empty driveway suggested no one was home. Brin had probably observed from this same spot the four times he'd written about his surveillance. Though there was an interesting pall over the neighborhood, nothing special stood out. That convinced Jarvis there must be something insidious to have kept Brin's attention. He killed the engine, settled back in his seat, and waited. The temperature quickly climbed half a dozen degrees, but the trees blocked enough sun that he knew it would be bearable for as long as he had to wait. The iPhone connected to the sound system continued to gently play.

Four hours passed and the sun was close enough to dusk that long shadows stretched across the street in front of the car. The temperature inside was down to 73. Jarvis had composed half a dozen post-slumber snippets, none of which would make it into the journal late that evening. He started making a grocery list in his mind and got as far as toilet paper when a late model Hyundai coming down the street toward him turned into the driveway. It idled for a moment before the engine cut and the driver-side door opened.

The young man wearing a white short-sleeved dress shirt was overtly Middle Eastern. He was slim and the briefcase he pulled from the passenger seat strained his slender muscles. Jarvis watched him fumble with keys and use a remote to lock the car then softly walk up the path to the newly painted front door and fumble again getting it open. He was unable to see past the young man into the house and the drawn curtains restricted any following of his movements once inside. Jarvis started his engine and drove slowly past the house, noting the license plate number on the Hyundai and debating whether to call Rayford for the trace or use a friend who had unrestricted and completely illegal access to the DMV registry. He needed the license plate; doing a search on the address would only give the owner and he had no way to know if the fellow Brin had been following was the owner, a renter, a squatter, or what. Unprepared for an unnecessary all-night vigil, he headed back to the Westside. Turning onto Reseda Boulevard where the cell reception would be better, he dialed his friend Peter, hoping Peter's mom wouldn't answer. She often tried to listen in on her son's calls, figuring that providing a private basement dwelling to her 41-year-old boy bought her certain privileges. Particularly with all the computer equipment and electronics he kept putting on the credit card she gave him that was supposed to be used for gas and incidentals. This time, Peter picked up.

"Dude, whaddaya need?"

Jarvis didn't bother asking how the recluse knew it was him despite the block Jarvis had on his cell phone.

"I've got a license plate. You ready?"

"Always ready, man. You carryin'?"

Jarvis laughed to himself. "Yup. How about two all-access passes in San Diego next month?" He could hear Peter's heart beat faster. That kind of pass to ComiCon meant he'd be able to go behind the scenes and maybe catch a glimpse of some of the booth babes – or, god forbid, some trampy B-movie chick – getting changed into alien garb or superhero costume.

Peter spit out a name, address, and social security number almost before Jarvis had finished giving him the last number of the plate.

"Can you text that, Peter? I'm driving."

"Sure, man, just make sure to get in the right lane and take Sepulveda in 100 feet – it's stop-and-go a mile up at Santa Monica." It didn't occur to Peter that it might freak someone out for them to know he could pinpoint their location based on a 30 second phone call.

"Say hi to your mom. I'll put the tickets in the mail." Jarvis disconnected before the boy-man could object to such an old-fashioned delivery mode.

He dialed another number. "Hey, Rayford. Another old lady drop?"

"No, just this one. Out of a coma. And dead."

Jarvis' mind went to Brin. Rayford felt the pause. "You got anything to tell me, you know, on the investigative front?"

A long pause. "Maybe. I'll let you know." He disconnected and took the next exit. He needed some quiet time. There was a wired Starbucks a mile further along Mulholland. He was there in forty seconds. Another minute and he was sitting in a quiet corner with just a couple of high school girls giggling as they waited for their order keeping him company on the other side of the café. He propped his iPad on the small table and pulled up a browser. It didn't take more than a couple minutes to get a picture of Azad Hekmatiar, the name Peter provided. The kid was on every social networking site Jarvis could think of and even though there wasn't much info on any of them, it was enough to tell a story. Facebook had him with twenty friends, light by the standards of anyone under thirty. His status was single and he didn't waste a lot of time listing his favorite movies and music. LinkedIn was a little more interesting, listing his current job as assistant store manager at Forever21. He'd fit right in with the teens buying low-end but cool clothes and knick-knacks. Azad named a high school and a local college as his alma maters. Nothing special to separate him from the hundreds of thousands of young men and women of Arabic descent living in the greater Los Angeles neighborhood.

Then Jarvis pulled up another browser window and typed in an address that challenged him with a password and warning saying the site was private government property and illegal access was a felony punishable by 25 years in prison and $1M fine. He risked being hit with the stiff ticket and slowly typed in a 14-character password comprising numbers and both upper- and lower-case letters. Almost instantly the screen changed to a clean, simple interface that would have made the designers of Google nod with appreciation. He entered Azad's full name and birthdate, conveniently provided by Peter, into the search field. A few thousand miles away, a government database accessed very highly protected information using the top secret clearance for the account belonging to a woman Jarvis had dated a year earlier. By "dated" he meant "slept with a few times," but long enough to inadvertently capture her account information from the keylogger that ran on his personal computer at home. She'd used it one morning while he was in the shower, unaware that every stroke was recorded. After they broke up, and by "broke up" he meant "she got tired of him not being as available as she'd like," he failed to inform her that he could now retrieve information from the Homeland Security files.

Azad Hekmatier was part of an immigration asylum program for youths caught in the struggles of their home country in Africa or the

Middle East. His originating country was not known, only his date of entry, two previous ports (Ghana and Newfoundland), and some school records. It wasn't enough to explain why Brin had been following him or why Brin was now in a coma. Jarvis shut down the iPad, drained his coffee cup, and headed back to Magnolia Avenue.

CHAPTER TWELVE

This time Jarvis pulled right into the driveway, blocking the shiny Hyundai. The Glock was tucked behind his back, just in case Brin wasn't following Hekmatier because of a string of parking violations. He knocked on the door and could smell baking bread and a mix of warm spices, bringing back olfactory memories as real as the door in front of him. A second knock and he could hear a chair scraping the floor somewhere beyond, probably the kitchen. No footsteps but he could feel someone approaching. He took a half step back to create a sense of safety, staying out of the kid's personal space. The door opened a few inches and Jarvis saw a gentle brown face, framed by curly black hair, peer out. Jarvis opened his mouth to say something but the young man's face went from curious to shocked. It stopped Jarvis before a word could come out. The kid, Azad, was the first to respond, by transforming the shock into something more emphatic and slamming the door shut. Jarvis had no idea what had freaked out the youngster. He knocked again and called out.

"Azad! Relax, I just want to talk to you for a minute." The boy looked innocent enough, nothing sinister, just a fish out of water gasping for air. Jarvis knocked again and tried the door handle; locked.

He stepped to the left and peered through a part of the window not obscured by drapes. He could see the kid fumbling through a closet about fifteen away, near the kitchen. Azad looked back at that exact moment and saw Jarvis peering through the glass. Even with the dimming light of dusk, Jarvis could see the expression on Azad's face and in that moment Jarivs realized what it was: recognition. Azad knew Jarvis. The young man found what he was looking for and pulled out a small portable boom box. If the smell of cooking food hadn't triggered in Jarvis such strong memories, he may not have made the connection. Instinctively he turned away from the window and took three long strides toward the front yard. He jumped and tucked into a ball, just as the first explosion blew out the windows and splintered the door. He rolled along the well-kept grass toward the street, shielding his face and neck with his arms. The second explosion blew a hole in the roof and started a fire that instantly consumed the living room and kitchen. A third explosion must have been pre-set; there was not enough of Azad left to hit a trigger. Jarvis felt the ground shake. The sound was deafening. His hands had been clasped over his ears while his forearms protected his face. It took just seconds for the roar to stop and be replaced by an echo and then the whoosh of the fire eating oxygen. Jarvis stayed on the ground, in case there were any more explosives, and watched the house be consumed. As he sat up and checked for any sprains or breaks from the sudden departure from the front door, he could hear a siren about a mile away. The fire station he'd passed while driving back and forth to Magnolia Avenue probably didn't need a 911 call to know there'd been a disaster or where it was. Jarvis mulled over for a moment the right move. He stood and watched the flames reach 30 feet in the air and dialed Rayford.

The fire was out and the neighbors remained entranced by the emergency team's activities. Jarvis had refused the blanket and medical exam from the EMT who had no one else to attend to. Rayford arrived fifteen minutes after getting Jarvis' call. His look was not one of camaraderie as he walked across the lawn after consulting with the West Valley detective whose case this was.

"There something you want to tell me now, maybe something you knew before but it slipped your mind when I asked earlier?"

The complexity of the sentence didn't obscure the sarcasm. It fell harmlessly after failing to pierce Jarvis' armor. "I was following up on a lead." He looked over at the smoldering house and raised his eyebrows.

Rayford almost laughed. "Okay, we'll discuss full disclosure later. What the hell happened?"

Jarvis walked toward the house, stepping over a hose that was plump with flowing water. The house looked like a giant had bent over and taken a huge bite out of it from above. "The kid blew himself up. The whole house and whatever was in it."

"Did you talk to him?" Rayford walked beside him, waving off the warning from the fire chief. "Do you have any idea what the hell was going on – meth lab? Pipe bombs?"

Jarvis stopped just at the spot where half an hour earlier he'd peered in the window and seen the young man fumble trying to locate the trigger. "There's going to be traces of something, whatever it is he wanted to get rid of. Including himself."

Rayford pursed his lips. "That's not an answer."

Jarvis turned to the detective. "I didn't get to say anything more than hello." He paused. "This is the guy Brin was following the day he was poisoned." He turned back to the crater that had been a living room and kitchen. "And he recognized me. As soon as he did, he did this."

Rayford looked back and forth between the gutted house and Jarvis. A storm gathered on his face. "And you didn't think you should tell me?"

Jarvis fixed the detective with a stare. He didn't blink for more than half a minute, then turned and walked away.

CHAPTER THIRTEEN

n the hospital room, an orange chair covered with something not quite as comfortable as vinyl was the only place to sit except the bed. Brin was off the respirator but still in a coma. Jarvis sat next to him, feet on the lower railing. He listened to the steady breathing and equally regular beat of the monitor. It was past visiting hours but the third nurse who'd tried to push him out had left them alone half an hour earlier. Jarvis looked at his friend and tried to picture what had happened in the restaurant. The waitress said Brin was eating alone. She didn't remember seeing a young Persian man there, but she'd made the point that was like trying to recall one ant from thousands scurrying around the ground. She'd worked at the Jewish deli for 35 years; it sounded more racist than it probably was. She only remembered Brin because he'd collapsed in his pastrami.

The kid recognized Jarvis but not vice versa. Maybe Brin had been more on the ball and put a place and a time to seeing him. Jarvis would work backwards and start with the most recent intersection of their lives. He needed to understand why Brin was following the kid who was now mostly bits and pieces mixed with smoking wood and ash. Rayford, despite his fury, would get the lab report to Jarvis if only to guilt him into sharing anything he knew. For now, Jarvis stared at Brin on the bed. Helpless; not how he'd ever seen him. Jarvis wasn't entirely certain that if someone ran in and tried to plunge a knife into Brin, the comatose Ranger wouldn't catch the killer's wrist an inch above his chest and then quickly break it and reverse the path of the knife back upward without opening his eyes. The daydream made Jarvis smile.

He'd brought his iPad with him and he used it to access Brin's journals. He re-read everything from earlier that day, pulling out the notes he'd made and smoothing the papers on the bed next to Brin's leg. The logs weren't comprehensive, weren't meant to be a diary. They read more like reminders for Brin. Triggers for things in his mind, so someone reading it wouldn't know too much, just get hints. The first mention of the young man was ten days ago but it wasn't clear who saw whom first. Jarvis wracked his memory to connect the kid's face with all the other faces he'd ever seen. The was no match, no flashing green light. Nothing.

The vibrating cell phone broke his reverie and disappointment. The number was Rayford's.

"Hey."

"They found a few interesting things in the mess, aside from an intact limb." He didn't sound as irritated as Jarvis expected.

"How interesting?"

There was a pause. "Twisted metal case, almost melted in the explosion. " Jarvis waited. "Not the kind you carry important papers in. More like the kind you use to protect a volatile or dangerous substance."

Jarvis looked at his sleeping friend. "Like poison, maybe?"

"There's not much to examine, but the lab will do what they can. I'll ring you when I have something."

"Yeah, thanks. I've got a couple things to run down. I'll get in touch." Rayford heard the truthfulness and hung up.

The iPad quickly pulled up Azad Hekmatier's Facebook page and LinkedIn account. Jarvis had the name of his workplace. He headed out.

CHAPTER FOURTEEN

Achingly stereotypical, the mini-mart/gas station where Azad worked was straight out of an episode of The Simpsons. A burly guy busting out of a worn, short-sleeved blue shirt stood behind the counter and telegraphed with his frown that he had a baseball bat within reach. Jarvis ignored the nonexistent line of customers and grabbed a pack of gum and a Slim Jim, just because he thought they were extinct.

Handing the guy a five, he tested the guy's language skills despite the apparent south-of-the-Mason-Dixon-line heritage. "Azad Hekmatier work here?" The clerk, probably night manager, didn't like being asked or he had trouble multi-tasking. He silently made change but raised his eyebrows to confirm he would be perfectly happy to swing the bat at a guy's head. Jarvis failed to convey extreme agitation or knee-weakening fear.

"There was an accident. I'm trying to find next of kin."

"Yeah? What kinda fuckin' accident? He pee on hisself?" This was apparently the funniest thing he'd heard in hours because he tilted his head back and laughed like a donkey objecting to being asked to pull a plow. Jarvis could see ancient silver fillings in otherwise gray teeth.

"Maybe. The explosion was pretty bad. Might've been enough to scare a kid into urinating."

The laugh ended and the clerk's head snapped forward. Curious, not concerned. "Don't tell me the little raghead was a terrorist? He blow sumpin' up with one a' them bomb vests?"

Jarvis resisted the urge to reach behind the counter for the bat. "Did he wear a turban?"

The guy shook his head. "Nah, not around me. He was just, ya know, obviously a Paki or somethin'. Whatever. So what explosion?"

"Gas line." He opened the gum, noticing now that it was Brin's brand. "He have friends, or people he hung out with?"

The laugh again. "Around here? Hey, the guy mopped the floor and wiped the toilet. When I was tired he ran the register. He was a scrub." He stopped for a second, scratching his belly through the shirt. "Always wearin' a suit, though, even plungin' the toilet. He was in school, or somethin'. Wanted to get a job or study some stupid fuckin' science or somethin'. I dunno."

Jarvis looked around the dump. Stepping stone, he thought. The kid had bigger plans, but for some reason they included poisoning Brin. "He have a locker or any place he kept his stuff?"

The clerk pointed to an opening leading to a storage room. "He had some shit in a locker back there. How'd you know?"

"You mind if a take a look? There might be something there to help find his family."

"Hey, is the little dick dead or somethin'? Is he comin' back? I mean, he's got a shift tonight."

Jarvis fantasized about the guy pulling the bat out and how easy it would be to take it from him. "No, he's hurt, won't be coming in. The locker?"

"Yeah, whatever, it's the third one. There's only three. Go 'head."

Jarvis went past the counter and into the back. It looked exactly like he'd expected. Apparently the clerk had never asked Azad to use his mop in this area. The locker was misnamed; it was closed but nothing interfered with changing that except pulling up on the bent metal slide that scraped as Jarvis gave it a hard yank. The only thing remarkable about the contents was the contrast between the mess outside the locker and the meticulous organization within. Clean, pressed shirt on a hanger, several books stacked neatly on the floor, an extra pair of well-shined shoes next to them. Jarvis picked up the books and flipped through them. A heavy textbook on civics, a slimmer one containing the plays of several modern but dead white men, and a lab primer for organic chemistry. They were all stamped with Cal State Northridge on the inside cover.

On the shelf, chin-level to Jarvis, papers in an equally neat pile lined up with pencils, pens, and a spray can of Axe Body Wash. The locker smelled faintly of the teen cologne. Atop the stack of papers, several receipts were held together by a plastic green triangle, one of those cool paperclips that didn't work as well as the old-fashioned metal curlicues. He picked it up and flipped through. Half a dozen from local sandwich shops. Three from a private postal service where people could rent boxes or have mail sent and held. They were COD, all for the same amount, with the sender somewhere in Wisconsin. Jarvis pocketed all the receipts and went back out into the store.

"You gonna buy somethin' else? Maybe know someone who might wanna job?" The clerk was obviously thinking about the double shift he was going to have to pull, probably saddened by all the poetry books he wasn't going to get to read tonight.

"The boy went to school. Did he talk about that? Mention any friends?"

Jarvis almost mouthed the words as they came out of the manager's mouth. "I don't know nothin' 'bout what he fuckin' did, 'cept wanna take a day off next week when he shoulda been plannin' on workin'."

Instead of walking out, Jarvis fixed him with his best "I'm a detective which is almost a cop so you better answer" stare. "Why did he need time off?"

The manager shrugged. "I dunno." Apparently that wasn't true. "Said he needed to go see some friend of his, outta town or somethin'. Probably another fuckin' a-rab terrorist."

He'd made his point and went back to scratching his belly. Jarvis left and didn't hear the man's parting comment.

CHAPTER FIFTEEN

Wisconsin was not known as a hotbed of radicalism. Jarvis went to the postal service storefront where Azad had collected his packages but they were closed. It was getting on to ten pm and there wasn't much that would be open and useful in the investigation. He thought about calling Rayford but there was nothing to say. Instead he pulled into the only Whole Foods market in the San Fernando Valley and used a hand basket to weave in and out of the yoginis, hippies, and painfully hot actresses who spent more time in the aisles here than on auditions. Very different vibe from the Ralphs where the old woman had been murdered. Jarvis picked up an organic, locally-grown, hand selected, lovingly packaged and displayed ready-to-eat salad along with a small carton of some brown tofu gunk. He sat on one of the benches out front and watched them start to shut the store down. Several patrons looked almost lost as they were gently ushered out into the parking lot and real world. Firing up the iPad and typing with one hand as he ate with the other, he peered at the receipt in the dim light and typed in the address of the sender. Google Maps gave him an intersection in Racine, Wisconsin, that looked about the same as any within ten miles of where he sat. But no business name. He switched the view from diagram to satellite and instantly the images went from the equivalent of stick figures to live portraits; the satellite images brought the neighborhood to life. Jarvis zoomed in and could easily make out a small strip mall. Even without a lot of detail, he was able to recognize a sandwich shop, nail/hair salon, and postal service office. Whoever had sent the packages to the kid did so from their own anonymous location.

Jarvis pulled up the Orbitz web site and did a search on flights from LAX to Racine. No non-stops – why would anyone want to get there quickly? He reserved a ticket for the next day and forced down the last two bites of tofu mud.

Back home he watched half an hour of late news, then played some online chess while Conan chattered with a girl Jarvis didn't recognize who was starring in a film he hadn't heard of. It was close to 1:00 a.m. when the first pangs of tiredness emerged, but not enough to be a distraction. He thought about Brin and how different life would have been if things in Afghanistan hadn't gone sideways that day. The bond wouldn't have been created and there were probably half a dozen times in the last ten years Jarvis would have come out on the wrong side in a fight or tough situation without his friend being there. It was time to return the favor, even if Brin felt he was still in debt.

Jarvis went into the bedroom and packed a light overnight bag. Mostly gym clothes and clean underwear. He didn't want to be in Wisconsin any longer than necessary. The clock flipped over to 2:15 a.m. and he stripped down to boxers and lay on top of the bedcover. He pulled out the journal and perched it on his stomach, clicked open the pen, and flipped to the page held by the bookmark. Jotting down the time, he closed his eyes and pictured Brin, pale and weak as he'd never seen him. He wrote out the night's prose.

Fuck Racine.

Jarvis put the journal on the other side of the bed and killed the light. When he opened his eyes the green illumination from the clock read 3:47 a.m. and he rolled out of bed, refreshed, rejuvenated, and ready for revenge.

CHAPTER SIXTEEN

erry's Deli in Venice was open 24 hours. In a row. It was one of half a dozen places that met Jarvis' unique needs. He drank his second cup of coffee and broke the yolk on an over-medium egg, mopping it up with lightly toasted sourdough bread. It was too early to call Rayford, barely past 5 a.m. as he dialed.

"Hey, I'll be out of town for a day or so."

The cop's voice was heavy with sleep. "Jesus. Are you a vampire?"

Jarvis chewed egg and toast in his ear. "I thought cops got up early."

"I've got a three-month old and he's got about two-hour naps going at best." A couple of deep breaths came over the phone. "Besides, no one sane is up at this hour, cop or not."

"I might have a lead on where the dead kid got the poison."

There was a long silence that wasn't Rayford pulling himself together. "I've got a dead woman that might be a murder, a guy in a coma who was probably poisoned, and a young man who may have blown himself up along with most of his house. You want to tell me how you're tying all that together?"

"Brin was following Hekmatier. I'm not sure why yet. That got him poisoned. When you get the tox report later this week it'll be the same thing that killed the woman. And it'll be the stuff you find in the case from the kid's house, if there's any trace." He paused. He could hear Rayford walking into another room and the crying of a baby starting up.

"Piece of work. Wanna tell me now what you've done the in just 18 hours to put this all together?" Irritation was present but Jarvis assumed it was grating nerves from an infant crying incessantly.

"I had a few leads from Brin. It doesn't really matter – you've got a murder investigation to deal with and I'm handing you the murderer and the evidence. You sure you want more?" Jarvis took a long sip of coffee and got up. He walked past the waiter's station on his way to the men's room and saw the woman who'd been filling his cup every few minutes for the last half hour. Covering the speaker on the phone, he gave her a heads-up "Back in a minute." She nodded without looking up and grabbed her coffee pot. She filled his mug before he'd made it as far as the urinal.

Rayford mulled it over. "What I want is to make sure you're not interfering with an investigation or tampering with evidence, and I don't want to get caught up in something that's none of my goddamn business." It was a fair set of goals. "And if it ties up nicely with the murderer killing himself, then that's great too." The sound of rushing water didn't bother him. "I've gotta change a diaper. Fly safe."

"If I find anything that helps you tie up the loose ends, it's all yours. Anything that'll make your life difficult…" He didn't finish the sentence.

Jarvis closed the phone and washed up. In the restaurant, a young man who might have passed as Azad Hekmatier's cousin walked slowly by Jarvis' empty table. He paused for a moment, as if to look at his cell phone and peck out a text message. With his body blocking anyone's view of the table, he took a small vial out of his pocket and pulled off the top. Without looking around, he spilled its contents into Jarvis' coffee cup and then sauntered further into the restaurant. As he circled past the tables to head out towards the door, he brushed by Jarvis emerging from the bathroom. The young man looked away and Jarvis passed without a glance. He was in his pickup truck and pulling out of the lot as Jarvis sat at the table, fingering the coffee cup. Instead of taking another pull and having to swing by the bathroom again, he put a twenty on the table and headed out. Jarvis walked through the nearly empty parking lot as dawn began to awake.

Twenty minutes later he was at the United terminal, overnight bag in hand.

CHAPTER SEVENTEEN

Racine, Wisconsin is not the armpit of the world – Trenton, NJ holds the honor. Racine is more like the left earlobe; nobody pays attention to it, but if it were gone you'd probably notice even if it didn't affect anything in any way that mattered. After a brief layover in Denver, Jarvis rented a car and was at the Racine Post-It Postal Service Center by 3:30 pm. Despite the name of the strip-mall store, no flock of attorney's from 3M huddled around plotting an infringement suit. Jarvis parked the Ford Escort, which was a mid-sized sedan according to Hertz, and unfolded himself from the front seat. He had planned out a clever ploy for getting the proprietor to divulge the information regarding the identity of the owner for Suite 129. Suite 129 was a 4X6 inch metal plate among a hundred others that looked the exact same on the left side of the store where people used almost identical little keys to open them up and collect their mail. The store was neat and clean. Mail was in the boxes by 7:30 a.m. and the last drop-off time was 5:00 pm, said the beautifully printed signs on the wall above the boxes and taped to the counter straight ahead. Another sign hanging from the ceiling said "Beautifully Printed Signs – Custom Made."

The owner/manager of the franchise was pulling on an overhead handle to release plastic peanuts into a box he was filling for a middle-aged man in overalls drumming his fingers on the counter. The packing

material filled a ten-foot wide swath of netting suspended from the ceiling
and a fat hose funneled it straight down when the handle was pulled. The
old guy filling the box had half a dozen of the white ovals clinging to his
plaid shirt and one on his hair.

"Be there in a sec, buddy." He looked from Jarvis to the customer.
"Harry, you don't worry about this. I'll get it all taped up and sent. Bill you
next month." Harry tipped his cap and grunted, heading out undoubtedly
to one of the eleven pickup trucks in the lot.

Todd – that was the name on his badge – interrupted his peanut
dispensing and walked over to Jarvis, dusting off the bits of plastic. "Help
you with something you wanna send?"

Jarvis made his first move, like in a chess game. It was an opening
and if everything went right, he'd be able to get the name of the box owner
before too long. "Well, to tell you the truth, I've kind of got a problem. I
got something in the mail, and it isn't mine, and I want to return it – but
it could be kind of expensive so I thought it would be better to return it
in person." He looked around. "The address was for here, but I kind of
thought it was going to be a store or something."

Todd kept smiling and Jarvis shifted the small plastic bag he carried
from one hand to the other, feeling the weight of the silver cufflinks he'd
bought as cover to show the owner that he was serious. There was also a
fake return address stamp in the bag, to prove he'd actually received the
item from here. It was going to take a little bit of fancy footwork. "It was
Suite 129. No name on it."

"That'd be Hector Gallego. He was just here 'bout fifteen minutes ago.
Here…" Todd pulled a pen from his shirt pocket and jotted something
down on a piece of discarded junk mail. "He probably won't be back 'til
tomorrow, so there's his address and phone number. Just give him a call
and swing by."

Jarvis refrained from gasping or laughing. He took the envelope and
shook Todd's hand. "Well, thanks very much. I'll do that – and give him
this myself." He raised the other hand holding the junk he'd bought at

the Racine airport and turned to the door before Todd could come to his senses and act like someone from LA. Jarvis was in his car and driving toward the hotel he'd book before he turned around to see if Todd was running after him. Nothing.

CHAPTER EIGHTEEN

The house was less modest than the one that exploded in Tarzana. The term "McMansion" leapt to mind. Jarvis cruised by the two-story modern stone residence. A wrought-iron fence protected a semi-circular drive, but more from nosy neighbors than anyone with havoc in mind – this was a home, not a fortress. An almost new Mini Cooper rested on the near side of the driveway. The gate was open. It wasn't the biggest house on the street, nor the smallest. Jarvis pictured Goldilocks sitting in the kitchen. He drove a block past and made a u-turn at the stop sign, parking half a block from the house. The direct approach seemed unwise this time. His shoulder still ached from hitting the ground a split second before the blast a day earlier. Repeating that scene would give him a monstrous headache. He settled down in the rental as best he could and watched the house. Dusk settled and began to be replaced by night.

Three hours later a blue Jaguar pulled up and turned crisply in. The driver emerged after gathering some things from the passenger seat. Jarvis easily watched from fifty feet away. The overlapping beams from the automatic floodlights were brighter than the afternoon sun. The man wore a tailored gray suit that cost more than Jarvis' entire wardrobe. He stood with his back to Jarvis, shifting a leather briefcase from one hand to another and putting a winter coat over his arm. The frost on Jarvis' windshield proved he wasn't in LA. As the man turned and shouldered the car door shut, he pulled from the front seat another case. This one glinted rays from the floodlights and Jarvis admired the clean metallic surface. He didn't need to send a picture to Rayford and the forensics lab to be reasonably confident the case was similar to tangled remnants found in Azad's charred living room. Jarvis quelled the urge to drive up onto the front lawn and pin the guy against the door and pepper him with questions. He decided a more subtle approach would be better. He took the five shot Beretta he'd bought earlier from the Gun 'n Smoke Shop out of the glove compartment and tucked it into his back. The guy with the briefcases turned briefly in his direction, reflexively but without seeing anything, and Jarvis took a mental snapshot. No recognition, nothing at all. Jarvis had never seen the man. Generic olive-complexioned, 55-year-old successful businessman. Or dentist, or terrorist. No way to know, except he was probably carrying a valise containing a poison that had killed at least one person, put Brin near death's door, and led to a young man immolating himself in front of Jarvis. Jarvis slowed his heart a few beats and waited until the man fumbled around with his armloads and keys, finally getting the front door open and slipping inside. Fifteen seconds later, Jarvis was at the window on the East side of the house, furthest from the floodlights and heaviest with shadow.

He was looking into a corridor that ran along the side of the house. The front foyer was straight ahead and a staircase a little to the right. Not that it resembled his modest, relatively shack-like home, but he figured the kitchen was down the corridor, a living room on the other side of the house from where he stood, and bedrooms upstairs. Too big for one person to live in, so there must be a family. Except the hallway was almost devoid of personal effects. No kids' shoes or overcoats, a dearth of women's clutter. Just slightly expensive artwork on the walls within view, nice carpet in the distance, and a distinctively man's touch even in the little he could see. Jarvis started to try the window, but stopped. Not because there was an alarm. Because he wanted to see if the man would blow up the house when he saw Jarvis. Better the direct approach. He went back to the front and knocked loudly on the door. He rang the bell a couple of times, just for good measure. It only took about twenty seconds for the handle to begin to turn.

The man must have been expecting someone. He opened the door willingly and without the hesitation. He held a drink in his hand, heavy glass and ice cubes surrounded by amber liquid. But whoever he was expecting, it wasn't Jarvis. The man's face froze, but did not scream out recognition. More mature and composed – and in control – than the kid in Tarzana. But Jarvis had no doubt the man knew his face as well as the kid had.

"May…may I help you?" He covered well enough to be an actor or excellent liar.

"Yeah, you could, thanks. My car broke down and my cell phone died. Can I use your land line to call triple A?" It was so clichéd Jarvis almost laughed out loud but suppressed it with a smile. The two men looked at one another and both played along despite the absolute transparency with which each knew the surface chatter was hiding some dangerous agenda. Only neither knew what the other was thinking. Jarvis hadn't a clue why this man knew him and had probably sent poison to be used to kill his friend Brin, and the man was unable to fathom how and why Jarvis had appeared at this door.

"Of course, please come in. There is a phone in the living room." Slight accent, Middle Eastern, could be metropolitan Tehran or something in Pakistan. Jarvis' ear was not sufficiently discerning. The guy could have been an Egyptian Pharaoh. "Let me get a phone book so you can get the number." He opened the door wider. Jarvis stepped through but didn't walk far enough ahead that he lost sight of the man.

"Thanks, you're very kind. I'll be just a minute and then get out of your hair." No one commented on the man's baldness.

They walked almost abreast past the staircase and into an enormous living room. The man indicated a chair on one side facing the window that gave a nice view of a rosebush shrouded in light and the hint of a large yard out back. "Just a moment, please. And may I get you some tea? They will undoubtedly take some time to get here."

Jarvis sat and put up a hand. "That would be too much, thank you, I couldn't impose."

"Tut, tut, it is nothing. I will be back in a moment." He stepped behind Jarvis and his footsteps moving away indicated he was not about to impale Jarvis with a knife. Two minutes passed and the footsteps came toward him. Jarvis turned with enough time to counter a blow if it came, but needed only to accept the cordless phone and a slip of paper with an 800 number on it. "Here, my friend, please call and I will be back in a moment with the tea."

Jarvis nodded and hit the Call button for a dial tone. He rang the number and gave his location to the operator along with a detailed description of the nonexistent problem. A truck would be there in 30 – 40 minutes. He hung up as the man returned with a silver tray holding two cups, a large glass samovar, and enough sugar to give most of Wisconsin diabetes. Definitely Persian or Afghani.

"My name is Mr. Marzani. Please, you must call me Zeb." He poured the tea and handed one of the cups to Jarvis.

"Thank you, Zeb. My name is Jarvis." He refrained from adding "as you know." He pretended to take a sip of the tea.

"So tell me, Mr. Jarvis, you are not from Wisconsin?" The accent was melodic. Zeb looked at Jarvis, then off to his right, then above, and then down at the ground. His question seemed rhetorical and it worried Jarvis. Zeb should have been far more curious.

"No, just visiting. I was looking for an old friend." Jarvis had a strategy in mind. He needn't have bothered. There was a flash of movement to his left, the spot Zeb had meticulously avoided looking. Before Jarvis could resolve the image as being of a hand holding something, he felt a tightening around his throat. The wire immediately cut into his neck, but instead of slicing through his windpipe and carotid artery, it just held him in place.

He could feel the presence of a large body behind him, one that apparently moved as silently as a cat but had the heft of a gorilla. The man's forearms held Jarvis against the chair and the wire kept him from struggling. The instantaneous and instinctive realization that he was being held for the moment, not yet murdered, kept him from clawing at the hands and scraping backwards to relieve the pressure.

Zeb remained seated and sipped his tea, which apparently contained no poison. "Why are you here, Mr. Jarvis? Did young Mr. Hekmatier tell you something before he martyred himself? I think not." Zeb was full of rhetorical questions.

Jarvis was pretty sure the questions would eventually require answers, and after that he would be killed. Racine was not where he wanted to die. Jarvis brought the hand holding the steaming cup of tea up and over his head, aiming for where his large captor's head probably was. The yelp of pain and release of pressure around his throat suggested success, though the man did not let go completely. Jarvis pushed backward with his legs, tilting the chair hard into the man's chest. There was a momentary relapse of pain as the wire tightened again with the backward momentum of the bodyguard but it ended as one of the guard's hands released so he could regain his balance. Jarvis assumed the discomfort from the scalding would not last and the man was already reaching for a weapon. Jarvis came out of the chair in a crouch, pulling at his lower back with his right hand. In one continuous move he brought the gun forward and fired three times into the back of the chair. It was mostly upholstery and all three bullets tore through the fabric losing little speed. He'd intended to catch the man in the torso or legs, but when Jarvis had pushed back with the chair it had knocked his attacker onto his backside. He was just getting up as Jarvis fired. One bullet tore into his left eye, another glanced off his forehead leaving just a scratch and the third plunged into this throat. Jarvis stood and was impressed with all the blood pouring out of him. He even admired the Glock in the dead guard's left hand. It was the new model, more expensive than the one Jarvis had at home.

Jarvis turned to Zeb, half expecting to see him holding a detonator. Instead, Zeb looked shocked, but it passed quickly. When Jarvis pointed the gun at his chest, Zeb relaxed. He even smiled.

"Please sit down, Mr. Jarvis. Before you interrogate me, please, finish your tea." The cup had fallen to the floor and Jarvis looked at it and raised his eyebrows. "Well, at least let me have mine before you begin asking your questions." Zeb leaned forward and spooned in half the contents of the sugar dish. Jarvis had seen worse during his tours in Afghanistan.

"Drink slowly. I have a lot of questions." Jarvis sat down in the chair that now had three holes and tufts of material sticking out.

Zeb laughed. "Of course you do." He took a long draw of the tea and pursed his lips as though he'd used lemon juice instead of water to steep the tea. Jarvis caught it too late. Zeb's eyes widened and the cup fell out of his hand. A choking noise emerged, with a little gurgle as a side note, and his eyes rolled up in his head until only whites were showing. He was dead before his forehead smacked into the samovar with a comedic clanging. Jarvis jumped up and reached over as if he was going to make some kind of resuscitative gesture but stopped before wasting any time.

"Goddammit." He put the gun in his belt, in the front in case there were other thugs waiting in the kitchen to pick up where the bodyguard still bleeding on the ground left off. "Goddammit." Jarvis looked around. If the place filled with cops, he'd have a lot of explaining to do and not much to show for it. He walked over to the bodyguard and confirmed all the bleeding was post-mortem. Only thing left to do was toss the place to see if he could figure out why the hell Wisconsin had suddenly become terrorism central.

The kitchen looked like the set from a daytime soap opera. It sparkled from expense and lack of use. He pulled out the drawer that looked like it would contain plastic bags and tin foil. He was right. Pulling a sandwich bag from the unopened box, he went back to the living room and tilted the sugar bowl into the mouth of the bag and shook gently until all the grainy material had been transferred. None had gotten on his hands, but after sealing the bag he returned to the kitchen, washed his hands, and rolled the bag into a ball before encasing it in another. With the deadly material in his pocket and another handwashing, he began his search. Upstairs there were three bedrooms. Only the master looked lived in, but barely. He methodically ransacked the closet, bed, dresser drawers, and found nothing. Next were the less obvious places; corners of the carpet, bedposts, window treatments. Finally, the really clever spots – wall panels, vents, faucets in the bathroom. Everything was clean and boring, as if for show. Jarvis went to each of the other bedrooms and repeated the process. A few minutes into the second bedroom, he heard a horn blaring. It was the guy from AAA.

He worked his way through two closets and the hallway. Nothing escaped his examination. The banister revealed nothing, nor the living room, other than two dead men. The kitchen gave just as little. Foyer, corridor, downstairs bathroom – all clean. Jarvis was getting bored, but not pessimistic. He was about to begin ransacking the garage when he felt a chill. A draft hit his legs and he went to the now-poorly-named living room. The flue was open in the fireplace. A clean, unused fireplace, which is what he would have expected in a show house like this. Except there was some debris beneath the unburned logs. Jarvis pulled out the metal rack and tugged at the uneven stones at the base of the fireplace. They were loose and gave way when he pulled hard. The space beneath was large enough to hold a box the size of a toaster, which is exactly what Jarvis found.

He undid the two clasps holding it shut and lifted back the lid. A thumb drive sat atop a manila envelope. He pulled the second baggie he'd been carrying and turned it inside out, using it as a glove to pick up the drive and turn the bag back right-side out, capturing the device like a dog-walker cleaning up after their charge pooped on the street. He sealed the bag and slipped it into his pockets. Fingerprints might prove interesting. The envelope he took out and opened. There were several sheets of paper, Arabic writing on two and English on the third. Going with the English, he skimmed the material. It didn't make sense, at least not to him. The words seemed random, sets of numbers without context, and spacing and punctuation non traditional. Some kind of code, probably Arabic as well he thought, and the thumb drive would likely be encrypted.

There was a flight in an hour and a quarter. He'd rented the car in his own name and the AAA guy would have it noted as being near the house. Jarvis knew he'd be getting a call about the bodies when they were found. But he didn't have time for Wisconsin police interrogations now. He went back to the dead guy who'd clearly recognized him and rolled the body over to check his wallet. There was cash, credit cards, and various pieces of paper that were not as interesting as the material in the envelope. The obviously fake name would be of no use. The man had a cover and Jarvis would only find out who he really was by figuring out what was on the paper and the flash drive. Jarvis left the house by a back door, avoiding the floodlights as he made his way to his car and drove to the airport.

CHAPTER NINETEEN

I t was after midnight by the time Jarvis collected his car from the Park
One lot next to the Southwest terminal at LAX. The valet had adjusted
his seat, apparently a necessity to drive the car fifty feet to the spot
where it had been sitting for less than a day. Jarvis hit the Memory button,
something he'd figured out after the 20th time this had happened, and settled
in. It would take him about 25 minutes this time of night to get to the east
LA neighborhood he'd punched into the GPS. He put the Glock under the
seat, appreciating the heft and familiarity after using the Beretta earlier.

In the middle of the night the 10 freeway was as empty as any freeway
in Los Angeles ever got and he reached the Florence off-ramp in half the
predicted time. Three turns and half a mile further and he might as well
have been in Beirut. There were more check cashing/payday advance
storefronts and nail salons than streetlights. Trash older than some of the
residents clung to sidewalks. Most of the cars on the street were either ten
years or more older than his, or they were newer and much more expensive
and tricked out. Jarvis turned down an alley to cut across to a small side
street and several large rats scurried out of the beam from the headlights.
As he rolled down the fifty feet of pavement, he passed huddled figures. At
least one was a drug deal, the players not bothering to look up, and he was
pretty sure a guy was getting a blow job from a hooker in one doorway.
He reached the end and turned left, onto a surprising street with several
well-kept homes amid the dotted landscape of drug houses and occasional

abandoned buildings. He pulled into the driveway of one of the former and stopped behind a late-model Charger with rims and a paint job that cost more than a year of Jarvis' payments on the Bimmer. Getting out of the car, his ears were assaulted by at least three different sets of rap music. The house to the left had a party going on; the one across the street looked deserted but the music was louder; and his destination emitted screaming lyrics in a language that wasn't English. He pulled the envelope from the front seat and headed toward the door.

He got as far as the walk leading to the house before a large shadow separated from the darkness by a pickup truck. A slimmer figure moved in from behind Jarvis, who felt more than saw it. His hand reached for the Glock but did not pull it out.

"Yo, mutha fucka, you in the wrong neighborhood!" The high-pitched voice probably led to a lot of schoolyard fights when the monster in front of him was a pre-teen. As the kid got older, the vocal squeal was more likely the instigator of a lot of beat-downs for anyone who said anything. Jarvis' attention was on the young man moving in from behind and not the hulk in front.

"Don' look 'way from me, milkman! I'm talkin' to you. Gimme your wallet or whatever shit you got on you. Maybe them car keys."

Jarvis' plan was to wait as long as necessary before pulling the gun and pointing at the kid behind him who was unaware Jarvis was tracking his every move. There was no one else visible on the street to watch the showdown, but he was sure there were eyes catching every move. The thug in front made a move to pull something from inside his jacket, but Jarvis recognized it as a distraction. The real threat was in his peripheral vision. Jarvis stepped to his left, toward the street, and began to make a move.

The music from the house they stood before suddenly got louder as the front door banged open. Before Jarvis could pull out his gun, a deep voice cut over the music and through the tension.

"Niggers, leave my boy alone. You scarin' all the upscale dudes who comin' to pay their respects."

The kid behind Jarvis laughed, thinking he'd had the white guy cowering. He was completely unaware that the only person in danger was himself.

"Yo, Moose, less' go. I gotta get some In 'n Out burger or I'm gonna pass out." The smaller man walked up to Jarvis and brushed by, but didn't give a shove. The two walked off into the darkness.

Jarvis turned to the house and headed to the door.

"Niggers? They let you get away with that?" He went up the couple of steps to the opening. The man who'd saved the kids the embarrassment of getting shown up on their own street smiled broadly. His olive skin and black hair, bits of premature gray flecking it, would have made him fit into the neighborhood if it weren't so clear he was Middle Eastern.

"Jarvis, amigo, nice to see you. Next time give a ring and I'll lock up the hounds."

Jarvis gave him a hug and Rini kept an arm around his shoulders as he ushered his friend into a living room that was twice as clean as one might have expected from the standard of the neighborhood and filled with the aromas of garlic, linseed, and pot. The couch in the living room contained multi-colored pillows, an expensive silk shawl, and a beautiful black woman so dark Jarvis almost didn't see her. Rini didn't introduce her and she didn't seem offended. The pot came from a very Persian looking bong in her hands.

Rini led him past a bathroom and small study/library that looked precisely as Jarvis had last seen it – tousled, filled with books in many languages spread on the desk and floor, and paintings of Che Guevera and Rosie the Riveter adorning the walls. In the kitchen Rini took a whistling pot off the stove and poured into a large glass bowl with a spout, steam painting droplets on his chin and cheeks. The tea instantly smelled familiar, reaching deep into Jarvi's throat and memory. Rini carried the bowl in two hands; Jarvis picked up the beautifully matching delicate cups and a tin full of sugar. They went back to the living room and the woman scooted over to make room. Rini stayed standing and poured the tea, starting with the spout near the cup and then straightening up. The waterfall he produced found its mark with precision and not a drop spilled as he brought the bowl back down, tilted it back, and repeated the procedure for the second, then third cup. Jarvis used what appeared to be a clean spoon on the misnamed coffee table to scoop three heaping piles of sugar from the tin and transfer them to the cups – three scoops per cup. His teeth ached in anticipation. The music wove between their unspoken ritual and only after the sugar had been stirred and dissolved did Rini sit down, Jarvis on one side, the stunner on the other, and turn to his friend.

"So, J-man, what brings you home?"

Jarvis looked over at Black Beauty and decided she posed no security threat. He opened the envelope and slipped out the two sheets of paper with Arabic writing and put them on the coffee table after moving the cups. "Mean anything to you?"

"Man, you just love me for my polyglotism." Rini opened a drawer under the table and pulled out a pair of heavy black-rimmed reading glasses. Back in Afghanistan he hadn't needed any. One time he'd saved Jarvis from great embarrassment by reading upside down and from about six feet away a note held by an old man whom Jarvis was sure was wearing a suicide vest. The shopping list saved the man's life as Rini translated the spices, fruits, and aphrodisiacs scrawled on the paper and Jarvis' finger was tightening on the trigger. Born in Pakistan, raised for his first ten years in Afghanistan, and a survivor of East Los Angeles for the next thirty years, Rini was the best translator and finder of prohibited alcohol in the entire 101st stationed in the Middle East. He peered at the papers.

"Yeah, there's really no word for it in Farsi, but I'd say the best fit is 'gibberish.' Bunch of random words, some numbers, and the dude was a terrible writer; didn't he use Word Autoformat?"

Jarvis pulled out the English sheet and put it next to the others.

"Yup, same shit as the English. Just junk." He picked up the English sheet and one of the Arabic. "Ya know, though, they're different, but there's some consistency."

Jarvis just nodded and let the guy whose IQ was a couple dozen points higher than the average summertime temperature in Afghanistan mull it over. "It's not total crap." Rini held the papers away from his face, peering over the glasses, then brought them in close. He got up and went deeper into the house. Jarvis spent the couple of minutes watching the girl. She'd curled up in a corner of the couch with a gossip rag in her hands, but he could see her eyes were unfocused as they pointed at the pages. He was pretty sure if he yelled "fire!" she'd just smile and look for a joint to light with it. She seemed totally oblivious yet entirely aware of him. Rini came back carrying a small book with a worn leather cover and some sheets of blank paper. Stepping over the table to get back to his seat between Jarvis and the girl, he laid the book in his lap and arranged the papers on the table top.

Rini began flipping through the book, stopping periodically and jotting down a few words in English and a few in Arabic. He consulted the pages Jarvis had brought. Back and forth, scribbling and reading. Jarvis watched quietly for a few minutes until Rini sat back and took the glasses off. Twirling them in one hand, he smiled at Jarvis.

"Man, this is very cool. It's kind of a cypher, not real complicated, but kinda smart." He held up the book. "Verses from the Quran, picking out specific words and numbers. Kinda hard to do since there's so many different translations, but it only uses sections that are old and don't change from one to the other. Stuff everyone agrees on."

Jarvis looked at the English scribble Rini had made. It made sense to his eye – a name and address, in Boston. Some other numbers next to it that didn't mean anything, at least not yet.

"Not sure why some is in English and some in Farsi, but it's all the same kind of code. I'd need an hour or so to get it all straightened out. You want a beer?" Rini was already up and heading to the kitchen. Jarvis picked up the papers. Calculating from what Rini had already done, he guessed there were about two dozen names and locations. The numbers next to them were probably amounts of poison sent to each. Racine was the hub and Jarvis was looking at the spokes – poison-tipped spokes that could kill a lot of people. When Rini came back, Jarvis drank deeply from the Corona bottle and clapped his friend on the shoulder.

"Thanks, buddy. I'm gonna owe you one."

Rini was already back at work and the girl was softly snoring, her head leaning far back on the arm of the sofa. "Ain't nothin', man. You already owe me too much to add another."

Jarvis closed his eyes and pictured the old woman in the grocery store, dead on the floor. His mind drifted to Brin, a breathing tube keeping his lungs moving up and down. Just before he dozed off, Jarvis began to compose a stanza, years of habit hard to break even if the one hour of sleep he'd be getting this night was on a crowded couch in a neighborhood he'd hesitate to walk through at mid-day. He'd just rhymed the second couplet when his mind hit REM and he started dreaming furiously. When he woke just under an hour later to the sounds of laughter and kissing, the poem had dissipated.

Rini and the woman were too stoned to make a real go of it, but Rini was doing his best. When he saw Jarvis quickly emerge from sleep, he left his hand on the girl's breast but gestured at the papers on the table with the other.

"'bout a dozen cities there, couple with more than one name. You've got some travelin' to do." The girl pulled his face back to her so she could get another kiss. Jarvis picked up the couple of sheets that had Rini's handwriting. He scanned the list of cities and the names next to them. The bigger cities, New York and Boston and DC, had two or three names and the numbers were higher for what were probably the units of poison. Smaller, second-rate cities like Des Moines and Cedar Rapids and Detroit had just one name. Jarvis scanned the non-alphabetical list. He found Los Angeles. Two names. One was of the dead young man he'd seen annihilated just the other day. The second was a woman's name. Her address was in a different part of town – West side of LA, nearer to Jarvis. He folded the papers and stood.

"Seriously, man, I owe you."

Rini waved a hand without turning around. He unlocked lips with the woman. "You let me know you need any more help on this." The woman looked over Rini's bent head and gave Jarvis a very clearly inviting look. Jarvis smiled his broadest, sexiest grin, which immediately led to her looking back at Rini and pulling his head down to her chest. Jarvis laughed and headed to the door, refreshed and ready to go find the address in Westwood his friend had deciphered.

CHAPTER TWENTY

3:00 a.m. on a Tuesday morning and the only people on Wilshire Boulevard were newspaper deliverers, trash haulers, grocery store truckers, and insomniacs. Jarvis turned up Gayley, one of the side streets just West of UCLA and took the windy road past a mix of frat houses, off-campus apartments, and regular family homes. Half a block south of Sunset Boulevard he turned left onto a small side street and squinted at the faded numbers painted on the curb in front of the houses. 12416 Clennan looked like a rental that had been used by groups of students moving in and out once a year for at least a decade. No lawn to speak of, walls in want of paint, and a roof that was a year or two past needing replacing. One car, an old Corolla, blocked the driveway. A new motorcycle leaned against the slightly warped garage door. Jarvis drove past and turned around in a driveway two blocks down, killed the lights, and came toward the house from the other side of the street. He parked across and cut the engine. The sounds of pre-dawn seeped through the window. He wouldn't make the mistake of knocking on the door.

Talk radio kept him company for the next three hours. He only had to pee in the large Pepsi bottle once. A little after six, a few cars on the block slid past with early risers and two joggers buzzed by, not giving him a glance. An hour later the door to the house opened and a college-aged young man, blonde and thin, came out. He backed the Toyota out and drove toward Sunset. Jarvis did not follow. Another hour passed and the door opened again. This kid was older, maybe a few years into his twenties. Dark hair, olive complexion, handsome and strong. He looked familiar, but not from the past – more recent. Jarvis couldn't place him. The young man pulled on a helmet that didn't cover his face and slung a backpack over his shoulder. When he gently rolled the motorcycle into the street and gunned it a little, Jarvis was pulling out of his spot.

The motorcyclist drove as though he'd just read the DMV rule book and was getting graded. It made him easy to follow. Jarvis hit speed dial on his phone and wasn't surprised when Rayford answered on the first ring.

"Where've you been?" He sounded as if he hadn't had a good clue on the killing since last he saw Jarvis.

"I had to make a quick trip to Wisconsin."

"Why the hell did you go there? No way you're working on another case. What's the connection?"

Jarvis turned left on Sunset and followed the bike along the windy road toward Pacific Palisades and the ocean. "Do you have any friends in the FBI?"

The derisive snort was as effective as if Rayford had been in the car with him. "This isn't some tv show where every cop has a buddy who runs the local office of a federal agency. I'm just a city detective." Jarvis sped up a little as the guy on the bike showed the first signs of exuberance by taking the twists on Sunset with a little extra gas. Rayford ended the pause. "My wife's sister is married to a guy in the LA field office. What the hell do you need the FBI for?"

Jarvis kept a hundred feet back from the motorcycle. The traffic was moderate and there weren't too many lights. If the kid turned off while he was around a curve, Jarvis would be able to see him up the side street in plenty of time. "I think the guy I visited in Racine was distributing doses of a poison. There's a list. You always curse so much in the morning?"

Rayford drew in his breath audibly. "You think this is some sort of home grown terrorism? Jesus, it isn't enough that I've got a murder, an attempted, and some kid who blew himself up."

"Well, it may not be home grown." He let that sit. "The list I've got is in English and Arabic."

"Shit. What about the guy you got it from? Is he talking"

Jarvis laughed to himself. "Nah, he won't be able to make any statements. I had to leave pretty quick. I'll probably need to have a chat with your FBI buddy about that."

"Shit. Okay, yeah, I'm cursing a lot, but you're bringing it on. Come on in so we can talk about this."

Jarvis rounded a bend and saw the motorcycle making a turn onto Amalfi Drive. He slowed and signaled, irritating the Escalade behind him that thought 65 in a 35 mph zone was not only reasonable but mandatory. "I'm in the middle of something, but I'll swing by when done."

"'Something'? Is it something I should be worried about seeing a report on later?" Irritated, but also an offer of help. "Tell me where you are."

"I'll be at the precinct in an hour. I'll fill you in." He disconnected and pulled to the side of the street as the motorcycle turned right on Pavia Rd and then left into one of the few modest houses on the street. The kid parked and walked to the front door, helmet and backpack still on. He opened the door without ringing or knocking and closed it behind him. Two minutes later he came out, helmet in his hand and no backpack. Jarvis flashed on the face. He'd seen it yesterday morning, early. Coming back from the bathroom at Jerry's deli to his table. He pictured the half dozen cups of coffee he'd drank and the full cup he'd almost sipped before leaving. The little prick had tried to poison him. Exact same as Brin. Jarvis' hands tightened on the steering wheel but he stayed put.

The kid burned just a little rubber coming up the street and passed Jarvis without a glance. Jarvis didn't give a single thought to following him, though fantasized about ripping his head off. He knew where to find him, and he would. Later. Five minutes passed and the front door opened again. A large, unpleasant man emerged. He wore khaki pants and a familiar shirt, black with a logo, and Jarvis couldn't place it. The backpack rested on his shoulder. He took a beaten up ten speed that had been leaning against the side of the house and swung a leg over. He pedaled the twenty feet down Pavia and then right on Amalfi, not passing Jarvis' car. His head was shaved and Jarvis could count the folds where his neck bunched. If he'd been a phrenologist, Jarvis could have read the bumps. The bicyclist was probably no more than 30 years old, but exuded the spite and anger of a much older, more cynical man. As he turned onto Amalfi and came within twenty feet of Jarvis, the logo on his shirt was easy to read. He worked at the Coffee Bean and Tea Leaf. He pedaled down Amalfi and Jarvis followed from 100 feet away, watching him turn right onto Sunset and toward the affluent beach town of Pacific Palisades. It was a small city that catered to tourists and locals, with plenty of antique shops, fancy restaurants, and coffee houses. Including a Coffee Bean. Jarvis waited until the bike was far enough away that he could get up to full speed when he passed. When the barista arrived and parked his bike on a newly painted rack on the sidewalk, Jarvis was already in the coffee shop holding a large Colombian drip.

Larry had clipped a black badge with gold lettering onto his chest – letting the waiting customers know they should call him Larry and confirming to Jarvis that the brooding thug was a douchebag. He was holding the backpack in both hands and pushed through the swinging door into the back, returning a minute later without the pack and carrying a carton of powdered vanilla flavoring favored by the Coffee Bean cognoscenti. Peete's used real vanilla and Jarvis scoffed at the substitute Larry put on a shelf below the prep counter. He also noticed Larry seemed a little excited to be getting ready to take orders from a bunch of sixteen year olds whose allowance was probably double his monthly wage. He tapped a tall black guy on the shoulder and replaced him as the drink maker. Larry watched the guy head out the front door, hauling a bag of trash and pulling a cigarette out of his pocket. The girl at the register called out a few orders and Larry unintentionally ignored her because he was looking at the clock above the door so hard. Jarvis followed his gaze. It was quarter to eight. He watched Larry glare at the girl when she scolded him with her tone in repeating the order and he began to mix the drinks. A couple of hot, complicated lattes and three large drips. One blended frapped thing and then a few hot chocolates and Jarvis lost track. Larry kept looking at the clock. It finally turned eight and Larry's gazed lowered from above the door to the sidewalk outside. As if on cue, a gaggle of pre-teens, five or six –it was hard to count, they moved and reconfigured so quickly – swept into the coffee shop. They giggled and laughed and Jarvis knew in Larry's mind every snicker or whoop was directed at him, was taunting him, even though they probably didn't even notice he existed. At least two of the girls ordered simultaneously, spitting out more than a dozen drinks, and Larry had already set up the four-cups-each carry-all cartons. They were regulars. He started steaming milk and gathering ice and coffee. Hot and cold drinks, for themselves and probably a couple of friends at school and maybe a mom or two car-pooling. One girl pulled a credit card from the pocket of her uniform and handed it to the girl while still giggling and managing to text with the other hand. Jarvis watched Larry. While steam was rising and blenders whirring, he passed over the glass container of off-white vanilla powder in front of him and bent down to the shelf underneath. He came back up with a large scoop, full to the brim, and started to distribute some into most of the cups and into the blender. Jarvis stiffened. Larry emptied the scoop and returned it under the counter, wiping his hands off on the green apron and rinsing them quickly but vigorously under running water in the sink next to the blender. With a series of flourishes that belied his otherwise hulking posture, he put dollops of foam where they belonged, poured frozen frappe into plastic cups, and lidded them all rapidly. He transferred the drinks to the cartons and lined them up on the pick-up counter. The girls collected them, continuing to ignore Larry as they inhabited a universe of their own making, and waltzed in pairs and triples out the door. The entire operation took under two minutes.

Jarvis watched the girls gather on the sidewalk and begin to move as a herd toward a waiting minivan. He looked back at the counter. Larry watched the girls too, an almost hungry look in his eyes though not leering or yearning. It was more of anticipation. His gazed shifted for a moment and involuntarily swept the coffee shop and as he passed Jarvis their eyes locked. There was a visceral, electric instant of recognition – not that he knew Jarvis or his face, as the first kid and the dealer in Racine had, but the kind of recognition a child makes when he has a hand in the cookie jar and an adult walks in. Or the gut-wrenching moment when a shoplifter realizes a security guard is looking directly at the cashmere sweater he's stuffed in his pants. Larry, already starting to take his apron off in preparation for a planned escape now that he'd played his final part in some plan of which he was a minor but deadly player, bolted for the back door. Jarvis was up before Larry'd made it halfway and he took a step toward the counter, but stopped and looked outside. The girls had resumed their movement to the van. One girl, the chattiest one during the ordering and waiting phase, was pulling a cold drink from one of the cardboard trays. She wrestled with it, tightly squeezed into a space too small for it. Jarvis changed his forward movement and hit the door hard, spilling onto the sidewalk and running the dozen steps to the girls. With a boxer's precision he punched the carriers from the hands of two of the girls, sending the drinks flying away from them and spilling mid-air before slamming against the closed door of the minivan. In one continuous motion, he slapped the drink from the hand of the girl who'd managed to get it from the carrier a second earlier and was bringing the straw to her lips. Shrieks arose and Jarvis was hit with a mix of icy cold frappe and droplets of steaming espresso as his momentum carried him into the mix of airborne liquids.

"Call the cops, now!" Jarvis shouted. The mother driving the van had more sense than the girls and was halfway out the driver's seat. Instead of panicking or berating the lunatic who'd accosted the girls – whose shrieks were more of excitement than fear and who were already calling Jarvis a variety of colorful euphemisms that seemed to come from a dialect he didn't speak – the woman pulled out her cell phone. She recognized the authority in his voice.

Jarvis turned back to the coffee shop and looked for the bike. It was still there. Larry was on foot. Jarvis ran quickly, efficiently around the back of the shop and could see Larry rumbling through the parking lot toward the grocery store on the far side. He was almost a hundred feet ahead. Jarvis adjusted his angle and put on some speed. His arms pumped and he established the rhythm of a sprint. If Larry got inside the large Ralph's he'd be harder to find and might be the kind of moron to take a hostage. Jarvis raced along a line of parked cars and imagined slamming Larry to the ground, grinding his face into the tar surface and beating the shit out of him until the cops arrived. He gained on him. Without warning the bumper of a car was blocking Jarvis' way. The silent electric motor in the hybrid gave no aural warning before cutting him off. He rolled to his left in a flash, hitting the back window and losing some speed but not his balance. He could hear the shouts of surprise and anger from inside the tiny Prius. Larry had picked up a few steps and Jarvis had to regain his speed. He was closing in and Larry looked back; the hairs on his neck must have stood up, like the prey in a National Geographic show feeling the approach of a hungry carnivore. He saw Jarvis and looked in front to gauge whether he'd make the grocery store door twenty feet away. His chances were good. Larry didn't bother to check both ways before crossing the nearly empty lane in front of the store. So he didn't see the motorcycle approaching slowly from his right. The driver gunned the engine and Jarvis was still thirty feet away when he saw it buzzing toward Larry, who got halfway across the lane. Six more feet to the sidewalk and the safety of the produce section. The rider on the motorcycle swung a baseball bat he was carrying while accelerating from twenty to forty miles per hour with the help of every horse in the 750cc engine. Jarvis heard the thud of the bat on Larry's skull and knew the thug was brain dead before the signals could reach there and scream in protest. Larry spun briefly to his left and crumpled to the ground, coming to a rest as the motorcycle whipped through a stop sign and grazed an elderly man carrying a single, heavy bag of groceries. It was the same motorcycle Jarvis had followed that morning. The driver was the kid he'd recognized from Jerry's Deli.

Jarvis got to Larry's body but did not slow down. He turned left toward the motorcycle. The kid tossed the bat off to the side. He goosed the gas and took one look back at Jarvis. Jarvis couldn't tell whether he was laughing or fearful. It didn't matter, as whatever look he wore disappeared when the SUV slammed into him. The woman behind the wheel looked up from the text she was reading, unaware she'd been going through the parking lot at 25 miles an hour, or that she'd ignored the stop sign gating traffic leaving the lot. Her initial irritation at bumping into the rear of a car was replaced by the horror of a body sprawled on her hood. Blood mixed with the drops of water from her recent car wash. Jarvis got there as she finally managed to parse the scene and turn the engine off. He rolled the guy off the hood, unconcerned about any permanent spinal injury – he just needed the guy alive and able to talk. The first part looked pretty good; the second was up in the air.

The faint whine of a police siren wafted over the sounds of people gasping and the motorcycle's engine still growling. The kid was out cold. Jarvis pulled out his phone and hit the last number dialed.

"I think I've got something. Maybe you should swing by Pacific Palisades' quaint little police station."

Rayford covered the 12 miles in fourteen minutes, heavy traffic offering no obstacle.

CHAPTER TWENTY-ONE

Jarvis was having coffee with the duty cop, sitting in an office much nicer than anything in downtown LA. There was no detective squad in the Palisades, just some good cops who liked to serve a population that didn't see a lot of murders or major felonies. For some inexplicable reason they had a state-of-the-art forensics collection department. The technicians were back at the scene, scraping samples of coffee and frappucino off the sidewalk while tourists looked on. Larry the poisoner was on a gurney in the back of one ambulance and the kid who'd smashed Larry's head in was in another heading toward Cedars Sinai. When Jarvis had left, it wasn't looking too good.

Rayford came into the office aggressively. "I've got a couple of detectives on their way, and a guy meeting the ambulance at the hospital. Wanna tell me what the hell happened?" The question was meant for Jarvis and the local cop didn't mind letting him answer. He blew into the mug emblazoned with Best Dad Ever.

"The dead guy tried to poison a pack of young girls, probably the same stuff they used on Brin. The kid on the motorcycle provided it. I saw him take it to the guy this morning."

Rayford's face got a little redder. "And you're telling me this now? Any reason we didn't have this conversation a couple of hours ago?"

Jarvis got up, holding the mug they'd let him use. It said Best Cop Ever. "Yeah, let's go have a chat with your FBI friend. He'll want to hear this." He looked Rayford over, unimpressed by the fury but sympathetic. "There's a good chance you could get your gold shield with this." He sipped from the cup and put it on the edge of the desk. "I just want to find who did this to Brin."

He shook the local cop's hand. "Hey, Bill, thanks for the coffee. Let me know if you need anything else. Just call." The cop nodded. He didn't argue about wanting to be in on the case more than just doing clean-up on Larry and the guy who'd killed him. That was plenty of excitement.

Rayford looked at the cop. A couple of breaths calmed him down. "Sergeant, my guys'll be here soon. They'll work with you on the details." Another nod from the cop and Jarvis and Rayford left.

They were silent until the parking lot. Jarvis understood the detective's frustration. The death of the woman at the grocery store, Brin's near murder, the exploding house, and now the mess in the Palisades parking lot all reflected on him. Jarvis felt sorry for him, which he hid. "I found a list when I was in Racine. Things got complicated before I found it." He gave Rayford a minute to ask what was meant by "complicated" and the detective passed. "Part of it was in English, the rest in Arabic." They arrived at Jarvis' car. "It was in code. A buddy of mine broke it."

"That's a lot going on in less than 24 hours."

"Yeah. The kid who blew himself up yesterday was on the list. And the guy on the motorcycle." Jarvis reached into the car and pulled out an unopened envelope. "Here's a copy of the list."

Rayford didn't take it. "A copy?"

"It's got all the information. I think your brother-in-law will want to take a look. I can probably get hold of the original if he needs it." Jarvis smiled, unreturned by Rayford.

"How exactly did you find it? Who'd you get it from?"

Jarvis shook his head. "No one you'll be able to talk to. They knew me, too, like the dead kid."

Rayford's patience ebbed. "Jesus, what's going on here? Are there going to be more of these?"

Jarvis leaned back against his car and crossed his arms. "I don't know what the hell's going on, but I think someone is distributing a fast-acting chemical weapon to operatives in different parts of the country. The kid in Tarzana, the guy here, they were part of that. The list has the rest. I didn't get to interrogate the guy in Wisconsin who I think is shipping the stuff out. He didn't seem to be very talkative while we were together."

Rayford rubbed his face. "This is way out of my jurisdiction. I don't wanna lose my cases to the Feds, brother-in-law or not, but I need help. There's an anti-terror department in LAPD. I'll make the call."

He pulled out his phone but stopped. "You know you're going to have to back off. You can't be mixed up in this. They'll run all over you – pull your license if you get in the way."

Jarvis stood and went around the door to get in the car. "All the guys I've met were Middle Eastern. They knew me. They must've known Brin. And we were in the Gulf together. It's no coincidence. This is going federal, but I'm in it either way." He started the car. "You need me, call. But you probably don't want to get too close."

Rayford started to argue, and stopped. "We'll have a sit-down with my brother-in-law, at least share the information. Then we'll see."

Jarvis closed the door and backed out of the spot. Another envelope containing the original sheets he got in Racine sat on the passenger seat. There were three pieces of paper in it. The envelope he'd given Rayford held two sheets.

CHAPTER TWENTY-TWO

J arvis held back one page because it contained a name he recognized. All the others would be hard to find by the FBI and cops – word had probably gone out about the explosion in Tarzana. And the deaths at the distribution center in Racine. The folly at the coffee shop would seal it and whoever was calling the shots would tell the other cells around the country to go underground. But only for a while. Once the investigation failed and attention turned to other news headlines, the poisoning would start again. Jarvis could stop it.

He headed home to pack a bag. He could make the 2:00 pm flight to JFK if he hurried. A black SUV parked in his driveway made him think the 7 o'clock non-stop was more likely. The front seat was empty; at least it appeared to be as Jarvis squinted through the tinted windows. The front door of his house, though, was open. The government plates on the SUV weren't forged so he left the Glock on his hip and went inside. He expected one Fed to be standing off to the side, positioned behind anyone coming into the room. The partner would be straight ahead, facing the door. They'd be cautious, but not paranoid since Rayford would have given them a heads-up on who Jarvis was. He swiveled his head left and right as he walked in. There was no one. Only one man, wearing a standard issue black suit, lace-up shoes, and black tie, sitting at Jarvis' small living room table blowing steam rising from a mug. It was Jarvis' favorite Colombian blend. The Fed's sunglasses were on the table and he sat with his side toward Jarvis instead of facing him. His knees were bent as he blew the steam and Jarvis caught a glimpse of checkered socks, black and gray and white. Not standard issue. The whole tableau was the equivalent of a lion rolling over on its back, exposing its belly to show vulnerability – to show trust.

"Can I get you a scone to go with that?"

The Fed looked up and over, as though he hadn't heard Jarvis' car pull up and every step he'd taken since. "I checked. Only some stale Oreos in the top shelf of the pantry."

Jarvis snickered. "They've been there since I moved in. Help yourself." He went into the kitchen and poured a mug of his own. There was an easy silence. Coming back to the dining room he took the seat to the agent's left. "Should I ask for a warrant? Or is breaking and entering SOP for Feds now?"

Leaning back in the chair, the black suit smiled. "Ahh, c'mon, the door was practically unlocked."

"So, FBI? NSA? Girl Scouts?"

"Hey, if I were the Girl Scouts I'd've brought better cookies." He looked Jarvis up and down. "Timmons. Anthony. Homeland Security. Bet that was your next guess." Timmons pulled out an ID wallet from his inside jacket pocket and flashed it briefly. Jarvis didn't look. Everything about Timmons screamed legitimacy.

"You guys move pretty quickly."

Timmons drank some more coffee, appreciatively. "Yeah, we got a flag when the old woman keeled over, plus the little fireworks in Tarzana. This morning the FBI station chief in town got the word from some local cop. Seemed to piece together pretty easily. Except for you."

Jarvis nodded.

Timmons leaned back and crossed his hands on his stomach. He looked at Jarvis a long time. Jarvis managed to still his racing heart. Or at least to keep from laughing at the intimidation attempt. He held the agent's stare, softly and unthreateningly, but inexorably. "I get that you're a war hero or something. And I get that your pal Brin is important enough to you that revenge seems like a natural course of action." He said 'course of action' as if he were teaching a class on business practices. "But you've already gotten yourself in pretty deep." Jarvis noted that 'pretty' seemed to be Timmons' favorite adverb. "Could be some trouble for you, going cowboy in the Palisades." Timmons looked for a reaction. Jarvis disappointed him. The disappointment elicited a sigh.

Jarvis drank some more of the coffee. So did Timmons.

"Y'know, a Fed trying to get to the bottom of this might want to haul you in for some serious questioning. Here in LA," and he paused for effect, "or out in Racine."

"You guys work really fast..." Jarvis assumed his guest knew about everything he'd done in the last forty-eight hours. "So what would keep that agent from wanting me to spend my evening in an interrogation room?"

Timmons smiled warmly. "Well, it'd be more than an evening, probably a few days, and might just result in the loss of a license to practice being a private detective here in California. Or anywhere covered by Homeland Security. And it's a pretty big homeland."

"I was thinking of making muffins, Special Agent. Would you like blueberry or banana nut?"

This got a laugh and Timmons came forward, setting the mug down on the table a little harder than he needed to. "Jarvis, do us both a favor – you more than me – stay outta the way. If this is a terror cell, you're gonna get stung hard if you obstruct or even look like you are. Let us do our jobs."

Timmons took another sip and stood. He slipped a card from his pocket and balanced it on top of the mug. "Give a ring if you think of anything you didn't tell the locals. Or if you get itchy to go out and try to do something to help your pal. I'll talk you out of it."

Jarvis let the Fed find his way out. He waited to hear the heavy thrum of the engine work its way down the street before he got up and headed upstairs to pack his bag. He could still make the early evening flight to NYC. Timmons' card went in his back pocket.

CHAPTER TWENTY-THREE

Tail winds cut thirty-five minutes off the flight. The taxi dropped Jarvis off on 57th between Sixth and Seventh Avenues. The back entrance to the Parker Meridien on 57th St. was subtle. A short awning protected an automatic sliding glass door. The cool autumn air on the street was immediately repelled by the blast of heat emerging as the doors slid open. The entry fed into a small vestibule with a second set of glass doors which didn't open until the first had closed behind a visitor, like a bank trying to ensure a horde of robbers didn't come bursting in at once. Instead, the second door opened into a narrow café lined on either side by dark, heavy furniture – benches and stuffed chairs – backed against walls. Even in the brightest of midday suns, it was dim and intimate. Tourists and locals came for sanctuary or temporary escape, sipping mixed drinks or hand-made hot chocolate. The path between the two sets of seating was narrow enough that two people walking abreast would barely miss brushing the knees of patrons. It was crowded, despite the late hour. Jarvis strode through and as he passed the bar to his left in the middle of the café, he nodded to the old man who'd worked there for a decade. As he reached the other end and was about to step through the open wrought iron doors leading into the cavernous hotel lobby, the waitress who'd been taking the order of a young couple at the last table stood. She turned just as he passed and they locked eyes. Neither stopped, but both smiled. He whispered as he passed.

"Penny."

She stepped past him in the opposite direction. "Jarvis."

He carried the smile along the marble floor and to the registration desk. The Dutch girl tapping on a computer looked up and smiled.

"I have a reservation for this evening. Maybe two nights. Jarvis." He pulled out a credit card.

"Yes, Mr. Jarvis. I have you in a Delightful Park View room, but was able to upgrade you to a Junior Suite, if that is acceptable."

"Yes, that is acceptable." He waved off the bellman after slipping him a five. The girl swiped his credit card and handed it back with two room keys and another huge smile.

"I hope you have a wonderful stay. My name is Jasmine. Please don't hesitate to call if there is anything I can do."

She was at least five years too young for the offer to mean anything other than excellent customer service and Jarvis avoided leering. He returned the smile and headed to the elevators. The 19th floor was for Platinum members of the hotel chain's frequent-guest program. Membership had its rewards. A private salon just off the elevator served everything from light breakfast to late night drinks – self-serve after 9:00 p.m. It was close to 12:30 a.m. and Jarvis opened the club room door with his key and found the fridge with a very cold Rolling Rock waiting. He carried it back to his suite which, despite the Junior moniker, was as big as his living room at home. Tossing his bag on the bed he twisted open the beer and sat in a newly upholstered chair facing a television screen larger than the one at home. He quickly found ESPN and put his feet up on the ottoman. Only the light from Sports Center and a glimmer of lamps in the park across the street nineteen stories below shining through the drapes cut the darkness of the room. He finished the beer and relaxed as the hockey highlights played. Sleep was still at least a couple hours away. As the credits ran across the screen, he got up and put the room keys in his back pocket. The ride down to the lobby was unbroken, as if he were the only resident in the enormous hotel. The narrow café had cleared out a little and he found a table closer to the outside door. His waitress started to come over from the bar and Penny tapped her on the shoulder. A brief conversation ensued and when the horse-trading ended he was smiling up at her as she put a scotch, neat, on the low table in front of him.

"I missed your call last week." There was no rancor in her voice, only playfulness. He hadn't called. Not last week and not since he'd been in NYC three months ago. But they'd already been through all that after the first time they'd met and he hadn't called the next day or when he'd returned to LA. Nor had she. Now it was a rhythm and neither one minded.

"Machine must have been broken."

She laughed. Only a few years older than front-desk Jasmine, she teased him. "What kind of machine? Oh, you mean one of those olden thingies, before voice mail."

He avoided making a crack and instead sipped the scotch. She bent down so her face was close to his and asked if she could get him anything else. Tiny, exquisite earrings caught the light from a chandelier above. The earrings he'd sent to her a few weeks earlier, making sure they arrived on her birthday. Casual didn't equal meaningless, no matter how infrequently he saw her.

"No, I'm good. Got everything I need right now."

Her laugh was a burst of warm, sweet air. She turned gracefully and put the leather folder containing the bill on the table. He watched her go and sipped again, two great pleasures. Signing his name and over tipping, he finished the scotch over the next few minutes and went back to his room.

He was ten minutes into a CNN broadcast at a little after 2:00 a.m. when he heard the soft rustle of a key card in the locking mechanism and the handle gently turn. He feigned sleep until he felt the weight of a knee on the bed next to him. With a sudden lunge, he sat upright and took her into his arms, startling Penny enough to elicit a squeal of surprise and then something more.

"Thank you for the earrings," she murmured into his neck as she melted to him.

Without taking his hands off her back, pulling her closer to him, Jarvis flipped off the television. The heavy white comforter cushioned their weight as he spun their bodies and suddenly he was on top of her, looming and predatory. She laid back and he leaned in close, kissing her neck, her collarbone, the round of her shoulder.

"I miss New York sometimes." He began to unbutton the starkly white shirt she wore in the café. She reached in with both hands and pulled the shirt apart, the sound of threads straining to hold buttons in place popping in succession. He laughed and ran a finger gently along the thin lace at the top of her bra. Jarvis made a guttural sound and he kissed the soft skin above one breast and she let out a breath.

The lights stayed on and an hour later Penny slept deeply curled in one corner of the bed, her back pressed against Jarvis' torso. His hands were behind his head and he stared into the ceiling. Brin and the name of the man he was here to see consumed his thoughts. Deep relaxation embraced him and gave him focus. Every so often, there was no sleep at all, not even the single hour that sustained him. It gave him great clarity when it happened, but also an edgy emotional state the next day. He listened to Penny breath, shallow and regular, as he planned his visit in a few hours to the loft in Greenwich Village.

CHAPTER TWENTY-FOUR

By 5:30 Jarvis was in the Starbucks across the street while Penny slept deeply, sprawled across the bed. He didn't need to look at the address on the sheet in his coat pocket. Three years earlier he'd been in NYC tracking a teenager who'd left LA either to make it on Broadway or punish her parents for being overly indulgent. She was staying with two other runaways and a guy who sold heroin during the day and beer in a dump on Houston St. at night. Skipping the subtleties, Jarvis had punched the guy in the nose hard enough to feel gristle dislodging and dragged the girl out by the scruff of her neck. She mewed and howled, but didn't really resist – he could sense relief under the protestations and unwashed hair. He was making his way down the hallway of the pre-war three story walk-up with the girl in tow when a door opened. A man popped his head out to check on the commotion and his eyes met Jarvis'. They recognized one another instantly. The man wasn't sporting a beard anymore and the Kalashnikov rifle was missing but Jarvis would know Mohan even if he'd been wearing a Halloween mask. The man pulled back quickly. Jarvis lengthened his stride, which resulted in the girl having to move her legs comically fast to keep up. He put a foot in Mohan's door before it could close. He didn't really want to have a chat with the man he'd last seen in an interrogation room in Afghanistan but he also didn't want to be shot in the back. This was one of those small-world coincidences he could have done without.

The door popped open easily because Mohan had pushed it shut quickly and moved back into the apartment before making sure it had latched. Jarvis had a hand on the borrowed gun in his belt, the other pushing the girl to the wall in the corridor. He didn't draw the gun. He saw Mohan in the middle of the one-room studio, heading toward a closet on the other side.

"How 'bout you just stay right there." Both stood still, the tableau interrupted only by the girl starting to whine that she was going to run away. Jarvis kept his eyes on the man.

"What are you going to do?" There was fear in the voice, stronger than the bluster of confidence Mohan was trying to convey.

Jarvis pulled the girl in from the hallway and pointed her to a chair on the right. "Sit." She opened her mouth but quietly sat. "What're you doing here, Mohan? You involved in this shit with the girls?"

No answer.   Jarvis put his hand more firmly on the .38 but did not pull it – the gesture was enough. "How's your leg?" It had been more than half a decade since Jarvis had shot Mohan while freeing Brin. Mohan wasn't holding the camera, or a blade to cut off Brin's head. He was just an asshole with a gun standing around and puffing out his chest. Jarvis had seen him being interrogated and hadn't been impressed with the man's intelligence or commitment.

Mohan's initial fear was subsiding and mostly what was left was hate. "Fuck you, Jarvis. You can't do anything here, I am not a prisoner of your shit country now."

Jarvis nodded. "Looks like you're doing pretty well for yourself." He looked around the room that resembled a junkie's shooting gallery more than a living space.   The girl was confused. She looked at Jarvis' hand, still on the gun. Like a tennis match, she shifted back to the man in the middle of the room who'd been heading to an open closet. "Why don't you go ahead and grab whatever you were going to get from in there?" Jarvis pointed his head to the junk-filled closet.

Mohan's face began to set like cement. Jarvis had seen the transition before on the faces of Mujahedeen in the street when an American walked by. Jarvis pulled his .38 out smoothly without looking away from Mohan. The girl gave a little screech and curled up in the chair. Mohan's eyes widened and for an instant he was a wild animal, deciding to attack rather than retreat. Momentum teetered in the room and he shifted his weight unconsciously toward the closet. Jarvis flicked off the safety hard, making a clicking noise that filled the room. Mohan's eyes transformed the animal anger into plain old fear and he was once again the cowardly accessory to an almost-murder in a basement in Kandahar.

"You have the number of Immigration? Thought I'd give them a call."

Mohan spit on the ground, but not too close to Jarvis. "I am legal, pig. You cannot harm me."

Jarvis laughed, the absurdity of the comment making even the trembling girl pay attention. Talking to the girl but looking at Mohan, "Go into the hall. Don't go past the stairs." He left the safety off the gun and walked backwards to the door as the girl scurried out.

"See you again, I hope."

Mohan couldn't answer. He half-growled something in Arabic but didn't move. Jarvis pulled the door closed as he left and half carried the girl out to the street.

It was three years later now and the building looked exactly the same, except for three more years of grime and neglect. The address on the sheet he'd gotten in Racine was the same building, but different apartment. Maybe Mohan was moving up in the world. Standing outside, Jarvis pushed in the door at the top of a half dozen red stone steps, cracked and littered with wrappers. The buzzer system had long ago stopped being repaired after frequent break-ins. A dingy foyer held a couple dozen scarred metal mailboxes set in the wall. Green and white striped tile, dirty and stained, covered the rest of the corridor. There were stairs immediately to his right. A heavy black banister was shiny from use, not cleaning. It was silent and empty. Jarvis took out the .38 and held it to his side. It was a different gun, but the similarity of the make and the surroundings generated a surprising hint of nostalgia. He suppressed it and moved down the stairs. Mohan's new unit was in the basement.

The walls were slick and in the dim light thrown by the couple remaining bulbs they looked wet. Urine stung his nostrils. Jarvis passed two doors on his right. Both had scratch marks and brand new locks. The first door on the left was padlocked, a sheriff's notice taped over the peephole. Mohan's place was the last apartment on the left. A trash bag that looked like it had been used more than once spilled over. Jarvis approached with his back against the wall, sliding the last few feet, knowing he'd have to dry clean the shirt. He raised the gun so it was pointing up, ready to swing forward quickly. With his left hand, he knocked on the door three times, loudly. In addition to the knob with a lock in it, there were at least two deadbolts visible. Probably a metal bar on the inside, too. He'd have better luck taking off the hinges than trying to knock down the door. But there was no window, no back exit. He'd checked, circling the building before. No escape. Completely illegal; ridiculously common in the city. He knocked again.

There was rustling behind the door. Papers shuffled and something banged against wood. Jarvis relaxed his grip on the gun, settling into the combat attitude he'd learned years earlier. The sound of a door handle squeaking mixed with the distinct meow of a cat. He was confused for a moment, the sounds overlapping but somehow wrong. He sorted them out and realized a cat was in the apartment but the sound of a door opening was coming from behind, where he had just been. Someone was coming in the front door of the building. He froze, taking deep, slow breaths, and listened for the steps. If they faded away, he would resume knocking. They didn't fade. Instead there was the squeak of a rubber sole on linoleum and the crackle of grocery bags rubbing against one another. The sound started to come closer and Jarvis could see a shadow at the top of the short staircase leading to the corridor he occupied. It was probably an old woman doing her shopping, or a drug addict tenant coming back from his morning score. There were five apartment doors in the hallway; eighty percent chance at least that it was someone other than Mohan. Legs appeared and the figure slowly descended, reluctantly. Both hands that emerged carried a couple of plastic bags from Fairway Markets, the orange emblem familiar to Jarvis. He lowered the gun, tucking it behind his leg and against the wall. The approaching man's head cleared the top and Jarvis could see a clean-shaven and gaunt Mohan. He raised the gun and aimed it at him for the second time in three years, before Mohan's eyes could adjust to the gloom and his brain sort out the scene in front of him. When it did, he was already on the bottom step. Mohan gasped. Instead of dropping the bags, he began to backpedal up the steps, rapidly but ineffectively. Almost tripping, he turned and scrambled, which was also ineffective because he hadn't let go of his bags. To Jarvis' eye, it was almost funny. Not quite, under the circumstances, but he couldn't help but think of a cartoon character spinning his legs like wheels trying to get out of a mess.

"Hold it, Mohan, I just want to have a chat." The gun belied the intent. Mohan was up the stairs in three strides and halfway through the front door. Jarvis wanted to chase him down, gun blazing, and take him out with a diving tackle and the applause of pedestrians. Instead, he holstered his gun and sprinted after Mohan.

It didn't take much effort. Mohan got only half a block before his wheezing and Jarvis' oft-exercised lungs were within a couple feet of one another. Jarvis could have jumped the last few steps for effect, but he decided it might mess up his knee. He gave Mohan a hard push from behind and the spindly legs couldn't keep up with the sudden and unintentional acceleration. Mohan fell forward and turned his shoulder inward to break his fall. The timing was perfect; half a dozen plastic garbage cans lining the brick wall broke his fall. It was still early, for Greenwich Village, and no heads turned as Jarvis straddled his quarry and put a gun to Mohan's temple.

"Nice to see you. Not sure you're so glad to see me, though."

"Fuck you! This is America you shit! You can't do this to…"

Jarvis hit him abruptly on the crown of the head. The gun made a dull thud. It would hurt like hell and leave a bump but not knock him unconscious. "Yeah, America. Land of the free and home of the terrorists."

Mohan didn't hear, the explosion in his head blotting out any sights and sounds for half a minute. He moaned and curled up in a ball until the wave of pain passed slowly, like an ice cream-induced headache. Jarvis put the gun away and waited. When the moaning stopped he grabbed Mohan by the back of the neck and dragged him into a sitting position.

"I'll shoot you right here, in the knee, and drag you back. Or you can man up and walk." Mohan looked up at Jarvis and any protestations disappeared. He struggled to stand, keeping his hands on the swelling spot on his head. Staggering like a drunk, he headed back to his apartment as Jarvis gave periodic encouraging pushes. A few people were on the street now and watched the two men walking. No one said anything. It wasn't that unusual a scene.

They made it to the apartment without incident, other than Mohan stumbling into the trash bag outside his front door and expanding the scope and eclecticism of the crap spilling out. Jarvis took the keys from Mohan's fumbling hands and opened the door, but pushed his captive through first. Just in case. The room was worse than the hole Mohan had lived in before. It only qualified as a studio rather than a closet because there was a tiny bathroom to the left and on the right a built-in stove and miniature counter. The smell was reminiscent of an alley in summertime when the trash hadn't been picked up for a week. The only thing missing was the scent of human excrement.   Wait, there it was. Jarvis pushed Mohan toward a sagging brown object that resembled a couch. He chose to stand. Ebola lurked on every surface. Mohan seemed unperturbed as he plopped onto the cushions. A puff of dust or something less innocuous wafted up. Jarvis held his breath until it settled.

"Been doing pretty well for yourself, huh?"

Mohan glared at him. He opened his mouth but before he could form a word, Jarvis interrupted.

"Yeah, I know, 'go fuck yourself.' You need to expand your comeback repertoire." Mohan didn't laugh appreciatively. "Let's cut to the chase. It'll save you some pain and me some time. What's up with Wisconsin?"

It sounded like a quiz show question but it made Mohan sit bolt upright, his headache forgotten. Whatever fear had been on his face before was just a warm-up. He looked instinctively toward the kitchen area, at a small refrigerator that barely deserved the name. Jarvis followed his gaze and when Mohan saw, he jumped up. The .38 was pointing at his groin before he had could take a step.

"Get on your knees." In Mohan's world, that was a precursor to a bullet in the head. Jarvis just wanted to keep him from leaping the handful of steps to the closet where there was probably a gun or two. He walked sideways to the kitchen area, not taking his eyes off Mohan who had gone down one knee at a time and clearly wasn't sure whether to be more afraid of Jarvis' pistol or what he imagined his handlers would do when they found out he'd been caught. Jarvis opened the tiny refrigerator door and flicked his eyes back and forth between the man in the center of the room, genuflecting, and the contents of the fridge. A Styrofoam container, Orange Crush, hummus, a very old lemon, and a very fancy silver cylinder, eight inches tall and outclassing anything else in the apartment or within a hundred feet. It looked like a high-tech nuclear device component. Jarvis switched the gun to his left hand and took out the metal container. It was surprisingly light. Mohan moaned, as if he'd held out some hope that Jarvis wouldn't find his secret in the sparsely populated second shelf. Looking at the container gave Jarvis a sick feeling in his stomach. He walked over to Mohan and handed it to him.

"Open it." Mohan looked at him as if opportunity had been presented suddenly. "If you spill what I think is in it, your blood will be mixed with it two seconds later."

Mohan twisted the top and bottom in opposite directions simultaneously. The cylinder was threaded but came apart quickly. The top pulled away to reveal a glass tube nestled tightly in a wrap of spongy foam. A drop from twenty feet would probably not have affected the glass.

There was a lightly yellow liquid sloshing in the partly filled tube. The sight of it turned Jarvis' sick feeling to anger. He pictured Brin sipping a cup of coffee laced with the stuff. He wanted to make Mohan crack open the vial and drink deeply. Instead he raised the gun to eye level and walked menacingly toward him.

"Who's running this? It isn't the guy in Wisconsin. He's a distribution point." Jarvis' voice was steady but strained. He was just a foot away from a quivering Mohan. He stopped and pulled back the hammer. "Who?"

Mohan's hands began to shake and the liquid sloshed. He was summoning up courage but it was like grabbing at drops of water as they faded into hot desert sand. He looked down at the vial and up at Jarvis. "I…no, no…don't shoot…but I can't…" His accent got heavier as he become more agitated.

Jarvis took the last step to close the distance between them. He put the gun to the man's forehead and could feel the tip of the barrel slip slightly on sweat. Mohan looked away and down. He began to mumble, maybe a prayer or maybe a pleading to be left alone.

"I'm going to stop all this. I've already got the list of everyone else, all the assholes like you who want to pretend to be martyrs. Killing civilians. But I need to know who's behind this – who has an antidote." Mohan looked up when he heard that. "That's right, moron. You think your handlers wouldn't have an antidote in case they needed it for themselves because one of you dumb shits decided to use it against each other? Now give me a goddamn name…" His voice was no longer strained. It was dead and it held no mercy. Jarvis knew Mohan was nothing more than a wannabe, a reluctant soldier trying to squirm ahead. He wasn't a leader or a believer.

Mohan's quivering stopped. He looked past the gun and into Jarvis' eyes. He saw the calm, the certainty, and it gave him strength over the fear. He opened his mouth as though to give Jarvis an answer. And then he cracked the vial open with his hands, spilling some of the poison on the ground and cutting his fingers on the glass. Before Jarvis could knock it from his hands, Mohan brought it to his open mouth and shoved the end onto his tongue. The jagged glass cut and the poison flowed over the gashes and down his throat. It was oily and tasteless. Jarvis was pushing the cylinder and broken glass away, grunting and knocking Mohan down and onto his side to get the liquid to come out of his mouth. But it was too late. Mohan smiled and tried to form words as the pain hit his gut and Jarvis' arms surrounded him in an attempt to squeeze the poison from his system.

Mohan silently mouthed "fuck you" but died halfway through, his body convulsing and a heavy foam mixed with blood coming out of his throat and onto the carpet. Jarvis stood and looked down at the body, his gun still in his hand, and he closed his eyes.

"Goddammit. Goddammit!" He fought the urge to kick Mohan, to pummel him, to beat him back to life. "Goddamn son of a…"

There was liquid from the vial on his hand and blood and sputum on his wrist from the dead man. He put the gun in his belt and washed off in the filthy sink.

CHAPTER TWENTY-FIVE

The street was busier now. Early browsers of the antique clothing stores mixed with tourists and guys with suits heading to a bank building two blocks away. Jarvis stood on the top step and surveyed the scene. The FBI was tracking down their list of poisoners and Jarvis still had half a dozen names on his stolen sheet. But by now most or all had probably destroyed any connection to whoever was behind the attacks or they had gone underground. More people would die when they spun the operation back up. Brin would be one of them. He watched a young couple strolling the sidewalk, ignoring the bustle around them. She hung on his arm and he pretended to be too cool to care, but he beamed. Jarvis followed them with his eyes as they passed, his mind on the FBI agent, on the man in Racine, on Brin in the hospital. And his thoughts flew upstairs to Mohan, another dead body that was a dead end. The couple was further down the street now and they kissed without stopping. Jarvis watched and his eyes widened. He turned and pushed the front door of the apartment building in so hard it crashed against the wall and the couple on the street turned, startled. Jarvis was already inside, taking the steps two at a time and pushing open the door behind which Mohan still lay motionless and dead on the floor. Jarvis closed the door and strode quickly the few steps to the body. He bent and grabbed Mohan's right arm. The limb moved like a heavy piece of rope. Jarvis turned the arm so the left hand flopped open. He didn't need to touch the hand. He could see the gold band on the third finger. Mohan had married. Maybe that's what had given him the courage to be a martyr.

Jarvis looked around the room again, with fresh eyes. The closet where a gun no doubt hid had a long coat, a scarf, and a man's hat. He pushed aside the coat and there it was – next to the shotgun a woman's raincoat. He looked across the room to the one piece of furniture that wasn't the couch, the Formica table, or the two chairs. He went across and pulled open the top two drawers of the dresser. The one on the right held unattractive, modest women's underwear. Mohan was married, and she lived here. Either she was his inspiration or his handler. Whichever it was, she would know something. Jarvis went to the front door and made sure it was properly closed and undisturbed. He took one of the folding chairs and put it to the left of the front door and across the small room. Anyone coming in would see him second, after the body on the floor. He settled into the chair, gun loosely in his lap, and waited.

It was three hours and fourteen minutes before he heard shuffling outside in the hallway. Jarvis didn't move as the walking stopped and the sound of grocery bags settling onto the ground crept under the open space at the bottom of the door. He waited until a key entered the lock and rattled a few seconds before catching, then he stood quietly and timed his crossing the room to coincide with the door swinging open. He let it hit him gently on the shoulder as he stood against the wall and waited for her to pick up the bags and come in. He saw her shoulder as she entered and stopped. She saw the body and read the scene immediately. The grocery bags dropped and she took a step forward, hand to her mouth in a silent scream. Jarvis swung the door shut behind her and she did not notice right away.

"Mohan! Mohan!" It was desperate, but not forlorn or shocked. She was angry. "Mohan! What have you done! You stupid…" She sensed even in her surprise she was not the only breathing person in the room. She whipped around, hands in a protective gesture.

Jarvis raised the gun to her just as he had done hours earlier to her husband. "Sit." He nodded to the chair he'd waited in for hours. "Now."

He felt none of the sympathy he might for a woman who'd lost her love. The venom in her face was meant for him, Jarvis, and it was undiluted with grief. She'd been a manipulator and Jarvis would treat her like the enemy. She glared but did as she was told. There was no recognition in her face. Jarvis was a stranger to her, unlike the reaction he'd gotten from the dead kid in Tarzana or the distributor in Racine.

"What do you want, pig, are you here to steal from us? Do we look like we have riches?" Her voice was husky, like it had been dry and raspy for years. The accent was distinctly Afghan, though Jarvis couldn't place the region. His ear was not as good as Rini's. "Did you think we had diamonds hidden in that?" She pointed disdainfully to the body on the floor and the cylinder still in Mohan's grasp. She might have been pointing at a safe in an otherwise unoccupied room. Despite the accent, her English was excellent, better than her American-born neighbors probably, and she was educated. Her clothes did not match her haughtiness. Faded jeans that did not flatter a generally unflattering figure. Hair in a worn scarf. Blouse difficult to describe because it was forgettable. She still wore her heavy brown coat, which may have been expensive before its first owner donated it to Good Will.

Jarvis didn't trust that the coat pockets were completely empty. His gun didn't waver as he instructed her to remove the coat and toss it on the ground in front of him. Her eyes widened for a moment as the idea flitted across her mind that the intruder had some sick sexual intention, but she abandoned the thought immediately. Jarvis was intent and angry, not bent on inflicting rape. She complied. He kicked it aside and his foot hit something heavy and metal within the fabric.

"Why are you here, bastard?" There were gutturals in her vowels and almost a trill on the "d" in bastard. She had none of the demureness that comes from years of wearing the habib. Mid-thirties, angry, confident; Mohan would have been putty.

Jarvis squatted in front of her, just out of range should she kick her legs up. His elbow rested on one knee, helping keep the gun aimed at her. "What was your target?" He didn't need to explain or to point at the dead man. Her face dissolved into understanding, though no less vehemently hateful.

"I see. You are a lazy American policeman. A detective maybe, thinking you have cracked a big case, yes?" She almost spit while saying 'American.' "There is nothing you can do. It is too late." She laughed and even though it was forced and fake it gave Jarvis a chill. He shot her in the right thigh. The retort of the gun was clean and quick and immediately absorbed by the ratty carpet and ancient couch. The woman sucked in her breath and paused in shock, then let out a cry and a string of epithets in Farsi. He recognized about half the words. He'd missed any arteries and the bullet had entered the meaty part of her leg. It would hurt like hell but there wouldn't be much blood. She would die of infection in a day or so if not treated. He pointed the gun at the middle of her face.

"Quiet. It'll hurt but you'll be fine if you get to a doctor in the next hour or so." He was surprised at how quickly she stifled any sobs. Anger beat out her pain.

"What...what do you want?"

"I'll ask again – who was the target?" This time he did nod toward Mohan. Her eyes did not follow.

"We did not..." She winced. It did hurt, a lot. "I did not have...I was not told where yet."

Jarvis nodded. "I need an antidote." Now she looked across at Mohan. "No, not for him." He almost laughed. "Who sends it to you? Where does it come from?"

She shook her head. "No. No, I will not tell...wh..." Her leg convulsed. The bullet might be touching some nerves.

Jarvis pointed the gun at her other leg. "I knew Mohan, from Afghanistan. He's an idiot, but not a killer." This got her attention and she peered at Jarvis. "You were his handler. You know where the poison is coming from."

She wasn't listening to his questions any more. "How did you know this man? From where did you meet Mohan?" It seemed very important to her, enough to ignore the historical evidence suggesting he would not hesitate to shoot her in the other leg.

"I met him briefly when he was about to help some of his pals behead a friend of mine."

At this the woman's face registered the recognition that had eluded her before. She moved faster than he would have guessed she could. She was up and out of the chair, a small knife pulled from somewhere near her waist, before Jarvis could come out of his crouching position. He shot her in the throat, almost randomly, as he angled the gun up and pulled the trigger. The bullet tore through her esophagus and blood splattered on her shirt and behind her. Momentum took her a few feet toward Jarvis and he spun, still crouching, out of her way. She fell to the ground, both hands clutching at her throat and neck. The knife remained in her right hand and cut into her cheek but the pain went unregistered. She hit the ground and rolled onto her back. Jarvis stood and leaned over her. She stared at him as blood poured onto the filthy carpet.

"Tell me how you know me. Who's behind this?"

She mouthed words but the only sounds were gurgling. There was a rush of blood out her mouth and she drew in half a breath. She tried to speak again. Her voice was even rougher, the words more accented, but they were clear.

"Murderer...murderer of my son, my Hakimi...murderer..." She died with the last syllable.

It was the fifth death in forty-eight hours Jarvis had watched; sixth if the woman at the grocery store counted. He figured she did. Jarvis pulled out his cell phone to call the cops but waited. It would be a long day and night of explanations and he was sure there wasn't a lot of time left. Instead, he unfolded the sheet he'd kept from the three he'd taken in Racine and looked at the names. There were seven. Two had red check marks next to them – one was Mohan's. The check couldn't mean they'd carried out their mission. He looked past the woman, blood still seeping into the carpet and looking more brown than red, at Mohan and the cylinder. The red checks meant the poison had been delivered. Five other people were waiting for their vials, and for their instructions. Instead of dialing 911, he called Timmons. He had a better chance explaining to Homeland Security why he was standing in yet another room with dead bodies.

CHAPTER TWENTY-SIX

Timmons didn't seem surprised to hear from Jarvis or by the content of his story.

"Yeah, I was pretty sure I'd hear from you. And it'd be after you'd done something I wouldn't like." Timmons was comfortable letting dead air fill the connection. So was Jarvis.

"The sheets you have with names, the ones with red ticks are the people who've already received vials of poison. Maybe you should focus on them, even though I think most have gone underground by now."

Timmons laughed, real humor infusing it. "You've made enough noise that they all know they might be compromised, unless maybe the guy in Racine didn't have enough time to reach them before you popped him." He paused. "How many on the sheet you have are marked in red?"

This caught Jarvis by surprise. Timmons cleared it up for him. "We spoke to Rini. Three sheets, and I've only got two."

"You guys are thorough." He looked down at his sheet. "Two with red, though one is...out of commission. Five others with no checks. I'll fax a copy."

"Thanks. And come on back. LA misses you."

Jarvis let the silence comfortably creep back in. There wasn't much he could do that would speed things up for Homeland Security. Getting to everyone on the list would take some time, and what he'd already done may have bought some more time by scaring the do-ers. Martyrs or misguided zealots or ideological morons, whatever they were, they would chill for a while. But it wouldn't stop there. He thought of the woman's dying words and Mohan's connection to Jarvis's past. Brin lying in a hospital bed. It was too late to find an antidote, at least one nearby. Brin would pull through on his own or Brin would die. The only thing Jarvis could do now was go to the source, to cut off the head.

"I've got a little vacation time coming."

Timmons thought about that. "Private detectives' benefits package includes paid time off nowadays?"

"I've got a trip coming up."

Timmons thought quietly. "You know, Homeland Security only operates within the borders of the United States. We've got sister agencies that have, uh, broader reach, but for the most part we're national only." It wasn't a threat or a suggestion. Just a fact.

"On an unrelated note, I always travel with my passport." Jarvis touched his back left pocket and felt the outline of the worn document he hadn't used much in the last couple years but was always within arm's reach. He started to do the mental calculations of a ticket, last-minute, for a very long flight. "I'll give you a ring in a few days."

"You do that. And travel safely." Timmons hung up and Jarvis headed back to the hotel to make some calls. Commercial flights into Karachi were limited given regional conditions. He needed to be more creative.

He hadn't packed for the desert so he walked a dozen blocks to a part of the Village that sold clothes other than black sweaters and pants and torn jeans. He picked out a few pairs of khakis, some good walking boots, several layers of sweaters, a light jacket to fend off the cool evenings, and several pairs of underwear. No one talked much about the real discomfort of sweating in 110 degree heat in Afghanistan. He found a decent duffel bag at an army surplus store. Walking among the gas masks, portable stoves, and laser sights, he fingered the camouflage outfits. Not a hint of nostalgia.

Back at the hotel, he began to make calls. Dozens of "consulting companies" provided security in the region, some acting as semi-legitimate armed forces augmenting US efforts. Others were private armies protecting companies still doing business in Afghanistan or aid agencies trying to help the locals while not being killed themselves. The recruiters reached out to ex-armed forces, offering good salaries, decent living conditions, and fewer rules than re-enlisting. Jarvis had never been tempted, but plenty former colleagues had. And one Colonel he'd served under had left the service a few years earlier and started his own company. He ran it like an arm of the military – boot camp training even for seasoned vets, strict rules of conduct, and zero tolerance for bullshit. Jarvis got him on his cell and didn't have to spend more than thirty seconds catching up on the six years since they'd last spoken. The Colonel didn't waste time – only the mission counted.

"Lieutenant, good to hear your voice. You looking for some work?"

Jarvis looked out his window at the park, dusk starting to settle and giving the city a false sense of calm. "No, sir. It's a little more complicated than that."

Two minutes later, the Colonel was giving Jarvis a series of telephone numbers and codes. Jarvis hadn't told him the details, just that he needed to get to Afghanistan and the mission, though private, was important. The Colonel's voice was clipped, clear, and hard. He'd help get Jarvis in-country. He didn't say anything more, but Jarvis knew if he needed anything else, he could make a call.

"Thank you, sir. I hope we get to cross paths again soon."

"Son, you do what you need to do." The line went dead.

CHAPTER TWENTY-SEVEN

The commercial flight on Lufthansa from JFK to Frankfurt was $2600 for coach. The gate agent was a vet who recognized the look on Jarvis' face and gave him an exit window seat. He looked slightly wistful handing Jarvis the boarding pass. A stint in the Gulf was more enticing than explaining to the fat woman next in line that she might have to buy two seats.

Jarvis put his one bag in the overhead bin and only got up once to stretch his legs and pee before they reached cruising altitude. Eight hours later he landed in late morning fog in Germany. He went through uncrowded customs and passport control lines then took a shuttle to a remote terminal where the planes were unmarked except for numbers on the fuselage. He got in line behind a dozen men who ran the gamut from Central Casting mercenary to left-wing aid worker. He fit right in. A courteous but no-nonsense security guard – private, not employed by either the US or German aviation agencies, directed each man in line through a metal detector and toward a second guard who escorted them to a private area. It was more like boot camp induction than flight prep. When it was Jarvis' turn, he went through the metal detector and then to his left, as directed. The guard took him to a bare space the size of a small doctor's examination room and pointed at his clothes. Jarvis wordlessly stripped naked and let the guard do his business after snapping on a surgical glove. The man's hands were cold.

Apparently not concealing any Uzis in his nether parts, Jarvis was permitted into the waiting area where several dozen people gathered. Against the advice of the signs, half the men smoked and no one objected. Duffel bags were lined up by a door leading to the tarmac. Three armed security guards roamed the room, not randomly but according to a clear sequence. Another two were on the tarmac on either side of the plain white 767. Half an hour passed and a guard opened the sliding glass door to the outside. Without any rush or bustling that accompanies businessmen and tourists jostling to get on a plane, the fifty-some-odd group naturally formed a line and worked their way up the mobile staircase.

The seats were less comfortable but much roomier than the commercial flight. There was no movie or hot meal service. All the travelers were used to government transport and quickly settled in for the seven-hour flight. Few people spoke and the guy next to Jarvis was asleep before the door closed. Jarvis waited until they were at cruising altitude and took a nap of just under an hour. No writing beforehand. He awoke refreshed and with a clear plan in mind. The guy to his left woke midway in the steep descent that felt like a Kamikaze attack – the angle of entry into Khandahar Airport was intended to minimize the amount of time the plane was potentially within reach of surface to air missiles. The g-forces felt familiar to Jarvis and put him in the right mindset. It was the mentality of war – heavy with anticipation, even during the stretches of unrelenting boredom, everyone knowing that a break in the calm was never minor, never just a bump in the road. Most of the passengers were up and holding their bags before the plane came to a stop. Jarvis was the last off the plane.

It was mid-morning and the sun had already baked away any coolness clinging to the ground from the evening. The tarmac was dry and dusty but as modern as any runway at LAX. The only differences were the rubble to the left that used to be the international terminal and the line of vehicles parked thirty feet from the plane. Two reinforced Humvees driven by security contractors, a government aid agency white van, two limos for the three men who'd sat in what passed for first class seats on the flight, and three taxis that looked like they'd crossed the dessert with Moses. All but the last taxi drove off. He wondered if the reason it stayed still was because it was waiting for him or was too dilapidated to take another breath and summon up the energy to move. It was the former. The driver got out with a creak of the door and waved as though Jarvis were a mile and a half away rather than fifteen steps. Jarvis pretended not to see, then not to recognize the driver, who took that as a sign to come around to the other side and almost jump up and down.

"Jar-vees! Jar-vees! Over here! It is me!"

Jarvis couldn't resist the impulse to smile any longer. He bee-lined to the driver and took off his sunglasses. They clasped hands, then hugged.

"Saleem, I see you got a new car."

The laugh was deep and real and was Jarvis' true welcome to a country he loved and feared. Saleem took the bag from Jarvis and tossed it through the windowless back seat door. He yanked open the passenger door, metal fighting metal as if it were a battle for existence. The ancient leather smelled of every food, every type of smoke, and every soul Jarvis had experienced in his two years in Afghanistan. He felt at home and afraid.

Saleem almost ran around to the driver's side and had the car in gear before his door closed. If the speedometer had been working Jarvis could have confirmed his estimate they were going fifty miles per hour before they'd made it the forty feet to the gate. The taxi entered a surprisingly dense stream of traffic headed out to the highway and into the dessert. They dropped in behind a quickly moving group of vans, small trucks, and old Mercedes that was following three US military Humvees. Saleem whistled, fired questions, and updated Jarvis on what had happened since the last time they had seen one another almost eight years ago. It was music to Jarvis' ears and he answered about one out of four questions, waiting for a pause in the monologue. He closed his eyes and breathed in, catching whiffs of diesel fuel, occasional animal smells as they passed a truck filled with chickens, and the unmistakable scent of war.

"Jar-vees, don't tell me you are here to fight some more the war? You

are not mercenary!!!" Saleem laughed but there was an undercurrent of
dead seriousness.

Jarvis opened his eyes and turned to his friend. "No, no habib. I have
some personal business." This time Saleem's laugh was undiluted.

"That woman, Fallah, she who took your heart back then?" Fallah
was an ancient prostitute who had crooked her finger at Jarvis many times
when he was on leave and traveling the city of Khandahar with his friend.
The first time he'd been disgusted, but by the twentieth it had become a
running joke. She was probably no older than 50 but looked as though she
were Methuselah's older sister.

There was silence and Saleem saw Jarvis' business was serious. "Where
will you stay, my friend? My home is open, you know this, but I think
maybe your business must happen from somewhere else."

Jarvis reached across the seat and clasped the driver on the shoulder.
"I'll need your help getting around, but it would be better if I stayed at
the Interconti."

Saleem watched the increasingly crowded road and nodded. They
were quiet for a moment and Saleem kept his eyes on the road. Below the
hubbub of the car and noise from passing vehicles, he nodded again and
whispered, "It is very bad here, my friend. Very bad for everyone, but very
very bad for Americans. Please you be careful." They rode in silence for
a mile and then Saleem began catching him up on what his three children
were studying in school and how his wife berated him for staying out too
late but always had a warm dinner waiting for him. They pulled to the
side of the road once to let a caravan of half a dozen Humvees whiz by.
Army issue, but under private label. Jarvis knew if they hadn't pulled over,
the vehicles would have either pushed them out of the way or a "security
consultant" riding in the lead car would have pointed a 50-caliber rifle at
them and not waited more than a couple seconds to fire off a few rounds.
Better safe than sorry. They were at the hotel twenty minutes later and
parted warmly but with foreboding in the air around.

CHAPTER TWENTY-EIGHT

The Intercontinental Hotel in Khandahar was where the war journalists stayed. It was also where the management of the US and European security firms lived when they were in Afghanistan overseeing the business operations of their private armies. In the old days, it was likely to house spies from allied countries and the few hostile ones with a more expansive travel budget. When Jarvis arrived, the lobby was filled mainly with dozens of men wearing cheap suits and too much cologne. They had nametags and paunches. A beautifully hand-written sign at the check-in desk welcomed the members of the International Congress on Infrastructure Redevelopment – Africa and Middle East Region. It could just as easily have read "Carpetbaggers and Country Rapers." Jarvis checked in and was surprised that the reservation he'd made the day before actually existed. A porter three times Jarvis' age took his bag to the room and Jarvis headed to the bar to find any foreign correspondents hanging around. Despite the movie cliché, it was the mostly likely place to find them. He crossed the lobby and walked under the wrought-iron arches giving entry to a hushed, carpeted, old-world bar that could have seated a hundred but held only three.

Jarvis sat down next to the only patron who could have passed as a US journalist. Not because he looked the part, but because the other two were a wealthy-looking middle-aged man and a woman just under half his age who probably took gold bullion along with cash and AMEX for her companionship. No newsman on a foreign beat could afford her.

"Another Scotch and soda, and none of the latter." The guy's nose suggested this was a lifelong favorite. More veins than Joan Rivers' legs. He looked at Jarvis and nodded. "You the Colonel's friend?"

Jarvis was probably half a dozen drinks behind so he ordered a cold beer. Technically, alcohol wasn't available for open purchase in Afghanistan. Neither were prostitutes nor drugs. "Yep."

The beer arrived and each man drank slowly and quietly. Jarvis was in no hurry and he'd never found rushing a man led to quick answers. The journalist drained his glass and signaled to the bartender who waited close by.

"I hear you've got a couple good stories from your time back in '03 when this crap started. I was in Darfur then, writing shit nobody read." He sounded less drunk than Jarvis figured he had to be. "I'm Harding."

They shook hands.

Jarvis didn't look for opportunities to tell war stories, but he didn't hesitate when talking to someone who understood. War correspondents often saw as much action as experienced soldiers.

"Maybe one or two. The one I wanted to share was in a shit town a hundred clicks from here. I walked in on a beheading."

That got Harding's attention. "Yeah, I know that story. Couple of RPGs took out a school. You saved a guy, sniper or somethin'. Ten more seconds and it would have been an internet highlight reel."

There wasn't much to add. Jarvis nodded over his drink. "One of the guys who was there, a wannabe, spent some time in interrogation at Abu Ghraib. I ran into him the other day."

The journalist looked around the bar as though a terrorist attack were imminent. It wasn't an entirely unfounded concern.

"Not here. In the States," Jarvis added.

Harding's attention went from gotten to enraptured. "Terrorism? Bomb or somethin'?" He was reaching for something to write about.

"Maybe. He was working with some other people, no one I've

identified. But there's more than a few."

"He 'was' working with some other folks? Past tense?" He got a look from Jarvis that didn't leave much room for doubt. "You workin' for the Colonel or the military?"

Jarvis took another cool sip and it felt like it rinsed hard sand from his throat even though he'd already done that. "No, I'm working it by myself. Helping out a friend, maybe a few more people."

Harding put a scowl on his face. "You're not gonna give me shit, are you?"

Jarvis turned to him. His glare cut through the scowl. "The Colonel said you'd help. If I get anything you can use, and you don't use it 'til I tell you it's okay, then you get a story."

The scowl was replaced by a moderately greedy smile. "A terrorism plot on US soil? Broken by a grizzled war correspondent in glamorous Khandahar? Okay, I'm in." He signaled for yet another Scotch. "Couple of the guys you interrupted back in 2003 have been doin' pretty well for themselves. They've got their own little Jihad Joes wreaking havoc. Not real big, but nasty. If your dead guy in the States was with them back then, maybe he was part of whatever you've gotten wind of."

Exhaustion was starting to creep in. Not needing sleep didn't mean Jarvis didn't suffer jet lag from being in three international cities in two days. His reading of Harding was that being succinct and informative was not his forte. Now that he'd hooked him, Jarvis could drop any false camaraderie. "You got a name for me? Some coordinates?"

Harding waited for the drink to arrive and he took a long pull as though it were his first of the day. "Sure, I'll shoot you a text. Little village 'bout thirty miles northwest. You'll stand out, but that's where the guys hang, their little base I think." He pulled out a Blackberry and began typing. Jarvis' iPhone buzzed with the incoming message.

He didn't look, just finished his drink and got up. "Thanks." He might need Harding later, so he gave a sincere smile and put out his hand. Harding took it and the grip was stronger than expected.

"I sent my number, too. And email. Remember our deal." The booze in his eyes didn't hide the hunger. His byline only appeared occasionally and his best reporting days were behind him. This could change the flat trajectory of his career.

Jarvis returned the squeeze and nodded. "I'll get in touch if I need anything else."

He let go and went up to his room. The air conditioning was on, his bag had been unpacked and stored in the closet, and there was a bottle of water and bowl of fruit by the dresser. It could have been a decent hotel in any city in the world. Except when he looked out the window from the 23rd floor he could see the sprawl of the city and on the horizon, northwest of the city, hills that hid thousands of men and women willing to kill anyone from a different tribe, a different region, or a country that was currently bombing and shooting at them. He lay down on the bed and stared at the ceiling. No sleep needed, but a little recuperative down time. He began to strategize his next move. Afghanistan didn't work quite the same as LA, but Jarvis was not entirely unfamiliar with the machinations. In a few hours he'd get a driver to take him out to the spot he hadn't seen for almost a decade, but whose images were painted in his mind's eye with a vividness and clarity that sometimes exceeded reality. He thought about Brin and started to call the hospital, not bothering to do the math for the time change. Before he could finish dialing, the cell phone rang. The caller ID was the unhelpful Blocked but he picked up anyway.

The Colonel did not wait for a greeting. "Captain, write down this address. You can pick up your equipment there. Your money won't be any good."

Jarvis reached for a pencil stub on the table next to the bed and jotted the coordinates onto a piece of hotel marketing material that welcomed the guest in five languages. "Thank you, sir."

That was the extent of the conversation. Jarvis listened to the cell phone equivalent of dead air then dialed a number. There was the strange beeping that passed for ringing in the Middle East and then laughter. A woman's voice from across a crowded room sang out. "Jarvis!" That was all she said but he recognized Saleem's wife. If he could have found the unmarried, American version of her he would have been wed years ago.

"You better come over or she is going to hit me for not telling her you were here, Jar-vees!" Saleem's voice was that of a happily married man. It wasn't a voice Jarvis had often heard other than from Saleem.

"When it's over. Can you pick me up in about three hours?"

Saleem said a number of things in Arabic of which Jarvis only caught the gist, but the room quieted down. "I will be there. Should I...bring anything?"

"No, I'm covered. And I don't want you getting caught buying anything you shouldn't." Jarvis was going to stir up enough shit; he didn't want to endanger his friend any more than necessary.

"Then I will see you. Rest, rest a little my sleepless friend." And the cellphone silence again.

CHAPTER TWENTY-NINE

Muezzins from half a dozen mosques called the faithful to prayers shortly after the sun came up. Kandahar woke like any city of hundreds of thousands, Sharia law notwithstanding. Jarvis could hear street cleaners, vendors setting up food, and some small arms fire in the distance. Tepid water from the shower cleared his head and erased any remaining jet lag. He put on the same clothes from the day before, adding clean underwear and socks. His shirt was loose, both for comfort and to hide anything he might want to tuck into his waistband or strap to his chest. Breakfast waited for him on a tray outside the door and he ate the figs, deep black coffee, and yogurt while standing at the window watching traffic begin to build. The hotel was in the equivalent of a Green Zone, similar to the semi-protected area in Baghdad where the military, their families, and trusted locals lived. But in Kandahar, it was more of a faded, foam green zone – little real protection from anyone with a true intent to cause damage.

Before prayers were over in the large mosque visible from his window, Jarvis was passing through the empty lobby and into the back seat of Saleem's cab. It smelled moderately cleaner than during the previous day's ride from the airport, the way yesterday's shirt, though unlaundered, used the airing from the night before to take a stab at being fresh. Saleem turned and greeted him with a warm clasp on the shoulder. "Today you are my passenger, not my friend?"

Jarvis pointed at the bustle of the street just beyond the driveway of the hotel, where several military vehicles – not US – idled. "Better for you that I look like a tourist taking a ride."

Saleem scowled but did not insist Jarvis change seats. He put the car in gear and rammed the car into traffic. He reached for something on the seat next to him and handed back to his passenger a heavy, sweet smelling cloth bundle. Jarvis took it and breathed deeply.

"Yes, Jar-vees, Melitha cooked for you this morning and you must eat every bite so I may tell her that is the real reason you returned to Kandahar."

Jarvis was halfway through the warm bread and meat filling before Saleem had finished talking. Saleem looked at him in the rear-view mirror. "I will not have to lie to her."

Jarvis choked on a mouthful of food as he laughed. The last time Saleem's wife had thought he lied she held a butcher's knife over his testicles, one hand on the blade and the other holding the penis out of the way. Fortunately, Saleem had been able to convince her of his veracity. He had told Jarvis the story with a mix of humor, fear, and respect, which fueled his love for his wife. Jarvis stayed with them several times, and Melitha's warmth, intellect, sincerity and strength made what otherwise would have been an ugly face into a portrait of an angel. Proof that beauty was far deeper than skin.

He gave Saleem the address provided by the Colonel and that put a halt to any lightness in the air. "That is not a neighborhood I would like to take you to." His voice had hardened, and Jarvis read it as a cover for fear; for both of them. It wasn't a no, just a warning. They drove in relative quiet – outside the taxi was a cacophony of city life, in the car they prepared for whatever lay ahead. Saleem had no illusions that the day would be anything near normal. He broke the silence after a few minutes and his voice was gentle and firm as he spoke to Jarvis.

"What you are doing, it must be done?"

Jarvis looked out the window and tried to count the number of men carrying weapons. He lost track at 20. "Yes."

A few minutes later they reached an intersection where all traffic was stopped. A disinterested uniformed man in his late 50s more or less directed traffic through the intersection, but not according to any rhythm or rules Jarvis could discern. To the right was a series of shops and restaurants. To the left was a building that looked as though it had been bombed, condemned, and abandoned, except a steady stream of people moved in and out. It was a secondary government building, not important enough to protect with military. It probably gave out permits for scooters or building stone walls. Jarvis tapped Saleem on the shoulder. They both knew the area.

"I'll get out here. Circle once. That should give me at least an hour." It was sadly funny that he was probably right. Saleem turned and didn't need to say how careful he wanted Jarvis to be.

Jarvis opened his door, narrowly missing a bicyclist who was ignoring the traffic cop along with most everybody else on the road, and stepped onto the hot, black pavement. He walked quickly toward the quasi-government building. Mostly men passed him on the sidewalk, some ignoring him, others glaring. But in Afghanistan a hard look was not always a challenge and Jarvis had learned to distinguish danger from curiosity. Just past the building whose doors were in perpetual motion a small alleyway opened to the left. He'd memorized the address but there were few markings. Instinct was more valuable than a map. The alley was wide enough for three people to walk abreast or a man to escort an ox without hitting either wall. Jarvis sidestepped the men and squeezed past the ox. There were openings and doorways on either side, some tightly bolted and others opening and closing in random patterns as people entered and emerged. The stone walk underfoot had as much loose rock as it had flat cement. A boy no older than 9 ran by kicking a soccer ball. It seemed out of place as Jarvis ventured further down the alley, which began to undulate and create blind turns. No more than 150 feet from the taxi he'd just left and it was a different world. A door on his left had a number 26, and he counted each of the next 7 so as to estimate where #33 was. The door was blackened with age and rusted with neglect. He raised a fist to knock when the boy with the soccer ball raced past again and kicked as if it were the winning goal, a perfect shot at the center of the door across the alley from where Jarvis stood. Jarvis recognized too late the boy was a lookout and the goal a signal. Before he could turn and assess the threat, there were two rifles pointing at him, one from either side. He'd seen the men, separately, a few moments earlier and neither had been armed. The door behind him, with the dirty mark from the soccer ball, opened. A man close to twice Jarvis' size emerged blinking in the sunlight that streamed into the narrow alley. He barked a few words and both men pressed their rifles into Jarvis, one in his neck the other in a kidney.

Jarvis knew enough Farsi to order in a restaurant and curse out a bad driver. He picked his words carefully. It came out more or less translatable as "Your whore mother fucked a pig to make you." He felt the rifles press harder against both parts of his body and sensed trigger fingers tightening.

The giant in the doorway barked again, and it sounded somewhere between a laugh and an order to rip Jarvis' organs from his body. Instead of lead-tipped bullets tearing into his back and skull, he felt the relief of gun barrels being pulled away. Andre the Giant's twin bent down and grabbed Jarvis by the scruff of the neck as though he were a doll. Jarvis didn't fight. The man leaned close to Jarvis' face and a cloud of garlic and untreatable gingivitis drifted toward him. In a whisper that was louder than a small airplane, the man said in passable English, "I eat you and shit out bones."

Jarvis wasn't sure whether it was a threat or historical account of the last person who'd crossed him. The monster half pulled, half carried Jarvis over the doorstep and into an instantly dark room where the air was stagnant and he could feel more than see heavy drapes covering the walls and the windows. The door shut behind him and he blinked to adjust as quickly as possible, in case there were threats other than the thyroid case who was finally letting Jarvis stand fully on his own two feet. The room settled into view as the rods and cones in his eyes deciphered the reduced light into familiar shapes and angles. It was small and mainly empty, except for a tiny, wizened figure on a stool straight ahead. He held a Kalashnikov rifle almost as long as he was tall. The air was warm and stale but the man did not sweat. The small door he guarded would require the giant looming over Jarvis to turn sideways to get through, and even then it was no guarantee. An arm pushed Jarvis toward the door and the diminutive guard's gun shifted just enough that pulling the trigger would eliminate any chance Jarvis could have children. Jarvis wasn't even sure the guard could see, but had probably killed enough Americans – and Russians before that and Iranians before that – that instinct was enough.

Jarvis stepped forward and turned the iron handle, which was surprisingly cool. The door opened inward and brightness spilled out, cutting through the murk in the outer room. Jarvis stepped into a space that was twice the length of the one he left, though narrow and empty. Empty except for a row of counters or shelving along each side. A long overhead incandescent light ran along the ceiling. The floor was cement but covered in a gray mat. Each of the two long shelves held dozens of plastic bags containing about a grapefruit-size lump of what looked like gray mud or clay. They were neatly tied at the neck with a red twist. Jarvis recognized the color and consistency of poppy extract mixed with wax and coloring, a common way for Afghan drug middle-men to transport their product. A sharp jab in his back proved the giant was, indeed, able to squeeze through the door. Jarvis moved along the center of the room toward an opening at the other end where even brighter light poured through. Behind him the wooden door shut and he heard a lock.

Jarvis moved quickly but cautiously toward the opening, glad to avoid another prodding by the enormous guard whose name appeared to have been Almak, a word used by the gun-toting watchmen outside and which Jarvis had thought meant "ostrich" and therefore wasn't sure why they had used it. Jarvis couldn't help but silently mouth the words "Big Bird" as he stepped through the entryway.

He knew what to expect and was neither disappointed nor surprised. To his right was a plastic sheet hanging from the low ceiling, blocking the entrance to a large but cramped room. It was cramped because there were two picnic-table sized surfaces surrounded by stools. The floor was covered in plastic along with the table. The walls were bright white and smooth and recently painted. A dozen men and women dressed for the streets of Kandahar also wore elbow-length rubber gloves and hospital masks. They used metal cups to take scoops of powder from a large pile in the middle of the table where they sat and then a handful of soft, white wax from a pile next to them and kneaded them together. It was quite an operation and if Jarvis' mental calculator was working properly, probably generated a few hundred thousand dollars worth of product a week.

Apparently that room was not his destination. No one looked up from their work when Big Bird smacked Jarvis on the shoulder to direct him to the left, where a staircase led down. The floor and walls were not as clean, so whatever was happening downstairs didn't require laboratory-like conditions. He could hear voices and movement. They went down the stairs and his minder had to bend over to avoid smacking the bridge of his nose as they passed under the lip of the floor overhead. The door at the bottom was unguarded and swung inward. It was heavy metal and the hinges were well-oiled and opened silently. Jarvis could see half a dozen locks and a bolt. It would take a rocket propelled grenade to open if the door were shut from the inside. He quickly saw why. The room filled the entire area under the house. They entered in the middle of the room. Straight ahead were crates lined on either side of the wide expanse and when he briefly twisted his head around, he could see a similar number of boxes and more crates in the equally-sized space behind him. The lighting was from bulbs hanging off the ceiling and no one had laid down any plastic or carpets. It smelled like the desert with a faint hint of old air conditioner. Directly in front was a scarred wooden table and three men sat. They glanced up briefly. The one counting money – American dollars – looked back at the stacks of bills in front of him. The man across the table from him kept cleaning a sparkling new AK-47, which competed for space on the large table with half a dozen handguns of various sizes. The man third man at the head of the table calmly smoked a cigar and kept his gaze on Jarvis.

Jarvis stole a quick glance to either side and was impressed with the polyglotism of the labels on the crates. Arms from around the world. The cigar guy wasn't pleased at his curiosity.

"You have pre-paid card, yes?" His voice was higher and lighter than Jarvis would have guessed if he'd been asked to do so. Western-style clothes, light wool pants and white shirt, sleeves rolled up, and a jacket over the back of his chair. The other two men holding guns were in native street garb.

Jarvis nodded at what he assumed was a joke. "Yeah, I hear you don't take cash." The man counting US currency didn't look up.

Cigar guy's beard was more like five-day stubble, a clean-shave compared to the long, straggly matts on the faces of the other two. Big bird was completely clean shaven, but Jarvis suspected it was genetics and not a razor. He didn't want to get distracted by looking around to check.

"You want gun. Two maybe. And lots of bullets. Yes." Not a question.

Jarvis had been thinking a tank would be useful, but might lose him the element of surprise on his mission. "Yes. I like the one you've got there."

The man put the cigar back in his mouth and smoke curled up on either side. "This one is mine. It has initials. You want to see?" He pointed it directly at Jarvis' face. Jarvis smiled.

"Yeah, it looks good on you. You have any that aren't personalized?"

Cigar guy waved the gun to Jarvis' left. "I got plenty. You have credit for one of these, maybe a little pistol, and as much bullets as you can carry."

The generosity convinced Jarvis the Colonel had probably paid for five times that much equipment, but that was the price of contraband.

"Amal!" Cigar guy shouted in the direction of where he was pointing the gun, behind Jarvis. There was some bumping around and shuffling from the other side of the staircase. He had to look around his enormous guard to see the man emerge. Amal was holding a small crate with Russian writing. He had a large pistol tucked into a belt holding up loose fitting pants and a rifle was slung over his shoulder. He looked like he had been living in a terrorist camp for the last year. Turns out he had been. Jarvis recognized Amal as one of the men from eight years earlier who had been holding Brin's head while the machete was poised over it. Amal had been young then and he was still young now, but the beard was darker, fuller, and in his eyes was the reflection of many deaths. They also flashed recognition an instant after Jarvis had placed him in the snapshot in his own mind.

Amal came to a full halt. The guy with the cigar looked quizzically at the tableau and Jarvis waited a heartbeat. The crate slipped from Amal's hands and he began to fumble for his pistol. Jarvis had only the time until his next heartbeat to decide. The guns on the table were five feet away and he wouldn't have time to wrestle with anyone for them. His guard had a couple of pistols strapped to his body but he might as well be trying to pull a thorn from the paw of an angry lion. There was only one not-entirely-suicidal option. He turned and kicked the big guard in the groin and spun like a half-back around him to cover the few feet to get to Amal. He passed the staircase but going up would only lead to several bullets in his back. He reached Amal just as the gun was coming out of his belt. There was fury in Amal's eyes and frustration that he couldn't point the gun at Jarvis and empty a full clip into the American. Jarvis hit him under the chin with his shoulder as he grasped at the gun. Amal was stronger than his slight frame suggested and Jarvis used both hands to twist the barrel toward Amal's torso. He drove Amal back to create space for the gun to turn away from himself. Jarvis could hear the huge guard with the sore testicles cursing and trying to catch his breath. Jarvis' attention was on not getting shot by Amal but he could hear shouts from the men at the table and the sound of rifle clips being loaded. Jarvis drove harder with his legs, holding onto Amal's arm and wrist. He could feel the man pounding on his head with his free arm and the rifle swinging from his shoulder wildly was hitting Jarvis in the hip. He gave one last hard twist and could hear Amal's wrist snap and all resistance give way. Amal tripped going backwards and Jarvis had the gun in his hand and was able to regain his balance and stayed standing. Amal hit the ground and Jarvis was over him, gun pointed at his forehead. He looked down at the terrorist and then quickly up and back to where he'd been standing a moment ago. The enormous guard seemed no worse for wear after having caught his breath and was literally growling as he walked toward Jarvis. The two subordinates of the cigar guy were coming at him with rifles and were speaking so quickly he couldn't understand any of the words. Cigar guy was still sitting, but holding his handgun now. Chaos was imminent. Jarvis pointed the gun at the large guard. It would probably take the entire clip to stop him. There was a sharp command from cigar guy that cut through the growing din and halted everyone in their tracks.

Cigar guy got up from the table and slowly walked toward Jarvis. Several of the men, including Jarvis, were breathing heavily. Everyone was quiet, only highlighting the tension. Jarvis calculated he could take out cigar guy, which would distract the others, then kill the two guards with guns in their hands. That left the giant, who would have enough time during the killing to get his hands on Jarvis. But if he started with the largest target, the others would shoot him dead. There was no cover and no good options. He decided he'd have to take his chances with Godzilla and shoot cigar guy first. Without looking, he fingered the safety to make sure it was off. It was. Before he could raise the gun, there was a scraping noise down and to his left. A movement caught his eye and as he turned away from the immediate threats in front of him, he saw Amal raising the rifle that had fallen off his shoulder. He pointed it at Jarvis. There was a single shot, loud and painful in the small space. Jarvis didn't wince, trying to determine where the bullet had entered his body. But Amal's face took on a shocked expression and he stiffened. The life drained almost immediately as a hole in his chest began to ooze blood. Jarvis whipped back around and began to raise his gun but cigar guy had already lowered his pistol. He blew smoke out of his nostrils.

"Fucking Taliban. Think they can come to me, do business, and ignore my rules. Scum."

Not the reaction Jarvis was expecting, a sentiment apparently shared by the other three men in the room. Cigar guy's volatility, though, seemed common. The other men lowered their guns and the tension dissipated.

"The small crate, it has what you came for. Take it and go." He waved the gun he'd just used on the bleeding Talib on the ground. Then he hardened and loosely held it pointing in Jarvis' direction. "But if you use anything against my men, I will see you again, yes?"

It seemed a rhetorical question so Jarvis stepped over the dead man and opened the loose top of the crate. He put one of the pistols in the band in the back of his pants and the other under the loose jacket he wore. The clips were conveniently packed into a belt, which he strapped beneath his shirt. Enough for a small assault, which was more or less what he had in mind. While arming himself, he kept an eye on everyone in the room who was still breathing. The three guards shifted uneasily once he had the guns in his hands but Cigar Guy seemed unconcerned.

Except for the look of murder in the giant guard's eyes, Jarvis thought there was a pretty good chance he'd get out. He backed his way to the staircase, coming close enough to the largest guard that he could hear his breathing and smell the fury on his skin. It wasn't from the pain in his groin, but from the frustration of not being able to rip Jarvis into small pieces.

"Thank you. I'll find my way out."

Cigar guy laughed. "If you leave alone, you will have a knife in your eye before you cross the alley." He pointed to the subordinate who'd been counting cash and gave a brief, sharp instruction. The man lowered his rifle, reluctantly, and walked toward Jarvis.

Without much in the way of options, Jarvis turned his back on the guns pointed in his direction and walked up the stairs. He passed the clean room and went through the small, secret opening guarded by the old elf who stiffened slightly until he saw the money-counting guard a step behind. A moment later Jarvis was back in the alley and everything looked perfectly normal, except he could pick out at least half a dozen men who would have been hacking him to pieces if he'd emerged alone. He headed back to the corner where Saleem would hopefully be waiting. Jarvis noticed for the first time in the last ten minutes that his heart was beating slightly faster than usual.

CHAPTER THIRTY

S aleem wasn't there but a small, angry mob of men in their twenties and thirties was. They were heading toward the opening to the alley, still about ten seconds away at their current brisk pace. Most wore traditional garb; a few were in Western clothes. All brandished some form of weapon. There were a couple of sticks that looked like they could hit a baseball further than a Louisville Slugger. Several rifles. One rolling pin. The men were all heavily bearded, observing Sharia law regarding facial hair and Taliban law regarding being angry and violent. Jarvis looked behind him toward the alley but he wouldn't get far, particularly if Cigar guy's men decided his hall pass had expired. Too much traffic to cut across the street. Running seemed cowardly. He looked up the street and could make out Saleem's taxi at a standstill, the wheels cutting toward another unmarked lane as he tried to work his way through the mass of cars to Jarvis. The men would get there long before Saleem did and Jarvis had no idea why they were bearing down on him with anger in their eyes. Jarvis reached behind his shirt for the larger gun hidden there and waited. Pulling it too soon would just agitate others near him and get him shot before the focused mob reached him. The men were only a few steps away now and Jarvis turned slightly to make himself a smaller target, also putting his shoulder against the building's stone wall for leverage. The mob got to the corner where he stood and their

voices were harsh, angry, violent. But they ignored Jarvis. They swept past
him as if he were no one of interest and continued another few feet down
the sidewalk. Jarvis did not relax his grip on the gun but looked ahead of
the passing crowd. He saw a woman, her rich, black hair bouncing on her
shoulders, the rest of her body covered by a heavy cloth down to the tops
of her shoes. She was walking without haste, looking at the vendors' stalls,
until she heard, or sensed, the furor behind her.

She turned just as the man leading the group reached her. He'd already
raised his arm, the thin, mean stick high above his head. He brought it
down across her face while he was in full stride. His momentum added
vicious weight to the blow and the woman's shock took a moment to
transform into pain. Inexplicably, she did not cringe or turn away. As if
mesmerized, she stared at the man even as an angry welt rose from her
forehead to chin. The man bumped into her as he came to a halt and
sprang back as if touching a hot stove. He raised the switch again and as he
did, the other men in his small mob surrounded the woman. Their timing
was impeccable, as the woman began to emerge from her surprised stupor
and look around for escape. There was none. A man behind her, younger
than the others but with a look of vengeful fervor in his eyes visible across
the distance to where Jarvis watched, had his rifle in his hands. He drew
it back, butt first, and brought it down toward the back of her head just as
the first man swung the switch again. It saved her life, temporarily at least,
as she tried to cover her face with her hands and bend away from the blow
from the switch. Her movements made the younger man miss what would
otherwise have been a devastating strike on the back of her skull.

All the men were shouting now and a crowd was beginning to
gather. Jarvis caught the words for "whore" and "blasphemy" or
something similar. This band, sanctioned or not, was patrolling
the streets for anyone violating Sharia law. She had gone out in
public without proper covering – not the only woman on the street
who failed to wear the head-to-toe burka, but something in her step
had caught the attention of the vigilantes. Too light-hearted, too

confident. Too happy. Other men in the group crowded in closer, striking the woman until she fell.

Jarvis itched to pull out the guns, to run over, to be the hero. He had seen this before but those times he had been with a squad of well-armed soldiers and it had been easy to intervene. Today, though, he would only be mobbed and maybe killed; at minimum he would end up in a prison. The woman probably wouldn't be killed, but she would suffer bruises, cuts, and at least a few broken bones. Her face, if the group was particularly fervent, might be sliced and made ugly, an inducement to cover it and her hair from now on. Jarvis' hands quavered and he made fists. They stayed clenched as he turned and walked toward where Saleem inched toward him. He cut across the barely moving cars and got in. His friend had seen what was happening a hundred feet away and there were tears in his eyes.

"This is not my country. This is not how I want my children to grow up. Taliban are strong again. It is…it is not what Allah wants."

Jarvis was grim-faced and tried not to look at the crowd watching the men as the taxi crept past the scene. But he did look, he stared hard. Some in the crowd cheered the abusers on. But a few, mostly older men and women but among them some youngsters, were quietly disgusted. They hid their outrage, fearful they might be next. Jarvis looked at them but could feel little optimism as the screams of the woman on the ground faded and she lost consciousness.

"We have a long drive. You can't come all the way, but if you get me as far as Bar-al-Akar I'll get a local driver." Jarvis touched the gun inside his jacket. In his mind, he dismantled it and put it back together. He did it in real-time, skipping no steps and not pretending to go faster than he was capable of – twenty seconds later he mentally stripped the larger pistol tucked in his belt.

"You know I want to help you more, my friend. To do more."

Jarvis looked at Saleem in the rear view mirror. "You have a family to take care of. You're already risking too much." The truth didn't ease Saleem's guilt over not taking up arms. He drove silently through the miasma of cars until they thinned at the outskirts of town. The road widened and traffic moved. It was late morning and the heat was beginning to build. Saleem closed the windows and turned on the air conditioning.

Jarvis thought back to the woman he shot in the throat in Mohan's New York apartment. She knew his name. She blamed Jarvis for the death of her son. It could have been one of the men he'd had to shoot during any one of a dozen firefights. A raid on a village where there'd been collateral damage. But Mohan had been there that day when the RPG hit the school. Children had died along with parents and at least a few of the Taliban who'd ambushed Jarvis. Mohan had been there, part of the capture and near-slaughter of Brin. It had to be connected. He directed Saleem toward the village, along the same road he'd ridden years earlier. This time though he wasn't in a Humvee, no armored plates or .50 caliber machine guns. No comrades who had his back except Saleem. And no idea what he was walking into except that it was part of the puzzle that led to people dying in the US and Brin struggling in the hospital.

CHAPTER THIRTY-ONE

They approached the village from the north this time. The day of the ambush the squad had entered from the south, the direction of the border. The view from this side of town was familiar to Jarvis but different, like the Mona Lisa hung upside down. If the recollection of small arms fire and explosions weren't burned into his olfactory memory, the village would be undistinguishable from hundreds of others.

He knew the length of the town was less than a mile as the crow flew, though the skies were devoid of any life. They'd driven out the day Brin was rescued. Two of the kidnappers were captured the same day, a couple more the next morning, including Mohan. If they weren't the masterminds then those behind the attack had never been caught. Jarvis directed Saleem a hundred yards along the road after they'd passed the first building and told him to pull over. Saleem did so, reluctantly.

"I will wait here." His voice was firm.

Jarvis opened the back door but did not get out. "No, head north two miles. The fuel stop, stay there. I'll call you and then you come – quick. Staying here doesn't do me any good if someone sees me getting out and decides you're a collaborator and ought to lose your head."

Several men drank coffee in a café across the street. Three women were turning up an alley fifty feet ahead. Saleem nodded. There was nothing useful he could say. Just keep his phone on and his foot near the gas pedal.

Jarvis gripped him once on the shoulder and was gone.

Saleem looked in his rear view mirror as he pulled away. Jarvis moved like a scout reconnoitering enemy territory.

The village had grown into a small town in the past eight years. There were fewer animals in the street, more buildings with signs indicating business was being conducted. Some of them had debris from explosions spread out front. He couldn't tell if the events causing the destruction were recent. He walked south, staying on the main drag but near the buildings, close to the entrances to alleyways if he needed them. Cars passed but they were sparse. The population walked, rode bikes, or sat atop work animals. The Southern mountains offered a hard life but there were no complaints on the faces of the people he passed. Outside the town food was grown, cows and goats tended, chickens raised. Within the informal boundary of the village food was prepared and sold, masonry was worked, clothing made. There was work for anyone who wanted it and unless an inhabitant was rich or busy shooting at Americans or rebels, the days were busy. Jarvis walked by open doors where men in long beards and women in full burka tended their business. All looked up as he passed, some with malice and others with disinterest. What Jarvis looked for was anyone who reached for a cell phone. Children played in the street, the occasional car swerving around them harmlessly. He turned a corner and to his right was an open bazaar with perhaps a hundred people milling about. There was price negotiating going on, a few disputes, and general camaraderie. There were also a lot of rifles, pistols, and large swords. Jarvis cut to his left and went up a small side street he remembered from the days when they had returned to the village and searched for collaborators to the ambush. He held a mental map of the maze of alleys and cutbacks that would take him to the open square he had raced into trying to find Brin. The walls were closer here and he brushed up against several people who did not yield as they passed. He turned his head frequently, checking that no one who had passed was circling back, showing more interest than necessary. The feel was more hostile than when he'd last been here, but it was subtler.

What he felt was not fury, but weariness. They were tired of the years of hostility. Afghanistan was always fighting a war and this was just the latest. Most didn't care about the Taliban one way or the other, it was just a reality of life. But the war forced them to make choices and even if they chose against the violence, the repression, and the daily death of the Taliban, they did not do it for love of the West. As he wound his way closer to the square, Jarvis knew the line between friend and foe had blurred here.

It took another ten minutes of crossing streets and alleys. Then with a jolt he turned a corner and the scene in front of him matched the picture in his head, only from a different angle. The square he'd raced into, but from across the way. The building he'd chased Brin's captors into, the second floor where guards had shouted warnings. The square was busier than it had been that day, but the feeling was the same. Commerce and life mingled. A few more balconies had been blasted away but even more new masonry was evident in a dozen spots – walls and doorways repaired, ruined, and repaired again. Jarvis scanned the square for lookouts. There was no US military presence, a few Afghan police in the far corner more than fifty yards away, and again, rifles slung on many shoulders. He looked for the protective spread favored by Taliban militants; one or two children seeming to play but more interested in scanning faces in the crowd. A long-scout as far away as possible and on high ground who could see anyone coming from a distance. And at least two armed soldiers near any entrance to a safe house or hideaway. Jarvis focused on the building where he'd chased Brin into, but aside from being nondescript it seemed to hold no attention for any of the dozens of people in the square. Children from kindergarten to teen played among the men and women doing business and socializing. A few kicked old soccer balls, others chased and played tag. A few held life-size wooden guns and played the Middle East version of cops-and-robbers. There seemed to be a lot of death and disagreements over wounds and whether they were mortal.

He stepped a few feet into the square. There was a handful of Western-looking men among the crowd. UN workers, foreign military or mercenaries. Afghanistan was a mélange. Jarvis did not draw as much attention as he would have in uniform. The new view gave him a better look. Thirty yards to his left, a café spilled out into the square. Half a dozen wooden tables were occupied by men drinking strong tea. Two had rifles that looked well-used. They drank and talked but spent more time looking around the square than at each other. A doorway ten more yards up from them captured their attention as well – one was always looking at it while the other kept an eye on the crowds. Jarvis turned his attention to the other side of the square to his right. All the way across the square but directly opposite the doorway the men found so interesting, a balcony hung off the second story of a building with few people going in and out the ground floor door. Jarvis squinted. A man with sunglasses paced the ten steps of the balcony, a rifle loosely in his hands. Jarvis cupped his hands over his eyes; there was a scope on the rifle. The sniper on the balcony, the two guards watching an entrance; he'd found a lair, though no way to know if it was the one he sought.

Jarvis stayed out of sight of the informal but effective security force and leaned against a wall. None of the guards could see him and he could keep an eye on the entrance until someone familiar entered or exited. The wait wasn't long. He'd barely worked up a sweat when the door under guard burst open and a small, ugly man emerged. The man shouted at the table of tea drinkers and pointed to the other side of the square. One of the seated men jumped up and grabbed his rifle. Jarvis looked toward the balcony across the way and could see the guard there take up a sniper's stance. The ugly man waited until the sentry from the café had made it over then he turned and barked another order. A larger, older guard came out with a pistol in his hand and bullets strapped bandolier-like across his chest. He moved confidently, as though he'd seen many gunfights. A few seconds later a tall, thin man emerged, moving slowly and without looking around. As if out for a stroll, he scratched his long beard, patches of gray making him look like an imam. Flowing robes and an ancient but sparkling clean head-dress made him stand out. He did not wait for the guard detail to fall into place; it did so as he moved. There was deference in the demeanor of the men who guarded him and as he stepped into the square, the bustle opened around him.

Jarvis knew the face, the angle of the walk. It was the man the US military had questioned repeatedly about the ambush and attack on the Americans eight years earlier. A clan leader, not exactly a religious icon but politically strong. No connection could be made then, but common knowledge was more credible than evidence. Mahmud Said had survived two decades as the strongman of this patch of Afghanistan and Jarvis was only mildly surprised to see he was still alive. There was a slight limp on Said's left side. Jarvis watched him cross the busy expanse and walk toward a break on one side of the square. He waited just a moment and then began to follow. His heart beat just a little faster as each step took him closer to the street where his Humvee had been destroyed and a building filled with children had crumbled.

The entourage around Said looked straight ahead; the sniper watched for threats further out. They weren't looking for a lone soldier. Anti-Taliban government forces, competing clans, businessmen with small armies at their disposal – that's where danger lay. Said seemed indifferent. The limp hadn't been there when Jarvis had seen him that one time, being treated deferentially by a military police liaison in front of a mosque filled with ready-to-be-violent followers. Jarvis imagined the scenarios that would have injured Said. None involved tripping over a bunny rabbit as he picked flowers in a field. Violence followed and emanated from Said. Jarvis stayed far enough back that he might lose the group but he was sufficiently sure where they were headed. The second prayer call of the day began shortly and the house of worship where Jarvis had first seen Said was a five-minute walk and only a couple hundred paces from the site of the ambush. Jarvis watched the group pass through an arch out of the square and onto a short walk that turned into an alleyway. He went to his right instead and stepped through a small shop that, like apparently every other building, had at least one table with men drinking tea. There was no clear distinction between the front and back of the store/café and Jarvis slipped into the heavily trafficked walkway on the other side. He turned right again and worked his way past men talking quickly and agitatedly, though not at or about him. He was circling around, working his way to the mosque he recollected was a couple hundred yards to his left. The buildings were too close together for him to look up and try to see the minaret. He relied on a mental map as he wound through this part of the village, finally turning left when he passed a woman in full niqab wringing out a large shirt while standing on a step leading to a narrow door. He could hear now the sound of the muezzin calling the faithful to worship. He followed the sound and the path matched where he had been heading. He turned one last corner and the voice filled the air, echoing in his ears and raising hairs on his neck. Jarvis had heard it hundreds of times, but it still brought forth an emotion that had nothing to do with war, or violence, or hatred. He ignored the feeling and looked at the entrance of the mosque. Said's guards knelt on rugs outside, guns by their knees. Said prayed inside.

Jarvis' plan was more of a loose notion of what he wanted to accomplish, less of a sequential series of steps on how to achieve it. He needed time with Said alone. A request for a personal audience wasn't likely to be well received, though. He watched the guards, who tempted the good will of Allah by regularly raising their heads to scan the streets for threats. Even if he got past the guards, he'd stand out like a wine stain on white carpet. He briefly considered a disguise and almost laughed out loud, the image of him wriggling into a burka leaping to mind. A couple of kids too young to be expected to pray ran by him, kicking a dilapidated soccer ball back and forth. He watched one boy run ten yards ahead as his friend kicked the ball up the street and the kid intersected the ball's path perfectly. Jarvis thought back to his football days and remembered the advice of the receivers' coach: go where the ball isn't – yet. He turned around and retraced his steps.

Five minutes later he entered the square at the spot where he'd started. The sniper was at his station, but more relaxed now, keeping an eye on where Said would return from the mosque. No other guards prowled the café or walkways. Jarvis joined a group of men who were either discussing the political events in Kandahar or creating a grocery list for dinner – his Farsi was limited. He crossed the square and entered a dried goods store next to the building containing the rooms from which Said had emerged. Like all the others, this place of commerce and gathering had more means of ingress and egress than a block of Swiss cheese. Jarvis passed through and out the back to a small walkway running behind the buildings.

Stragglers from the square edged past Jarvis, carrying bags of fruit or bundles of clothes. No one seemed interested in him or the scarred wooden door leading to Said's lair. That didn't seem right. He walked past the door, as disinterested as anyone else and continued ten yards to the back entry of a stall selling fabric. He acted the tourist, fingering a heavy wool shawl and watching the alley. One of the men he'd passed, holding some fruit and with the ubiquitous rifle over one shoulder, had stopped in a doorway further down and pulled out a fig. Leaning back to get out of the sun, he bit it in half. The guard had abandoned his post during the prayers to go get a snack.

Unless Jarvis wanted to wait for the man to need a bathroom break or he wanted to take on the sniper, this was his best chance. Two people walked down the alley past the guard, otherwise it was empty. Jarvis waited but as they turned the far corner, two women emerged from the same shop Jarvis had used to enter the alley. He waited for them to leave. The walk was empty. He took a deep breath, grabbed the shawl unnoticed, and started toward the guard.

Noise from the shops floated into the alley but they were alone. The guard looked casually toward Jarvis as he put the rest of the fig into his mouth then turned to look the other way, sensing no danger. Jarvis quickened his step and covered the fifteen feet in seconds. As the man turned forward and looked down into the bag to pull out something else to eat, he felt a mass moving toward him. Instinct propelled him back against the wall and his hands reached for the rifle. Before he could untangle the bag and grab for the gun, Jarvis was on him. With the momentum of his full weight moving at a fast walk, he threw his left elbow into the guard's face. The nose broke immediately. Jarvis turned his shoulders hard toward the man and punched him in the center of the diaphragm before the pain from the broken cartilage could reach the guard's brain. It hit him simultaneously – the surprise of the attack, the agony in his face, and the sudden inability to draw a breath. Stunned and confused, his hands went to whatever part of his body they could reach. Jarvis quickly looked up and down the alley for any observers and saw none. He took the guard's head in both his hands and jerked it backwards, short and hard. The dull sound of the skull against the stone wall was lost in the man's rattling breath. Jarvis embraced him and slid him down to the ground, unconscious and rasping for air through his mouth.

Hunching over him, Jarvis arranged the gun across the guard's lap and folded his legs in front. He leaned him back and put the bag with several pieces of fruit remaining atop the gun. The piece of cloth he'd taken from the shop went over the man's head and shoulders, hanging down on either side. Jarvis arranged the guard's head so his chin rested on his chest. Slightly obscured by the cloth, he looked like a hard-working sentry who was taking a much-needed siesta. It wouldn't fool too many people for long, and if another member of Said's entourage arrived all hell would break loose. Jarvis got up and walked across to the door going into Said's safe house just as three young men came around the far corner. They were too interested in pushing one another hard back and forth and laughing to worry about Jarvis. He waited until they passed and then put his hand on the warm metal handle. Expecting he would have to pick a lock or smash open the door, he gave a cursory twist. It opened silently and with a slight push he let the light into a small, cluttered room. He stepped in and shut the door quickly, waiting for his eyes to adjust and hoping there wasn't someone else in a corner of the room training a gun on him. Ten seconds passed and there was no sound of gunfire nor the feeling of metal ripping into his body. He could now make out the surroundings. It was more broom closet than entryway into a secret hideaway of a powerful Taliban clan leader.

The door at the other end of the messy room was closed but loose on its hinges. He could see light coming from the cracks. Jarvis drew his gun and went to the wall beside the door. Peering through a small gap he could see the room beyond. It was a kitchen, simple but clean. Vegetables sat on a wooden table in the center. A stove was to the right. Two pots steamed on gas burners. A late lunch would be ready for Said after his prayers, but the cook was not present. Either she was in a different room or the guards doubled as food preparers. It was the former, proven by the door on the other side of the kitchen swinging open and a young woman wearing far less than a burka coming in carrying the carcass of a recently killed chicken. Despite being little older than eighteen, she swung the chicken onto the table and started hacking at it with the cleaver in her other hand with such precision she could have worked at a Brooklyn butcher shop.

Being that age and that brazen, she could only be a daughter of Said's. Anyone else would be too deferential, too afraid, to move with such confidence even alone. Jarvis decided there was only one way to find out. He swung open the door and pointed the pistol at her. The cleaver stopped in mid air and her eyes widened but she did not look afraid. Surprise was quickly replaced by anger. She turned her shoulders and Jarvis pictured Tom Brady getting ready to throw the ball downfield, except the pigskin in this case was a large, flat, dangerous knife.

"Stop! No!" Not in Farsi, but universal in its meaning. He repeated the words in her language and audibly cocked the gun. She got angrier but the tension in her throwing arm lessened and she let it fall to her side. She spit out several expletives, two of which he recognized.

Jarvis moved a few steps closer but still out of cleaving range. He motioned with the gun for her to put it down. She complied but didn't put it out of reach. He used a similar waving motion with the gun to make her back away and stand near the sink. The thought flitted across his mind that if he had a daughter, he hoped she'd act with the same boldness displayed by this girl. He hoped he wouldn't have to kill her.

"English? Speak any English?"

She almost spit at him when she realized he was an American. Through clenched teeth she said in Farsi something along the lines of not speaking the language favored by marauders, invaders, murderers and pigs. Jarvis' Arabic was getting better by the minute. He needed her to stay calm and be a good hostage. When Said returned, if the sequence in which the guards left was reversed upon entering the house, he would leave two guards outside and be preceded into the house by the small ugly man while the larger, dangerous bodyguard stayed with his boss until the coast was clear. If they looked out back first, Jarvis was screwed.

Keeping an eye on the girl to make sure she didn't pick up some vegetables on the counter and hurl them at him, he pushed open the door to the rest of the house and took a quick look. It was not dissimilar to the many others he'd seen, including the one where Brin had been held and almost executed. He closed the door and motioned for the girl to come toward him. She complied but eyed the cleaver as she passed. He tut-tutted her and she kept her hands to her sides. Jarvis pushed the door open again and motioned her through, following closely. Her hair smelled of flowery shampoo – unusual for an Afghan woman who was forced to follow Sharia law which barely permitted soap. In the large room Jarvis could take a closer look at the setup. The front door was twenty feet straight ahead. To his right was a small door next to a larger closet door. He knew it led to a basement. He passed the girl without taking his eyes off her and tried the door handle. It was unlocked. Opening it slowly, he peered down into the darkness. A short staircase and the feeling of a large expanse below. Silent, lightless, unoccupied. He tilted his head toward it but the girl didn't move. He raised the gun to her again and gave her a grim look. No time for games. She held his stare and moved toward the door. As she passed him, she said clearly and distinctly, with little accent:

"You will die, American pig. Today, here, with your yellow blood all over my floor."

Jarvis wasn't surprised that her English was almost as good as his. "Maybe. But if you're a good girl, your father won't be the one bleeding today." He felt her fury and her desire to turn and rip his eyes out with her fingers. Instead she went through the door, down two steps and turned around. Jarvis put a finger to his lips and said "shhh." And closed the door. It locked from the outside and he turned the small bolt. It wouldn't hold if she really wanted to get out but it would give him enough notice if she did.

Prayers were almost over. Jarvis went to the other end of the room, with the front door on his left and kitchen on this right. There was a hard wooden chair next to the wall, out of place with the large sofa and three comfortable stuffed chairs placed around the room. It was where the guard sat. Jarvis settled in, holding the pistol lightly in his right hand. With his left, he took out the other gun and put it on the ground next to him. Loose, relaxed, and ready, he waited for the front door to open.

Ten minutes passed and Jarvis heard steps on the wooden platform in front of the building. There hadn't been a peep from the door leading downstairs. Men's voices discussed something about tea and whether there were any cookies in the kitchen. They stopped outside the door and Jarvis stood and moved to his left, putting the gun from the floor onto the chair. Anyone opening the front door would have to come all the way in to see him. He held the other pistol in his right hand, aimed chest-high. If he had to shoot his way out, he had enough ammunition for the two guards – a few bullets for the big guy and one for the smaller one. Said would be unarmed. Escape would be out the back, but he'd be hard pressed to get away from the two guys at the café if they decided to go around back. The voices stopped and the door handle began to turn. Working backwards from the routine when they'd left, Jarvis expected the big guard to come in first with Said close behind. His plan was to tell the guard Said's daughter was being held downstairs by a colleague and would die if he warned his boss; so would he. Jarvis had practiced words that would convey the idea, if not with precision then at least with vigor when spoken in concert with the gun. He hoped fear of getting Said's daughter killed would convince the guard to bring Said in and have a chat.

The door opened and Jarvis immediately realized he was holding the gun too high. Instead of pointing at the tall guard's chest, it was leveled at Said's head. The clan leader had come in first, pushing the door partly open and turning back to give an instruction to the men outside, then shutting it. He did not look into the room until the door was closed. When he did, he walked straight ahead to the couch, not seeing Jarvis. He went to the small door leading downstairs and unlocked it, pulling the door open and calling gently to the darkness.

"Sylia."

She came bolting up the last few steps and into her father's arms. Jarvis was confused. Said turned to him for the first time. He was calm, in charge, and dangerous all in one look. His English was excellent.

"I heard you had come to Kandahar, Lieutenant Jarvis." He was unafraid, despite the gun in Jarvis' hand. "I was not expecting you to come looking for me." He stopped in the middle of the room.

Jarvis' gun was still trained on Said. He looked at the daughter, trying to figure out how the father had known he was here. Jarvis scanned the room for cameras. There was nothing. Then he took a closer look at the girl. A small bulge in her skirt. She'd called her father on a cell phone.

"She told you someone was here, an American. How'd you know it was me?"

Said turned toward the window. "You went to Wisconsin. And New York. I know you were trying to avenge your friend, the butcher Brin who killed many of my people." He looked at Jarvis again. His voice became steely. "It is too late. For every brave Afghan you have killed, for every child crushed by the rockets you fired that day and the parents left to their grief, a hundred of your comrades will die. A thousand. You did not stop anything."

Jarvis shook his head. "That was sad. I lose sleep over it even today. But that was war. You're killing innocents now."

Said pointed a finger at him. Anger infused his accusation. "No one is innocent!"

Jarvis moved the gun toward the girl. "No one? No one is safe? Stop whatever you're doing in the States. Call it off, all of them." Said's eyes widened but he did not move other than to turn the finger he'd been pointing at Jarvis instead to the window. It instantly shattered and Jarvis' gun flew like lightning from his hand. Said barely flinched. The sniper's aim was flawless. Jarvis leapt for the second gun on the chair as Said brought out a pistol from under his robes and pointed it at Jarvis. Everyone froze.

The front door opened and the large guard barreled in, rifle pointing ahead. At the same time, the door to the basement flew open and the older man holding an ugly handgun came up the last steps and around the girl. They closed in on Jarvis and formed a semi-circle from which he could not escape. All three would put bullets in him before he could reach the chair.

"My daughter. She had a brother. He died in the school that day. The day your military bombed a room of innocent children." His voice rose and the gun wavered.

The girl went up to him and took his arm. "This man, this Jarvis, he was there?" Her father nodded. If she'd wanted to kill him before for taking her hostage, now she emanated a blood lust. "Kill him, Papa. Let me do it."

He held her back, but not for Jarvis' safety. Said tilted the gun toward the guard on his right with the rifle and said in Farsi an innocuous sounding word: "now." The man raised the rifle and aimed it at Jarvis' head. There was a cracking sound, familiar but odd, and Jarvis tightened. He was surprised for the second time that day not to feel a bullet. Instead, blood spurted out of the guard's left eye and there was a popping sound. A second bullet from a high powered rifle had knifed through the window and entered the guard's skull, passing through brain tissue and following the optic nerve before exiting through the eye. Everyone was shocked and for a moment no one could decide what to do. The reverie was broken by the old guard cocking his handgun. The next bullet passed directly through his heart after making a large hole in the window but far less noise than the other two. The guard was dead before the gun dropped from his hand. Said and the girl were still frozen in surprise and incredulity. The father came to his senses first and pushed his daughter back, out of the line of the window. He kept the gun trained on Jarvis but was afraid to shoot, not sure where the next bullet would come from. He looked expectantly at the door, knowing the two other guards at the café would have heard at least the window breaking and come running. No more than a minute had passed since the first shot knocked Jarvis' gun away; only seconds since the two guards in the room were killed. Silence prevailed. Steps came toward them. Steady, cautious. Said couldn't decide where to point his gun. He kept it on Jarvis, knowing his outside sentries would back him up so he didn't need to aim at the door, just keep Jarvis covered. It was the wrong choice.

The door swung open evenly. The tip of a rifle, then a scope, entered the room, followed by Brin. Said moved his gun toward the door but Brin had the rifle inches from his face before the surprised elder could adjust.

"Hiya, pal."

Jarvis was at least slightly more surprised than Said. "Seriously? Two days ago you were in a coma." He picked up the gun from the seat of the chair.

Brin tapped the gun still in Said's hand. "On the ground, buddy. Fast." Said let the gun slip from his hand and clatter to the ground. The girl looked confused.

"I woke up. Felt better. Got pissed. "

Jarvis shook his head, checked the slide to make sure there was a bullet in the chamber. He turned to the window. "And you decided to go on vacation to Afghanistan?"

Brin kept his eyes on the father and daughter but answered Jarvis' implied question about how the hell he'd made it through the door just now. "Sniper wasn't covered by a back-up. He's dead. The two guys in the café are just resting. They might need medical attention." He peeked a glance at Jarvis. "You left a pretty obvious trail. Wasn't very hard to find you."

That got a laugh. "I wasn't expecting to be followed."

Brin poked at Said. "Whaddya want to do with them? I'm okay with executing another Taliban group leader." The girl's eyes widened and her earlier bravado was replaced with fear for her father, but also confusion.

"You'll kill me anyway, I know, you ignorant American. But I am not Taliban. They are as mindless and violent as you, but they at least respect and love Allah."

Jarvis held his gun at his side, but kept a close eye on the door. "I don't care about your politics. I only care that you sent people to kill in my country. Me and Brin to start." That got Brin's attention. He hadn't put much thought into the politics of why he had almost died, only that he needed to find Jarvis and make sure he was okay.

Said laughed abruptly and brutally. "WE go to YOUR country and kill?" It didn't take a Sunday news show pundit to explain the irony. "I am glad to have revenge on my son's death, but I did not send anyone. Others decided to do that."

Lying seemed pointless so Jarvis believed him. "Then who?"

Ignoring the rifle pointed at him, Said turned and kissed his daughter on her head and faced Brin and Jarvis again. "Your rocket in the street that day killed many, not just my son. The Taliban protect us, they feed the people, and they make vengeance. Kill me now if that is what you are here to do."

Brin raised the rifle to Said's head. "Okay." He chambered a round with a loud click. "But it wasn't our RPG that hit that school, pal. It was one of yours."

"Liar. Liar!" Said's face reddened, rage distorting it.

Jarvis knew Brin would shoot, but only if he got a nod from him. He let it play out, because anyone looking into a rifle barrel with Brin at the other end knew with certainty he'd just met the Angel of Death. Whatever emotions played in Brin's complicated brain, compassion wasn't in the game.

"Whatever, man. I saw it. The guys who grabbed me fired one into the truck and one at the building. Same RPG profile. You ready to die now, kind of for nothin'?"

Brin's lack of compassion made room for a compelling veracity. Even under the circumstances, Said heard the truth in his voice. Rage abated and confusion wrote on his face. And then Jarvis saw it all melt away as Said came to a realization.

"Tell me. Now. What is it?" Jarvis demanded.

Said turned to his daughter and for the first time in her life she saw him cry. It was just a couple tears, silent on his stony face. "I am sorry, my daughter, I am sorry for what I have made you, in hate." She didn't understand.

He looked away from his daughter in shame but was defiant facing Jarvis. "They said it was you. It was the Americans killing our children, ripping bodies of parents apart. It was you that day. And now they are taking revenge. They used their own mistake to drive hate into our hearts."

Jarvis lowered his gun. "They sent men to kill Americans. Who did it? Why did they wait so many years?"

Said shook his head, not in denial but sadness. "Taliban. They say they save us, they want my help to have the heart of my people. But they lied, lied about a horrible mistake. They accidentally destroyed the school, and used it to blame you."

Jarvis watched the realization creep over the daughter's face. "I need a name."

Said's gaze swept the two dead men on the floor. "You are bloodthirsty and soulless beasts. I will not help you."

His daughter's hand on his arm surprised him. Her grip was hard and her shock had grown to anger. "Papa, it is true? The Americans did not kill Alar?" She already knew the answer. "If you do not tell them, then you are saying you hate them more than you love him!"

The clash between duty to his followers and the truth of his daughter's words made him grimace. He made the wrong choice and stayed silent. The girl's grip tightened and her head whipped toward Jarvis. "The local Taliban leader is Akba Mudar. Whatever you are trying to stop, he is the one."

The name was not unfamiliar to Jarvis. In that earlier time, Mudar had been known as a brutal henchman to the Taliban regional chief. He must have graduated and a lot of people had probably died for him to get his degree. Said did not react, though there may have been a hint of relief in his downturned mouth.

Jarvis spoke to Brin. "Mudar must've set up cells in the States. I don't know why they waited so long to activate them. But I get why they went after you. Only one who could say it was friendly fire that day."

Brin still hadn't lowered the rifle. "Seems like a lot of work. And kind of dumb – they just pissed us off."

Jarvis raised his eyebrows in agreement. "Let's go have a chat with Mudar. See if we can't talk him out of poisoning a bunch of innocent people." Back to Said and his daughter. "I don't think he's in the Yellow Pages." The reference was lost on them. "How about you give him a ring and invite him over." He looked down at the bodies. "Yeah, maybe you should tell him you've got a couple hostages – let him know it's us."

This woke Said out of his reverie. "No! I will not be a traitor!"

Brin swung the rifle toward the girl. "Call him." There didn't need to be a threat. Brin would pull the trigger unless Jarvis said something. Jarvis was silent. Said's hand moved under his robe and Jarvis raised his gun just in case. A cell phone appeared and Said started to dial. Jarvis wondered if the connection was any better than his crappy AT&T service back home.

There was a rapid discussion that involved Said being deferential then angry, then thankful. Jarvis couldn't make out any of the words in the dialect they spoke. Said disconnected and returned the phone to his pocket. "He will be here in an hour. He will have men with him."

Jarvis looked around the room and his eyes rested on the door to the basement. "We should make sure there's nothing in here to spook him - or outside. Brin, where'd you put the guys from the café?"

Brin looked a little mournful. "I didn't have much time, just a bunch of duct tape. Had to bring it from the States." He pointed to the basement door with his rifle. "There's an entrance to the downstairs from the place next door. Kind of hidden, but no one was around and I had three guys to stash." Jarvis figured the third was the guy he'd incapacitated in the alley. "They're all there. That's why I was out of breath a little – lots of running around."

Jarvis pictured Brin moving around the square in the open but seen by no one, taking out the sniper first, then the two guards as they returned, and getting into position to take the shot through the window. A ghost. A very fast ghost.

"Okay, we've got less than an hour before an armed Taliban entourage shows up. Should be enough time to come up with a plan. Figure out what the hell they're up to and how to stop it."

Brin raised his eyebrows questioningly. "What plan? Let's shoot these guys so we don't have to watch our backs and then the other guys when they get here. After we interrogate them, for sure."

Nodding, Jarvis gave it due consideration. "I think you're on the right track, but tactically I'd make some modifications." He tried to sound thoughtful and not laugh. "Let's start with Said and his daughter. They live. And Mudar is a thug and heartless prick, but he'd probably love to die a martyr. We won't get much from him with a straight-on approach." Jarvis looked at Said and the girl, wondering if they'd followed the nuance of him saving their lives. "If you two help, this will go a lot better. I know we're not going to be pals and after we're gone, you'll get back to riling up the crowds so they think we're all devils, but on this thing you're wrong. We didn't blow up the school – it was just a horrible mistake, one made by your team."

He waited. Said was torn, but not the girl. "Do it, Father. Help them. I don't fear death," which she spat in Brin's direction, "but I won't die for no reason. Help them."

Said looked closely at her and Jarvis could see the decision shift. "Yes. I will help." Brin lowered the rifle, but not his guard.

Looking around the room for something to work with, Jarvis stopped at Brin. "You have any of that duct tape left?"

CHAPTER THIRTY-TWO

Twenty minutes later everyone was in the basement in a tableau very different from the one upstairs. The space was large and mostly barren, a room where men could meet and talk without distraction. Chairs were scattered around the room and a makeshift podium was pushed up against a wall. The stairs leading down had a large storage space beneath, enough to hold four bodies as it now did although two were still breathing. In the center of the room two scarred wooden chairs were back-to-back. Brin and Jarvis were identically bound – ankles to the thick wood legs of the chairs, waists encircled by the same duct tape to the backs of the chairs, and hands bound uncomfortably behind them. Said watched as his daughter tore two more pieces off with her teeth. She was focused and efficient.

"Get him down here. Try to keep the guards upstairs." Said nodded. The sound of banging echoed from upstairs through the open door at the top of the stairs. Mudar had arrived. Out of courtesy to Said he would not burst in, at least not until after a decent interval. Said turned to the stairs.

"No, not you. Her." Jarvis nodded at the girl. Said began to object but Brin craned his neck around and gave a look. The daughter understood why it had to be her.

"I will bring them." She put a piece of tape over Brin's mouth and then Jarvis, who smiled just before she did. She was disarmed for a moment, then turned and went up the stairs. She did not acknowledge her father as she passed. When she reached the top, she closed the door. Brin turned around, unhappy. The sounds above were now muffled. Until a sharp, angry voice cut through the door and several sets of feet crossed the floor. Jarvis could hear the girl alternately demanding and pleading, though the words were unclear. She was trying to keep the guards upstairs. From the amount of pounding, he guessed three men in room – Mudar and two guards. There would be at least a few more out front for show. The door opened and Said stood at the bottom of the stairs, waiting. Sandals hit the steps and a weathered young man in desert garb defiantly descended, brandishing an old Kalashnikov. He looked past Said and at the bound men in the chairs. Said ignored the guard, who went around him and shouted a few words up the stairs. The next set of footsteps echoed haughtily in the basement. Mudar entered like a sultan, nodding at Said and not pausing, assuming the older man would get out of the way. He was ugly, not in the way that made him almost handsome. In the way that got him women only because he was a killer and had power. Said stepped aside deferentially. His daughter followed a few steps behind and looked chastened for allowing one of the guards to have gotten past her.

"You are not dead!" Mudar was equally surprised and angry. His powers of observation made Jarvis smile under the tape. "Why are you here?" He waited for an answer, convincing Brin and Jarvis that he gained his power through violence, not intellect. He caught on and pointed at his bodyguard who leaned in and ripped the duct tape off Brin's mouth first, then Jarvis'. It hurt.

"Why are you here? Why are you not dead?" as if they could now understand the question with their mouths unencumbered.

Jarvis licked his lips. "Brin almost died. And your morons couldn't get to me."

Mudar moved quickly. He slapped Jarvis, hard, in the face almost before Jarvis could brace himself. It was not just a threat, but a sign of disrespect. "Then you'll die here instead. You came here to stop me?

Stupid Americans, think they can come five thousand miles and start a war. You have a war now, pigs!"

Jarvis was fairly certain Mudar would saw off their heads right now if he had a steak knife. "You sent men to poison innocent people. Even a scumbag like you could have the decency to go after military targets, not women and children."

Mudar's anger dissipated into laughter. "No one is innocent. Tell me why you are here and I will kill you quickly."

Brin couldn't resist. "To kill you, asshole, before you hurt anyone else."

Mudar raised his hand to slap Brin but the angle would have resulted in him smacking Brin in the ear. Instead he spat in Brin's face. He got laughter in return. Brin wasn't fearless – he just didn't know what fear was.

Before it could deteriorate further, Jarvis cut in. "I followed the trail. The kid who poisoned Brin and a couple others, the guy in Wisconsin who received and distributed the stuff, and your pal Said here," he nodded unpleasantly at Said to keep up appearances.

"Then you are truly fools. You will wish you had died that day when the school fell, or by poison back in your despicable home." Mudar's voice began to rise, a sermon on his lips.

"No, dumbass, you're the fool. You're taking revenge on something we didn't do." That stopped Mudar. He looked surprised. Jarvis kept him off balance. "The rockets that hit the school and killed those kids and parents, it wasn't ours. It came from your guys."

"Lousy frickin' aim."

Mudar's face squinted in confusion. "You know that? You know the bomb was from us?"

The wording caught Jarvis' attention. The English wasn't perfect, but good enough that he knew Mudar picked his words. And he figured it out. "You already knew. You knew your own RPGs hit the school and you used it to get people riled up."

Said looked at Mudar quizzically but Mudar ignored him. A look of pain came over the daughter's face. Mudar laughed again, only this time it was cold and dark.

"You are the fools. It was no accident. We waited for you, at that spot. We ambushed you in front of the school. We fired on the school as if we were shooting at you. It was a plan. A brilliant plan in praise of Allah!"

The room was silent except for the sound of breathing and the almost audible thumping of hearts as realization spread. Jarvis broke the reverie.

"You killed those kids, those mothers, to get sympathy?" He was incredulous but something was still off.

Mudar leaned in close, almost nose to nose with Jarvis. "I did not want sympathy. I wanted fury. The fury of orphans, children who lost everything because of the Americans. Children who would do anything for revenge, even grow up and go to America and raise the sword of Allah to smite the heathen!"

Even Brin was mildly surprised. "You're a freakin' psycho."

The slang may have been foreign to Mudar, but he understood the sentiment. "Tell me what you have learned. Tell me what you know of the glorious plan! If you do, you will die honorably." His inconsistency on method of death did not comfort Jarvis.

Said's eyes were closed. Thoughts of his son dying so Mudar could carry out a plot to increase his power and influence tore at him. His knees weakened. Mudar barked an order at his guard who raised the rifle and pointed it at Jarvis' head.

"Tell me now."

Jarvis looked at the guard whose eyes were lining up on the sight of the rifle. With a startle, the guard's gaze moved away from the rifle and back to Mudar, a sudden movement catching his attention. The daughter's arm was making a wide arc and the small knife she'd hidden under her scarf flashed above her head before she plunged it into Mudar's neck. Blood instantly shot out and hit Jarvis' face. Mudar made a high-pitched squeal and clawed at his throat. Jarvis turned back to the guard, expecting a bullet to either hit him in the forehead or whiz by on its way to the girl. The rifle wavered as the guard overcame surprise and tried to regain his composure and prepare for a fight. He didn't have time to make the transition. Brin and Jarvis simultaneously reached under their chairs, the duct tape on their wrists entirely for show and not restricting their movements. Each came out with a pistol and Brin's shot rang first, entering the guard's left eye and killing him instantly. Jarvi's shot was a heartbeat behind, piercing the guard's chest and stopping any last-minute pumping of the organ with the brain already dead. Both men stood, the tape on their chest as much a ruse as that on the their wrists, and pointed the guns at Mudar. He was already on the ground, but much further from death than his bodyguard. Blood had stopped spurting and was oozing now. The daughter stood over him and cursed in Arabic. She put her face close to his and growled the name of her brother, then plunged the short knife into Mudar's chest at the diaphragm. Unable to breathe his last, Mudar choked and fell into unconsciousness and died quickly from loss of blood and lack of oxygen.

The two shots had not gone unnoticed and the flurry of activity didn't distract Brin or Jarvis. Footsteps came to the top of the stairs and started down. The second guard was confident the sounds had been of an execution. He was just unaware of the identity of the victims. He did not find out, as Brin put a bullet in his right kneecap as soon as the guard's legs came into view. As the man fell forward in agony, Jarvis shot him twice in the head. The body rolled noisily down the stairs and came to a rest next to Said, who still had not said a word. He was the only confused one in the room, the only one unable to act.

The girl was unfazed by the death around her. The gunshots had barely distracted her intense study of Mudar's body. Now she turned to her father.

"How could you let this happen? They killed my brother. They killed your son!"

Jarvis reached gently but quickly for the knife still in her hand. She didn't notice. Upbringing wouldn't let her harm her father, but she could hate him with a hot fury.

Brin's tone was the same as when he'd been facing Mudar and imminent

death. "Your father didn't know." It was a fact. He turned to Jarvis, with
the body of Mudar curled in a bloody ball between them, "there're some
other guys out there. We should take off."

It was excellent advice. Killing a Taliban leader was several notches
worse than any of the other killing they'd done that day.

"I need to be sure they won't send anyone else to the States. Someone'll
pick up where he left off." He pointed at Mudar on the floor. "I've got a
list of the others, but was hoping we'd get him to call them off. Don't think
we'll get him to do it now. Unless he's got a boss." He said it like a question.
Said did not register it but his daughter did.

"Who else? Who else is doing this?" Her voice was near hysteria and
her hands were in fists, ready to pummel her father. The tone broke his
catatonia. He turned and looked past her, to Jarvis.

"There is no one else. This was Mudar's plan. Not from the beginning.
Sheikh Kalid plotted it. Mudar was his right-hand man, until Kalid was killed.
Now it is just Mudar and his men. I did not know they were so evil. I did
not...I did not know..." His voice broke and it was sad and inexcusable.

Brin spoke directly to Jarvis. "It'll keep on. His men will want revenge
and they'll keep going."

Said's voice interrupted and it was stronger. "No, they will not. I won't
let them. I'll tell everyone what happened. They will be pariahs."

Jarvis looked over the scene. "We don't have a lot of choice. We need
to get back to the States and hunt down the rest of these guys. They're
hiding after I got a couple, but they'll start up again."

There was some sort of emotional, cathartic exchange threatening to
overtake the group, the girl forgiving her father or Said pledging to help the
Americans. Instead, Brin turned and headed for the back door leading out
to the alley. Jarvis took one final look around, picked up the pistol from the
belt of the guard who'd tumbled down the stairs, and followed Brin without
looking back. There was silence behind him as he ducked through the
door. He mentally counted the bodies who'd taken their last breaths in the
half-day since he'd been in Afghanistan. He felt no sorrow for any.

CHAPTER THIRTY-THREE

"You want to explain how you got out of the hospital and made it to Afghanistan thirty-six hours after I figured you were brain dead?"

They could hear shouts coming from the square but that was almost a hundred yards away. They were working their way through the back alleys and toward the East side of the town. Jarvis pulled his cell phone out of his pocket and squinted at the display. One bar, which appeared and disappeared.

"I woke up, asked a few questions and took off before they could quiz me about my social security number. I don't like hospitals."

Brin had spent approximately three hours at Landstuhl hospital in Germany after almost being beheaded; which was a little less than the seven days of recovery and observation the doctors had ordered. Since then, Jarvis knew from direct experience that a sewing kit was as close to medical treatment as Brin had seen in a decade, excluding his recent coma.

"Yeah, okay." He looked at the phone again as they picked up their pace along with the volume of noise coming from the square. "But now we're even." Brin smiled without breaking pace or looking over at Jarvis. They both were vigilant, looking for threats from any direction including above. They rounded a corner and saw a group of armed men smoking outside yet another coffee drinking spot haphazardly set up in the middle of the small road. Brin and Jarvis didn't stop, which would have drawn more attention to themselves. They kept moving and the men shot them dirty looks but nothing more.

They took a hard right at the corner. It was the wrong direction but they didn't want to pass too closely to the men. Jarvis saw a solid bar on the phone and hit speed dial. The phone barely rang before Saleem picked up.

"You are ready? I can come now?" Jarvis could hear the feigned calm in the voice.

"Yeah, now would be a good time. Same spot, and make sure the car is turned around – and gassed up." He cut the connection as they turned left on another small side street to get heading back in the right direction. Behind them a hubbub boiled up. There were steps on the stone underfoot and the pace was increasing. Interested parties were getting closer. Voices shouted now, and Jarvis knew word had gone out. The men they'd passed were looking for them or had told Mudar's followers about the two American's who'd hustled by. Brin looked at Jarvis and pulled out the gun he'd kept under his jacket.

"Think we'll need to shoot our way out?" Brin was mostly nonchalant.

"Not today, Butch. I'd like to make it back to the States in one piece." They broke into a trot, each taking a turn looking back while the other looked forward. It was a natural, well-orchestrated partnership that might keep them both alive.

Neither had to tell the other which turn to make. They went left twice, then right, and cut across another alley. They were getting closer to the street near the edge of town but there was no way to know if a posse was waiting for them. The Taliban network could be tightly woven or full of gaping holes. Jarvis crossed his fingers for the latter. They reached a small intersection. Straight ahead was the main road and a hundred yards west was where Saleem would appear in another minute or two. Straight ahead also was a two-man guard walking down the middle of the narrow street. Shoulder-to-shoulder, they had rifles pointed in front of them – the silver lining being that they were walking away from Brin and Jarvis instead of toward them. Jarvis looked to his right and the street curved back the way they had come with no openings in the building to let them cut through. To the left was just a wall. Only one good choice. He took a deep breath and nodded toward the guards who were talking excitedly and angrily. At any moment they could turn around and see the Americans standing like tourists. Brin and Jarvis bent over to make themselves smaller targets and moved quickly and quietly toward the main street and the guards.

Brin was stealthy but Jarvis was faster. He reached the guard on the left just as the men sensed someone behind them. It was too late. The butt of Jarvis' gun made a dull, angry sound against the man's skull. He fell limply to the ground without a sound. Brin's approach was more time consuming. He threw an arm around the other guard's neck before he was able to do anything more than look in surprise at his companion's body drifting to the ground. Brin locked his forearm across the man's throat and used his left hand to hold it in place, the gun still in his right hand. The guard struggled heavily for a moment until lack of oxygen to his brain put him to sleep. Brin gave an extra tug for good measure and he heard cartilage strain. He gently laid the man on the ground. Seconds had passed and the alley was now empty of anyone standing except Brin and Jarvis. They trotted to the corner where the wider street passed and peered around the corner. Normal activity, men and women walking and talking, none appearing to be on the lookout for foreign murderers.

Jarvis did not see Saleem but knew he would be there. They walked briskly onto the broken cement and turned right. They avoided looking like killers on the run and moved cautiously but steadily toward the spot a hundred yards away where Saleem would soon be. There were people on the street, residents trying to live their lives. No one looked too closely at them, but the hair on the back of Jarvis' neck stood up despite the sweat that now soaked his shirt. He and Brin moved like hunters being hunted. They were halfway to the spot when they heard an engine gunning and shouts from a side road. They didn't break stride but both men looked back as a pickup truck careened onto the main street from the left. The bed of the truck banged into the stone wall of a building as the driver over-corrected. He hit the gas and the back corner of the truck scraped a few feet before it got onto the street, forcing a woman carrying a three-year-old to almost dive into the middle of the road. Brin and Jarvis picked up their pace, but they wouldn't be able to outrun the pick-up. They'd both seen in one glance what was chasing them – one driver, a passenger with a handgun hanging out the window, and a man with what looked like an automatic weapon in the truck bed. The driver's inept maneuver hadn't thrown the outside shooter off, but banged him around enough to keep the gunfire from erupting. Jarvis calculated they had about 30 seconds and the truck would run them over; even odds on whether their bodies would be riddled with .50 caliber bullets when that happened. They ran faster.

Wheels screeched and an engine strained. This time, though, it came from up ahead. Thirty more feet and there wouldn't be any buildings on either side as the street broke into open space. Saleem's cab raced toward them, a hundred feet away. If he came too far, there wouldn't be room to turn around quickly enough. The pick-up occupants wouldn't watch patiently while Saleem executed a 3-point u-turn. Jarvis raised his arm and made a circular motion like a blender. It must have pissed off the guy with the automatic because there was a crack of gunfire and bullets sprayed the wall to their left. His aim improved slightly and the next round hit the stone to their right. Brin and Jarvis instinctively began zigzagging in counterpoint to each other, making the target smaller but increasing the risk that one would be hit. Jarvis kept his eye on the taxi. Saleem didn't need any instruction. His motivation to get to his friend as quickly as possible was quelled by his desire save his life; he spun the wheel hard and the car did a smooth 180…and kept going around. The front wiped out a small cart holding multi-colored fruits, shocking the vendor who was suddenly holding a large melon above empty space, but the impact corrected Saleem's turn and he was skidding backwards. He'd been accelerating, hitting 60 mph before turning the wheel, and his momentum kept him sliding another thirty feet, trunk first, toward Brin and Jarvis –

and the pick-up truck spitting bullets. It deserved to be filmed and added to a James Bond movie.

Brin and Jarvis needed another ten seconds to reach the taxi. It would be close. They could feel the truck getting closer. They split, Jarvis going left and Brin right. Running along the wall, they forced the gunmen to pick one. Jarvis figured their odds had increased to a 25% chance of survival. They pushed for the final sprint and ten feet from the car they saw the taxi's trunk hit by half a dozen rounds. Brin shouted "go, go, go!" and Saleem hit the gas. He started to accelerate forward and Brin and Jarvis gave it one more push. They hit max foot speed as Saleem got the taxi up to ten miles per hour. They reached the doors on either side and grabbed the handles. In unison they dove in and the doors slammed shut behind them from the force of the taxi's acceleration. Bullets shattered the back window and several continued forward, creating spidery cracks in the windshield. The pick-up truck was straight behind them and the passengers' aim was truer.

The men in the taxi did not exchange words; there was no confusion about next steps. Saleem jammed his foot on the gas and both Brin and Jarvis pulled out their guns. Jarvis had one in each hand. They turned, knees on the back seat, and fired out the space where the window had been. Jarvis got off half a dozen shots from both guns, taking out a headlight and cracking the truck's windshield but mainly trying to keep the pursuers from being able to take close aim. Brin, even in the heat of a deadly chase, remained the marksman. He lined up his shot, accounting for the swaying of both vehicles and jarring up and down from the poorly paved road. He pulled the trigger twice in rapid succession. The man with the automatic rifle in the bed of the pick-up didn't feel the second shot shatter his jaw because the first had entered his skull just about in the middle of his forehead and destroyed enough brain tissue that pain had no time to register. He did a cartoonish back flip off the truck and the shooting stopped instantly.

"Shit. Remind me never to piss you off."

Brin smiled at the compliment but did not take his eyes off the truck.

The primary threat neutralized, he took a deep breath and exhaled. He pulled the trigger three times in succession. The first finished the job on the truck's windshield Jarvis had started. The second hit the driver in the shoulder. Before he could react to the pain and swerve, the third bullet crashed through his chest breaking two ribs and tearing a lung, lodging next to his spinal cord. He did not die instantly. The truck cut right as his arm jerked back from the pain. The driver fell forward and to his left, turning the wheel that direction and sending the truck to the other side of the street. The wheels caught a crack in the road and the truck, now sideways, went airborne and began to flip. At sixty miles an hour there was enough force to complete two and a half turns. It hit the ground upside down and slid another twenty feet. Fuel being the only thing in abundance in Afghanistan other than Taliban, the tank was full and ready to create an impressive explosion. It did. Brin and Jarvis ducked instinctively in anticipation of shrapnel outracing the taxi despite the increasing distance they were putting between themselves and the mess. A few shards of glass and bits of unidentifiable metal, perhaps mixed with some remains of either the driver or his not yet dead passenger embedded themselves into the cab's trunk and a few rained down on the roof.

Saleem took a quick glance in the mirror and saw the destruction but did not slow down. He was at fifty miles per hour and heading toward seventy. Brin and Jarvis turned back around and sat facing forward. Both started to reload their weapons.

"Nice clustering."

"I was off with the second shot on the driver. I'm still a little woozy from the coma." Brin did not speak with irony, just explaining his subpar performance.

Jarvis leaned forward and put a hand on Saleem's shoulder. "Very good timing. There's a race in the States called the Daytona 500. I'm going to enter you in it. But slow down now. We don't want any more attention then we've already earned."

CHAPTER THIRTY-FOUR

Jarvis caught Saleem's eye in the mirror. "We need to find a place for you, at least until they sort out whether the town decides Mudar's a martyr or a nut." It seemed pretty obvious to Jarvis but he wasn't an expert on geopolitical clanship and Narcissism.

Saleem managed a weak grin. "I'm not the one shooting the town up and killing the spiritual leader of the local Taliban." His irony slightly lessened the heaviness associated with racing away from the scene of multiple killings, hundreds of rounds fired, and at least one RPG. "I've got a cousin north of the city. We'll be okay for a month or two." His expression, which Jarvis could hear more than see, went grim. "How are you two going to get out of Afghanistan? Or is there more to do here?" This time when he looked in the mirror he was checking out the still burning truck even as it receded into the distance.

"I could stick around and do some more stuff." Brin's idea of 'stuff' differed from how Jarvis wanted to spend his time. Brin was good at killing and mildly indifferent to the circumstances. Jarvis was good and less indifferent.

"You could always re-up for a tour."

That drew a rare laugh from Brin. He could get work as a contractor but the military wasn't allowed to touch him. As much as they valued his talent, there had been too many off-the-record civilian missions in the past decade where he'd pissed off people, some with pull in offices at the Defense Department.

"The Colonel arranged extraction in case things heated up. And if I managed to leave not in a body bag." He looked over at Brin. "I'm sure there'll be a second seat, but I don't suppose he was expecting you'd be here."

They drove in relative silence a few miles, the wind whistling through a couple dozen bullet holes and the glassless back window. A few cars passed going in the other direction. A horn unexpectedly blared behind them. Fifty feet back and coming up fast was a large, ancient Mercedes sedan. Saleem pressed the gas pedal. Jarvis and Brin turned and readied their guns. The car must have been going more than 100 mph, closing the distance in seconds.

"Take it easy!" Jarvis ordered, "don't speed up."

Saleem looked wildly in the mirror at his friend but obeyed. The Mercedes was on them and Saleem braced for ramming or gunfire. Instead the driver of the car flashed its lights and moved into the lane for oncoming traffic. It passed by without any of the four occupants looking over. They were engaged in animated conversation and swerved back in front of the taxi three or four seconds before instigating a head-on collision with a large, open truck carrying fruit coming from the other direction.

"Women drivers." Brin's deadpan cracked up Jarvis and broke through Saleem's tension. No woman had driven in Afghanistan since the first Model T rolled off the production line, except for US military personnel. A beating or worse would be the penalty.

They moved along at an unremarkable speed for another two miles, the men in the back seat keeping an eye out for anyone looking like they were pursuing and not just driving like crazy people. Both also looked out to the desert. The Taliban had almost as much equipment as the Afghan army and a Humvee coming from the desert could be a patrol summoned by Mudar's men. Saleem saw trouble first.

"Up ahead, about a mile." On clear days, with no dust storms or smoke from explosions, visibility was almost endless.

Brin and Jarvis peered through the cracked windshield. They could make out three military vehicles, but not their markings. Two blocked the road, one idled on the side facing them. Cars coming in their direction did not stop, only slowing down to go around the vehicles. But cars going out of the town were being stopped and men with rifles were peering into windows. Saleem slowed down.

"Keep moving, don't slow!" Jarvis checked his ammunition.

Brin looked to either side but already knew the answer. There were no side roads, and the taxi wouldn't make it more than a half mile on the sand. He didn't need to count how many bullets he had left.

"We run it." Jarvis knew the likely outcome, but it was the lowest risk option. Behind them they were guaranteed to be wildly outnumbered. "Get ready."

Brin interrupted the preparation. "Seven o'clock."

Jarvis looked to his left and back a little. A cloud of dust fifty yards away in the desert was getting closer. "We're fucked. Speed up."

Saleem hit the gas. There were two civilian cars waiting to get through the checkpoint and the guards were waving them along laconically after a quick glance. Brin and Jarvis put bullets in the chambers of their handguns and the rifle.

"Head to the right, then veer left when we're twenty feet away – play chicken with the oncoming cars when you go around the Humvee. Don't give ground…" Jarvis' expectations of surviving dropped.

The lead guard at the roadblock looked up as he heard the taxi's engine rev. Jarvis could see they were Afghan regulars. That was little comfort. Some were allies, trained by the US and committed to freeing their country. Others secretly harbored hatred for the invaders and stayed in the military instead of becoming Taliban marauders because it gave them free reign to commit mayhem. Like now.

"I'll take out three – front guy, driver on the far left, and the one taking a piss on the side of the road." Brin would have said five if they weren't only twenty seconds from contact. Even he had limits.

The vehicle coming in from the desert was on a collision course with the taxi and its speed was impressive. Fifteen seconds to contact and Brin put his rifle out the passenger side window. The guards at the roadblock were signaling one another wildly, reaching for their guns and trying to decide whether to stand firm or run from the crazy driver who looked like he was going to ram them. Two elected to head to their vehicles for cover. The Humvee coming from the desert was close now but the dust kept Jarvis from being able to make out the driver or other occupants. Under other circumstances he'd have Saleem hit the brakes hard and let the Humvee pass, but that would make them sitting ducks for the other mercenaries.

"Back off the speed for a couple seconds, then gun it!" He hoped this would be enough to throw off the other driver's timing.

Saleem did the maneuver and Brin lined up his first shot. The taxi's acceleration wasn't enough, the engine straining and unable to get up the verve to jump forward. The Humvee from their left was just about on them. It hit the semi-paved road and impact was less than a second away. Jarvis turned his gun toward the oncoming car and aimed around Brin to try to take a shot and throw off the driver. His finger began to tighten on the trigger and the Humvee neatly swerved to its left, the back wheels sliding a few feet but righting immediately and suddenly it was driving alongside the taxi at the same speed, in the other lane. It left the dust behind and Jarvis could see a driver and one passenger. He instinctively aimed at the driver while his mind registered the sight.

"Could you pull over, Captain Jarvis!" the corporal in the passenger seat shouted over the two roaring engines.

Jarvis eased his finger off the trigger. If it was a Taliban trick then they'd gotten very good at impersonating a Nebraska accent.

Brin had already assessed the situation but Saleem needed some direction. "Ease up, Saleem. It's my escort." He had to lean forward and shout in his ear, not just because of the noise but because the driver's attention was riveted. He had emotionally braced for what was probably impending death. It wasn't as common an experience for him as for Jarvis and Brin. Jarvis' voice broke through and Saleem hit the brakes. A little too hard and the taxi swerved precariously almost sideswiping the Humvee but the Army driver was good and avoided a collision. The taxi burned some rubber but righted and came to a halt before smashing into the second car in line at the blockade. The Army vehicle pulled alongside. The two vehicles blocking the road were regular Afghan military. Not a huge vote of confidence, but in this case they appeared to be protecting against violence, not instigating it.

"Chopper waiting for you, sir. I was only expecting one passenger." The corporal stood outside the taxi, weapon at rest but vigilant to anyone approaching. "We can take all three, sir."

Jarvis looked at Brin. "The Colonel's got eyes everywhere."

"Sir, there's a report of two armored vehicles and a pickup truck with hostiles heading this way."

Jarvis and Brin got out on either side of the taxi. No time for long goodbyes. "Stay away at least a month. They don't know who you are, but they'll be looking for the car." Jarvis looked over the vehicle. "Hope you've got a good body man."

Saleem was still shaken but sufficiently calm to smile. "It will be good as new next time you visit." Visit.

Jarvis reached through the window and shook his hand a long moment. "Thank you." He let go and trotted to the Humvee. Brin was already in the back, scanning the horizon in all directions. He looked hungry for something else to shoot. The corporal gave a wave to the Afghan guards who had emerged cautiously from their vehicles, glad the crazy Americans weren't going to run them over. Jarvis joined Brin in the back and they split the perimeter, each taking 180 degrees. The driver pulled away quickly, heading out to the desert and toward a spot just over the horizon where a transport helo awaited them. No one followed, no bullets plinked the armor. Five minutes and they were in the 12-man helicopter and kicking up an even bigger dust cloud. The airport was a fifteen minute flight. Jarvis hadn't checked the outbound schedule for commercial flights. There'd be a charter heading out at some point in the next twelve hours and the international airport would be safe for that long – the Taliban wouldn't launch an assault just for him and break the day-to-day low level insurgency with an open attack. But the helicopter veered north instead of vectoring to the Kandahar airport. Brin gave him a thumbs-up and a smile. Over the noise he shouted:

"VIPs, huh?"

CHAPTER THIRTY-FIVE

The US military base for the southern region came into view a couple minutes later. The Colonel had gone above and beyond. Jarvis figured he must know more about what was going on than Jarvis realized. They landed near three other helicopters, but much larger and meaner – bristling with weapons. The corporal who'd escorted them to the transport earlier had put them in the company of a sergeant who looked at them quizzically but respectfully when he'd led them into the helicopter. Now he jumped out and signaled toward a permanent looking tent.

"Sirs, you can clean up in there. Transport plane heads to Frankfurt at 1600 hours. Commercial flight to Los Angeles after a couple hour layover."

Jarvis nodded. "Thank you, Sergeant. I'll mention your hospitality." Nothing rewarded a career military man like recognition with a higher up who could support early promotion.

They headed to the tent and the noise from the enormous rotor lessened. Brin looked like he'd just arrived home after a long stay away. Jarvis glanced over and could only think, "pig in shit."

They opened the metal door to the tent, which was more portable barracks than camping accoutrement. A couple thousand square feet, separated into rooms by wood paneling, and a shower and full bathroom at the far end. It was empty and the rations on the table up against the wall were a couple notches better than MREs. Brin looked slightly disappointed – probably had in mind a good tube of steak mush and freeze-dried mac and cheese. The fresh sandwiches were too civilized.

He rested the rifle that was still in his left hand on the ground and cocked his head at Jarvis. "What next, Kimosabe?"

Jarvis laughed abruptly. "Kimosabe? You watching TVLand in your hut in the woods?" He went over to grab a sandwich; he hadn't eaten in sixteen hours, a rookie mistake. No way to know when the next meal was coming or when he'd need a burst of energy. "Next we've got some hunting to do." He took a bottle of water and sat in a folding chair at a small table in the center of the room.

Brin took water but eschewed the sandwiches and sat down across from Jarvis. "Keep going."

Jarvis thoughtfully chewed a reasonably good egg salad on rye. He pulled a sheet of paper from his breast pocket and unfolded it in front of Brin. It had names, addresses, and some numbers on it.

"Mudar was running an operation to poison people in the States. Sick fucker blew up the school and blamed it on us so he could foment fury and vengeance in the kids who lived and the parents of the ones killed."

Brin didn't look at the paper. "Foment?"

Jarvis choked on a bite of sandwich and held back another laugh. "I found a couple of 'em, and most of the rest probably went underground. FBI has the list – well, they have part of the list." Now Brin looked down at the sheet.

"Why'd you hold back on these?"

Jarvis fingered the corner of the paper. "The sleepers out in the boonies were probably their second-raters. They'll stay hidden and the Feds will track them down. Timmons has them. But the A-list crazies are going to be in the big city where they can do more damage. They won't stay quiet for long. We're gonna find them. You in?"

"Try and stop me. Kimosabe."

"Careful or I'll start calling you Tonto. Or worse – Robin."

That got a solid laugh out of Brin. They looked at the list and began to map out a strategy: Chicago, New York, San Francisco. Jarvis had already terminated the threats in LA. New York was down one after his visit to Mohan. That left one more in NY and one each in Boston and San Francisco. The Terrorist A-Team. He and Brin were now a kill squad of two. Word would get out about Mudar being dead and the cells would either disappear forever or accelerate their pace. If they were still awaiting instructions, they'd be confused and the FBI would have time to track them down. But if timetables had already been established, they'd eventually bull forward. They were kids, turned by hatred and set on a path in a country they were told had ruined their lives. But as kids they were still impressionable – and unpredictable. He and Brin would need to focus on the major cities.

Jarvis pulled out his satellite mobile. Among the various emails was one from Lufthansa. It was an electronic boarding pass for FRA to JFK. "Looks like we really are VIPs. Business class across the Atlantic. I've got yours here – guess the Colonel didn't have your email address." Brin probably had a few dozen addresses, none traceable to him.

"Great, I can catch up on my tv shows."

Jarvis wasn't entirely certain his friend was kidding. He planned on getting at least two nights' worth of sleep on the military plane to Germany. There was planning to do and the comfort of a smooth-flying commercial flight with food and drink was the perfect setting. They sat quietly for a few minutes, very different emotions about the job ahead but almost identical strategizing going on their minds.

"I'm going to grab a shower. We've got a couple of hours."

Brin looked up. "I was gonna say something, but…"

Jarvis laughed as he headed to the back of the building. His friend still smelled of hospital and sweat. He hoped there was enough hot water for Brin after he took his own 30 minutes to wash the sand, the grime, and the scent of death off his body.

CHAPTER THIRTY-SIX

I t was a seven hour ride to Frankfurt am Main Airport. The converted DC-10 was almost as loud as the helicopter and much bumpier. The seats were slightly more comfortable than aluminum beach chairs. Jarvis settled across from Brin who promptly fell asleep and snored lightly for six and a half hours. Jarvis had no doubt that if a gun were cocked within fifty feet, Brin would instantly awaken and have the target in his sights. But all other noises were filtered out.

Jarvis pulled out a tiny spiral notebook, smaller than a cop's beat notes. A shard of pencil stuck out the metal rings. He flipped open to an empty page as the plane sharply ascended. The first five thousand feet kept them in range of any shoulder missiles the Taliban might have acquired, so the quicker they made it out of that altitude the happier everyone was. Descents were even more interesting since gravity was working in their favor.

He doodled for a moment, creating an intricate and meaningless design along one row of the lined paper. The shapes didn't form anything in particular, but resembled a geometric prison. His mind wandered to Wisconsin, then New York, and finally the ground falling away below.

Movie idea: A girl raised in Afghanistan learns to hate the invaders, her father a leader of the insurgency. She meets a soldier, who she believes is responsible for the death of her father, only to learn her own countrymen did it for political reasons. She questions her allegiance as she falls in love with the soldier.

Ending?

His pre-sleep ritual sometimes took the form of movie ideas. He re-read it and tried to picture Brin with a family, but kept seeing him like Tarzan living in tree-tops instead.

Jarvis stretched his legs out, leaned back, and watched Brin breathing deeply half a dozen times before his own eyes fell heavily. He slept for two hours, double his norm, making up for the previous night of no sleep at all. He cycled through two periods of REM and the dreams were vivid and shocking, but they didn't interfere with his rest. He awoke refreshed and peered out the window into the dark sky knowing the sun was chasing them westward. Below was the first hint of Europe and in a couple of hours they'd land in Germany. He looked over at Brin who didn't appear to have moved in the slightest.

Jarvis pulled out the piece of paper with the names of the remaining terrorists who were still loose on American soil. He ran his finger along each name, trying to imagine their emotional state right now. Then he took his thoughts back in time, when they'd been radicalized by a horror blamed on him and his comrades, but in reality perpetrated by these children's own people. They were still children today, though hardened and filled with hatred. And the instigators were not truly their people, but a mutation, a false family who preyed on the fears and the patriotism of the innocent. Jarvis had to stop these children. He probably had to kill them. Little comfort came from knowing Mudar was dead. There would be another to replace him.

Ninety minutes later the plane made a slow, lazy circle and landed on a special runway far from the commercial tarmacs. Brin woke instantly and ready for combat seconds before the wheels touched the pavement. A narrow, stubby bus with tinted windows and plush seats carried the two men along with five other passengers to an unobtrusive gate at the main terminal a mile away. No one spoke except for the driver, a corporal in NATO uniform, who thanked Brin and Jarvis as they gave up their weapons before stepping off the bus. The transition was serene and bizarre; one minute a rifle and handgun were as normal as a laptop bag and bottle of water. Now they would cause hysteria and get both men arrested. Jarvis momentarily felt naked. He shook it off as he and Brin clambered up the metal staircase to the terminal building filled with regular travelers. In a few hours he would be armed and on the hunt again in New York.

The business class seats on Lufthansa fully reclined and Brin was asleep again before the chimes went off at ten thousand feet indicating it was safe to turn on approved electronic devices. Jarvis pulled out the iPad that was miraculously still in the duffle bag the corporal had handed him a couple hours earlier. He hadn't bothered asking who had gone to the hotel room and collected his things. Jarvis pulled up a map of New York City and plotted the location on the sheet indicating the address of the poisoner. The plane had wi-fi so he could overlay museums, stadiums, outdoor markets, shopping centers, and any other heavily traversed spot or gathering place where people were likely to consume food or drink. He also added supermarkets. Assuming the poison hadn't been aerosolized – a technically complicated process and one that diluted the potency of the agent that needed to be ingested – the killer would need to get it into some food supply. The rinky-dink Starbucks attempt would only have killed half a dozen people. That made sense if the goal were to create uncertainty and fear among the populace. But New York had heavy, dense population centers so a bigger splash would be easier. And maybe with most of the cells now out of commission or hiding, a big hit was in the plan. Jarvis rolled the dice and assumed the murders would be big and showy.

He wrote ideas and the broad strokes of a plan in the Notes app and linked them to different locations on the map. When they landed, the first thing they'd have to do was get armed. He pulled up Outlook and shot a couple of emails to former colleagues in the area. Shutting off the iPad, he settled back and flipped on the large screen embedded in the seat in front of him. There were twenty-four movies, sixty-three televisions shows, a hundred and sixteen music tracks, and a dozen games available on-demand. He narrowed it down to one film he thought he could put up with and accepted the offer of wine and dinner from the flight attendant who seemed to want to stay and chat. He started the movie and figured by the time the protagonist got the girl, saved the day, and rode off into the sunset he'd have some answers to his emails.

Seven hours passed quickly. Jarvis watched the business travelers sleep through most of it. He had no recollection of his sleep patterns as an infant or toddler, but he vividly remembered long nights in elementary school when his father would catch him reading with a flashlight under the covers or watching a portable television at 2 a.m. in the closet. College was when he decided it was a blessing instead of a burden. Getting into an Ivy League school surprised his parents because they never paid attention to his grades and assumed a smartass kid who spent all his spare time playing basketball and chasing girls was making up for being dumb. He never tried to distinguish whether he excelled because of talent in the classroom or an extra six hours of study time every night. In college he just knew he could take more classes, ones he liked and not just the ones for his major. Biology for the latter, and anything related to history, criminal justice, and war that he could get his hands on. He could have graduated in two years if he'd focused on bio but staying the full four cost his father another sixty grand and he figured it was a fair trade for almost two decades of having to live with the prick. The chain of thought was not transparent to him as he looked at the slumbering passengers and he was unaware of rubbing the spot on his collarbone where his father had slammed the frying pan one Saturday morning breaking it – the bone, not the pan – clean in half. The acceptance letter along with first year tuition information had just arrived. Jarvis' mother reminded his dad about a promise he'd made a dozen years earlier – he'd pay for any school the kid got into. So sure his son was a moron, he laughed and even signed with his scribble on a sheet of yellow legal paper she provided. She hadn't pulled it out since then, half in hope and half because over the years she'd moved inexorably toward her husband's way of thinking that her son was never going to amount to much. The father's incessant cynicism, code for what others might call emotional abuse, wore at her and Jarvis. It was easier to give in and not fight. But when the letter came, a shadow of her former self emerged and she insisted.

When the frying pan hit and Jarvis bent over in pain as he heard the bone snap, he kept his legs beneath him. It took thirty seconds for the blinding agony to stop and when it did, he rose up. Still a couple inches shorter than his father, a growth spurt still a year or so ahead, and forty pounds lighter, he single-mindedly aimed himself at his father who had already turned back to the dish of eggs he'd made. Jarvis' mother saw the look and stepped between them before the father could know what was in Jarvis' eyes and heart. She took Jarvis to the hospital instead of calling the police and used this new leverage to whisper to her husband, "every penny the boy needs."

They never spoke of it and Jarvis did not see his father for six years.

The plane circled New York as it descended to five thousand feet and Jarvis looked out the window. They flew along the Hudson and it seemed the plane was tracing the outline of the gaping, empty hole that was still ground zero. Construction crews, scaffolds, trucks – they were all dwarfed by the enormity of what was no longer there. The flight attendant tried gently to wake Brin to tell him to return his bed to the upright position. She got as far as reaching a hand out to his shoulder before he was fully alert and instantly assessing the situation. He did so quickly enough to avoid grabbing her hand in mid air. Instead he turned to Jarvis.

"Get a good night's sleep?" He yawned and cracked open a bottle of water. "Let's go hunting."

Thirty minutes later they were in a taxi heading to Brooklyn. A pawnshop run by a Ranger Jarvis knew had a back room and wide selection of weaponry.

CHAPTER THIRTY-SEVEN

Both men felt better walking down 7th Avenue with weapons tucked in their waistbands. Brin wanted a couple more items but couldn't think of a good way to avoid getting attention carrying a high-powered sniper rifle in Manhattan. He'd settled for a beautiful knife with a brutal seven-inch serrated blade. It added weight to his ankle and felt good. They passed three Starbucks in two blocks and picked the next one that was mostly empty. Jarvis' tall drip fought back some of the jet lag and he was surprised at Brin's caramel macchiato and blueberry scone. They picked a couple seats in the back with a small table and no onlookers. Jarvis spread the sheet with the poisoners' names and the map he'd drawn.

Brin got crumbs on the map as he gestured with the scone. A piece of blueberry landed on Yankee Stadium. "You think they'll go for a high value target?"

Jarvis brushed off the blueberry. He peered at the map and the list. "Only one name on our sheet with a red mark. One guy with poison, the other five don't have it yet." He shook his head. "Unless we missed something and Said and his pal weren't the only suppliers. Yeah, I think he'll hit something big if he isn't scared off."

Brin washed some scone down with sugary coffee. "Let's go get this guy."

"Yup. And I'll check in with Timmons and see if they've made progress on the rest of the list." He pulled out his phone. "I've got to make a call first."

He scrolled through the text messages he'd received in the past few days. One was from Penny at the Parker Meridien. It made him smile but it was a little too dirty to share. He found the one he wanted and hit "Dial number."

Harding answered on the fourth ring. The journalist sounded like he'd been sleeping or drinking. It was both and Jarvis could hear the creak of the bed as Harding sat up and rubbed his hand over his face. "Yeah, yeah… Jarvis, finally, huh? What the hell'd you do? Shit's been flying for the last 24 hours."

The voice could be heard across the table and Brin smiled at the flying shit they'd caused.

"I'm going to send you a file. It's a narrative, a story about a Taliban plot to murder their own people and blame the US, radicalize some kids, send 'em to the States as moles for half a decade, then activate them so they start poisoning innocent people around the country. Sound interesting?"

There was dead silence on the phone for ten seconds and then sounds of scrambling as Harding pulled himself together, grabbed his computer, pulled on a pair of boxers, and reached for an almost empty bottle of Scotch, all at the same time.

"Goddammit, you better have some names to give me!" It sounded more to Jarvis like he was saying *"I'm gonna get a Pulitzer for this!"* He hung up and raised his eyebrows to Brin.

"I think I made his day."

Harding didn't care the line had gone dead. He sat at the desk facing the window onto the street in front of the Intercontinental Hotel and connected to the satellite broadband signal. He launched a secure VPN and logged into his paper's account. A dozen emails of increasing agitation from this editor, but nothing from Jarvis yet. He strummed his fingers on the desk and watched his belly shake in rhythm. He hadn't visited the gym on the second floor in the three months he'd been there. Or any gym for about twenty years. He took the bottle of Scotch by the neck and washed away any lingering regrets over the state of his flabby gut. A knock on the door didn't dissuade him.

"Housekeeping?" The chambermaids were Afghani, timid, and very efficient. He wasn't sure if they hated Americans or loved the money. He left a ten dollar bill on his pillow every other day so he figured it was the latter.

"Yeah, sure, c'mon in." He retried the email and nothing appeared. The door opened behind him and the maid came in carrying towels, leaving the enormous cart holding every conceivable cleaning item known to mankind and available on the black market. She averted her eyes and went straight to the bathroom. Harding gave her a mild wave.

The carpet in the hallway muffled the footsteps of the man who'd been pretending to open the door next to Harding's room. He didn't hesitate as he caught the door the maid had pushed to swing shut as she headed to the bathroom. It was only three long strides to cross the room and the Glock in his left hand rose smoothly as he covered the distance. The movement reflected on the laptop screen but was indecipherable to Harding, who half turned out of instinct. The result was the .38 caliber bullet entering his left ear instead of the back of his head. A second shot was unnecessary but entered his temple at an angle and destroyed the bulk of his frontal lobe tissue. His brain never registered the sound of the shot. The maid's, however, did. She came out of the bathroom, eyes wide and a scream on her lips. She saw only a man in camouflage with a black ski mask, a large gun now pointed directly at her chest. The scream stayed on hold. The man shook his head slowly and put a finger to his lips. The girl, who had seen much worse even in just the last week on her walk home from work, understood. She knew if death had not come yet, it would not be delivered on her by this man at this moment. She turned her eyes to the ground and walked quietly to the door. She would clean another room for now and come back later.

The gunmen kept his weapon on her as she walked and waited for the door to shut tight behind her. He looked back at the dead journalist. The irony and convenience of the dead man's last, inadvertent act was not lost on him. Harding's head had hit the keyboard just right – he'd refreshed the screen and a new email sat atop his inbox. It was from Jarvis. The killer pushed Harding off the chair and with gloved hands opened the email, read the two page summary of the Taliban escapade, and deleted everything. He emptied the computer's trash for good measure, then closed down the laptop and took it with him. The ski mask came off after he was in the hallway and heading for the elevator. He passed the cleaning cart halfway down the hall and noted the maid was not in view. The gun went back into the holster on his hip.

In the Starbucks in New York, Jarvis opened his iPad. "Our guy lives in Princeton. Want to drive or take the train?"

Brin cocked his head. "Isn't that where you...?"

"I'll rent a car. Shouldn't take more than forty-five minutes to get there." He'd made the drive hundreds of times while in school. He gathered the papers from the table and both men drained their cups as they stood. There was a Hertz location six blocks away. Half an hour later they were headed to the Lincoln Tunnel in a Ford SUV whose model Jarvis didn't recognize. The smell of stale smoke was covered by generous amounts of industrial lavender or periwinkle spray. Despite the bumper-to-bumper crawl through the tunnel, in twenty minutes they were cruising down the New Jersey Turnpike headed for exit 9. As the industrial landscape fell away to the lush, tree-filled sections of central New Jersey, Jarvis got a whiff of nostalgia over the periwinkle and smoke. He pushed it far down to where it belonged.

CHAPTER THIRTY-EIGHT

Brin had his window down and arm outside in the 80 mph wind, his hand snaking up and down as though it were swimming upstream. Jarvis watched, feeling like a father on a road trip with a playful kid. A kid who could eviscerate an enemy soldier with a three-inch knife before the man was aware he'd been attacked. He picked up his phone and scrolled through the contacts, hitting Timmon's number with his thumb. New Jersey law demanded use of hands-free systems while driving, so as to avoid unnecessary distractions. Jarvis held the phone to his ear. The Homeland Security agent picked up before the first ring was done.

"How was your trip?" Timmons' voice, even over the roar from the open car window, held as much humor as professionalism.

"Productive." He had to shout a little and Brin closed the window with only mild reluctance. "I think we may have irritated the suppliers."

"Yes, I heard you had some company with you. Brin disappeared from the hospital. The body count in Afghanistan is still a little unclear."

Jarvis hit the Speaker button, less to avoid a ticket and more to let Brin listen. "You Homeland Security guys seem pretty up to date on things happening outside the Homeland."

Timmons paused and the sounds of Turnpike churning beneath the wheels filled the air. "A lot of people are worried about the group you hit."

There was no humor in the voice now. "What you two did is going to save a lot of lives. And we couldn't have done it as quickly – or with as little red tape or repercussions."

"Does this mean we get a medal?"

Timmons' laugh was instantaneous and sincere. "I'll try to make sure you don't get arrested for almost causing an international incident. But let's wait until all the clean-up is done. Where are you two now?"

Brin looked across the seat with concern. He didn't like his existence to be known to anyone in the government, much less his precise whereabouts. Jarvis appreciated his pal's paranoia. "I'm heading to the guy in New York I think has some of the stuff. He was the only one with a red check against his name, and I don't think anyone else will be getting deliveries soon."

"Perfect. I'm in DC and have a helicopter waiting. I'll meet you. What's the location?"

Brin shook his head vigorously. Jarvis concurred. "We're fine. It's probably a kid, scared and insecure because his handlers aren't calling anymore and his tweets to Afghanistan are ignored. I'll try to take this one alive."

"Yeah, your track record's been pretty spotty on that." Timmons didn't sound like he was going to be put off. "You can't cowboy it on US soil anymore. The only reason you didn't get pulled off the plane heading out of the country was because we were busy with the people on the pages you gave us. But now you have our full attention."

Neither Brin nor Jarivs were fans of the "our" in Timmons' comment. "Okay, the address is 2257 Prettybrooke Lane in Princeton. Not sure where the helipad is." Jarvis hit the Mute button. "Better to let them in now. He'll just be on our asses if we don't." Brin didn't visibly nod but understood Jarvis was right. The Mute button went off. "We'll meet you two blocks east on the main road. Easy to find us, you'll smell the rental car."

He clicked off and they rode in silence for a moment. "I don't think this means you can't shoot the terrorist if that's needed."

Brin looked temporarily assuaged. A hundred and fifty miles to the south Timmons used an encrypted cell phone to tell his aide to get the

helo spinning now. He walked out of his boss's office in the Homeland
Security Department's headquarters three blocks from the Capitol, leaving
the sheets from Jarvis on the desk. Every name had several notes next to it.
His boss's voice echoed in his head: clean this up now.

CHAPTER THIRTY-NINE

The air in the rental car cleared out a bit as they drove through downtown Princeton. They didn't need to go down the main drag to get where they were going, but Jarvis succumbed to the tugs of nostalgia. The town was on one side, the stunningly idyllic university on the other. They coexisted symbiotically, unlike other college towns that relied on the school and students for their identities. Princeton was a town in and of itself. Jarvis looked at the enormous wrought iron gates, massive stone buildings, and cute brainy chicks going in the doors. Brin punched him on the shoulder.

"Thinking about going back to grad school?"

They stopped at the main light and watched half a dozen kids crossed the street to the Hoagie Haven that already had a line out the door. Jarvis could taste the overly-mayonnaised tuna two decades later.

"Yeah, thought I'd get a PhD in foreign relations, since that's going so well. Travel the world, conduct diplomacy in faraway lands."

Brin tapped the handle of the automatic pistol in his pocket. "Sure, diplomacy. I'm in."

They passed through the north edge of town and entered a tree-lined section that was lush and fertile. People came to live here because of the beautiful homes, quiet streets, and easy access to New York. And because they had a few million to spend on the homes that spilled over the quarter acres they sat on. There were also more modest houses that hadn't been torn down and rebuilt yet. Prettybrooke Road had both – large, well-maintained family homes paid for by Wall Streeters who could live where they wanted and rentals for students. Jarvis rolled past the address where the poisoner lived and a hundred yards later turned onto another side street that looped around and put him back on the larger road where he could again see the sign to Prettybrooke. He pulled off to the side and killed the engine.

"We'll wait for Timmons and see what's what."

Brin looked up and down the street. One car every couple of minutes. "Remind me why we're waiting for the suit to show?"

Jarvis pulled out his Glock and checked the clip. "It doesn't matter much to you because you're a ghost, but I've got to deal with things like licenses, taxes, and other shit that keeps me in the life to which I've become accustomed." Brin laughed. "So I'd like to keep on his good side. Besides, he's cleaned up the part of the mess we don't want to deal with, picking up the rest of the list. Wouldn't be fair to keep him from the fun part."

That got a nod from Brin, who appreciated the fun stuff.

There must have been a helipad within striking distance. A black Escalade rolled over the hill a hundred yards behind them. It broke the local speed limit and was parked behind Jarvis' crappy rental in seconds. No doors opened for more than a minute.

"Careful guys." Brin appreciated caution as well.

Jarvis opened his door. "Let's go break the ice. Keep your hands in the open." Both men sniggered. Jarvis was pretty sure if he had a gun held to Brin's head he couldn't pull the trigger faster than Brin could reach into his pocket, flip the safety, and put two between his eyes before the hammer on Jarvis' gun had moved.

Brin waited until Jarvis had stood, then opened his door and followed suit. The Escalade was ten feet behind the rental, close enough to ram them if need be, and far enough away to get around them if a quick exit were needed. Careful. The back door behind the driver opened and Timmons go out. Brin didn't watch him, eyes on the driver's door instead. The tinted windows didn't reveal the number or intent of the occupants.

"Kind of cliché, huh?" Jarvis nodded at the vehicle.

Timmons agreed from where he stood. "Need to keep up appearances." He looked over at Brin. "Glad to see you're doing well."

Brin still didn't avert his gaze. "Brought some friends?"

Timmons pointed to the car. "Just a driver. I figured the three of us could take care of it."

Brin was unconvinced, but Jarvis broke the moment. He walked over to Timmons and shook his hand. "Guess you're pretty much bi-coastal."

Timmons smiled and tilted his head at the Escalade. "Let's take your car. Mine's a little…conspicuous." They walked to the rental and Brin watched carefully as the black SUV pulled back onto the road and sped off. Brin's hand never left the gun in his pocket, despite Jarvis' suggestion.

"You're looking pretty healthy considering…" Timmons was giving Brin a detailed once-over, like he was assessing a foe.

"I'll call shotgun for you." Brin opened the front passenger door and nodded. Timmons looked at Jarvis and shrugged.

"Nothing wrong with a little paranoia, especially when someone's after you." He got in the car, then Jarvis, and finally Brin in the back seat. Timmons wrinkled his nose. "Wish I'd brought you guys one of those little fresheners to hang from the rearview."

Jarvis started the engine to get the air conditioner going. It was still warm, Indian summer keeping the Princeton girls in shorts for a few more weeks. It was late afternoon and the setting sun heated the leather seats and the men's cheeks. "The house is too nice for some kid from Afghanistan to own. Maybe it's a share, bunch of guys living together to save a few bucks. No cars in the driveway and no bikes near the door. Don't think anyone's home."

Timmons pulled out his cell phone and flipped through a couple of screens. "You're close. The kid who lives here rents, but he's got some cash. He picked up a masters from Princeton a couple years ago. In biological engineering. He works at a pharma company in Edison. He shares the place with another guy who came over from Afghanistan with him." He looked at Jarvis and back at Brin, both of whom wore silent questions on their faces."

"I looked up the address you gave me and did a little research." Still silence from his car mates. Timmons drew a deep breath, like he was about to sing an aria. "Yeah, it's a little more complicated than that."

Brin's gaze switched to Jarvis but his attention stayed on the Homeland Security guy. "What do you mean, 'complicated'?"

"I went through the list you gave me – the partial list." There was a slight chastisement in that. "All the names except two were part of a program. Mohan and the supplier in Racine weren't."

"What kind of program? The 'Come to America and Kill People' initiative?" Jarvis' voice was flat.

"We have an asylum program. For people, mostly kids, who lose their homes, or families. Or who helped us out and are in danger." Timmons looked out the window toward the street sign. Prettybrooke. Seemed painfully ironic at this moment. "All these kids came over after they lost family. No way we could know it was a plot."

"Goddamn, buddy." Brin was irritated. "You know what we found in Afghanistan. These kids lost family because the Taliban killed a bunch of their parents and friends, making it look like we did it, and now they've turned them into little time bombs. And you let them in. Congrats."

Timmons turned to Brin and smiled. It was patient, and a touch condescending. "These things are complicated."

"Okay, fellas, no geopolitical debate right now. We've got to find this kid, Khalid Brown." Jarvis looked back at Timmons. "Some old-style Ellis Island name change on that one?"

No answer was needed. "Brown finishes work at six. Unless he's planning on poisoning a bunch of people during happy hour, he should be home soon." Timmons sounded sure of his intel. Brin was less impressed.

"You tracking these guys or did you just Google the kid on the way over?"

Timmons' patience continued, but Jarvis sensed it was fraying. "Both. I pulled the records on Brown when you gave me the address and I got the file."

Jarvis surveyed the street quietly but his mind raced. "Khalid works at a pharmaceutical company? Could he be making the stuff? If he is, then he knows what's going on because his handlers probably contacted him and he went to ground."

"No, not yet. He's at work today. I called." He looked straight at Brin. "From the air."

"You're a little bit of a dick, aren't you?"

Timmons laughed at Brin, which didn't break the tension like he'd wanted. "Let's set up just past the house, wait for him to come in."

"Do you have field training?" Jarvis' question was neutral. Timmons wasn't offended.

"I'm not a decorated vet like you guys, but I put some time into a few operations before becoming a desk jockey." He opened his jacket and flashed the butt of a Sig that looked like it hadn't spent its entire life in a holster. "I can shoot straight enough."

Brin snorted but kept his tongue. Jarvis started up the engine and drove the trio to the lane where Khalid lived, turned up the street, and went past the house to the curve that would circle them back to the main road. Just past the point where they lost line of sight to Khalid's house, he pulled into a driveway and turned around. He drove toward the bend from the other direction and stopped just as Khalid's house came into view. He cut the engine again. "6:23. Shouldn't be too long – if you're right."

The three men sat quietly, the ticking of the engine pronounced in the warming air. Timmons coughed unselfconsciously. Jarvis pulled out the sheet with names of terrorists on it, Khalid and one other name marked with red. "We'll take care of this one, and the other guy, Jaleel Mekrobi. If we can get to him before he blows himself up maybe we can convince him to tell us if anyone else has the poison. But that still leaves a lot of name just on this sheet. You've got a couple dozen on yours."

The implied question left Timmons silent for a moment. A sharing mood came over him. "Once I got word of your escapades in Kandahar, I pulled the asylum records and matched them with the list – or at least the names you gave me." No irritation in his voice, perhaps even a little amusement. "There were entry patterns."

Brin was derisive. "They were all carrying duffel bags marked 'Hazardous Material' and chanting 'Allah Akbar'?

Amusement evaporated from Timmons' voice. "They were from the same town, even though they were spread out in time, and all were involved in an Allies-related collateral damage event." It sounded much softer than 'bombing.'

Jarvis wanted to save the testosterone for the confrontation with Khalid. "So what's the op?"

"We located and neutralized everyone on the list. The analysts figured out the ones on yours and are working on that, too." Jarvis raised his eyebrows. Timmons clarified. "We only took out the ones who resisted. Seven were detained and are on their way to Gitmo or Saudi Arabia. Or somewhere else."

There were half a dozen countries that still participated in rendition of foreign terrorist suspects in the US; several were still unknown to the press and Congress. The convenience of being able to send someone to another country where the rules of interrogation and detention were looser than in the States outweighed the risk of social or legal repercussion. Jarvis was just surprised Homeland Security had moved so quickly. So decisively. It was also disturbing they would let him and Brin participate now. It meant they were worried about taking more risks. That didn't bode well for the government's concern over Brin and Jarvis' well-being. Jarvis found that oddly exhilarating. He knew Brin would find it positively heart-thumping.

"That's a lot of action in just a couple of days." Jarvis hadn't heard anything in the papers, which wasn't an entire surprise, and he hadn't really been glued to CNN for the last seventy-two hours.

"Seemed wise to move quickly," Timmons shot back. "A lot of lives at stake."

The ensuing debate on operational policy was interrupted by a Scion B flying up the road and pulling into Khalid's house. The driver's door opened almost before the car came to a full stop and the tall, thin, exceedingly handsome Khalid sprang out as though he'd been ejected. Black curly hair passed just under the front door frame.

All three men silently checked weapons and open their doors simultaneously.

CHAPTER FORTY

B rin didn't wait for instructions, crossing the street and slipping behind the house next door to Khalid's. He would position himself in the back, to catch the kid if he tried to escape or to enter if the other two were able to establish an interrogation. Timmons gave Jarvis a concerned look.

"Don't worry, he's not setting up for a kill shot. Just keeping the kid from rabbitting."

"I'll come from the west, you from the east. Just so we don't draw attention." Which meant separating so it would be harder for anyone in the house to kill them both. Jarvis nodded agreement and pulled the gun to hold at his side. There were no neighbors peeking out windows, no cars interrupting the early evening, though that wouldn't last long as the work day wound to a close and residents headed home.

They crossed the street near the spot Brin had disappeared into and Timmons split off and jogged thirty feet further. They were now on either side of the house, still on the sidewalk. Timmons had pulled his Sig and kept it near his side, loose in his hand. They approached the small front yard and came toward the front door at an angle. They met on either side of the door.

"Your asylum seekers all seem to know me. Better if he sees you first. He'll probably think Homeland Security is just checking up on him to see if he needs anything, you know, groceries or a massage."

There was no rancor in his comment and Timmons took no offense. "I know the files, but the registrants don't know me. It may take some convincing, especially if he's gotten word from his handlers. He'll be skittish."

Jarvis was quiet for a moment. "You know, if he'd heard the cells had been exposed, why would he be following his regular routine?"

Timmons gave it some thought. "Maybe they told him to be sure not to act suspiciously. But he sure was in a hurry just now. Like he'd gotten instructions or something."

It seemed late to be debating. Jarivs nodded and Timmons rang the bell. "Khalid! Khalid Argami! Special Agent Timmons from Homeland Security – open up please!"

They listened carefully. Not a sound. Timmons knocked and the door pushed open an inch. Khalid had swung it shut but not hard enough for the latch to grab. Incautious move for a potential mass murderer. But they were grateful. Timmons pushed the door further and led with his gun. Jarvis followed him in, in a slight crouch and swinging from the Glock from side to side.

The front door opened into a small foyer. A closet to the right was closed. Straight ahead a small corridor lead back to what was probably the kitchen. A staircase waited ahead and to the right. The house was silent. Timmons nodded to the stairs and Jarvis agreed. Before he could step ahead of Timmons, the sound of rushing water broke the calm. It came from a door in the corridor leading to the kitchen. Both men turned toward the sound. Beyond the spot where the sound emitted there was a glimpse of movement and Brin came into sight. His gun was trained on the door in the corridor as well.

The door opened and Jarvis saw a mirror in the background reflecting a toilet. Khalid had something in his hands and a look of relief on his face. The time it took him to take two steps out of the bathroom was the amount of time he needed to register two men in front of him holding guns. Surprise was his first reaction, then recognition – a look Jarvis was beginning to be tiresomely familiar with. The kid had nowhere to go and before he could do something stupid, Jarvis wanted to get him under control. He took a step toward Khalid but was interrupted by a the explosion of a gun firing and the whisper of a breeze passing his ear. A bullet slammed into Khalid's chest. A second bullet tore a chunk out of his forehead and he would never be pretty again.

Timmons was pointing his Sig at Khalid and shouting, "In his hands! Get what's in his hands!" Jarvis covered the falling body of the kid with his. Khalid was dead but Jarvis treated him as though he were dangerous and intent on killing them – if he held a switch to an explosive, he might still succeed. Jarvis stood over the body and kicked with his foot. He moved the kid's arms and legs, pushing back the trouser legs and the jacket. Nothing. In his hands were a towel and a magazine. No poison. No gun.

Jarvis looked back at Timmons, the source of the shots that killed Khalid. "What the hell? The kid was taking a dump. That's why he was in a hurry."

Brin passed by the tableau and gave Timmons a hard look before going up the stairs, like a hunter checking to see if the cub they'd just killed had a pissed off mama bear on the way to maul them. He went to the second floor and cleared all the rooms while Jarvis stared at Timmons.

"What the hell good was that?"

Timmons didn't look apologetic. "I thought he was holding a weapon. Better safe than sorry." He holstered his gun. "It doesn't really matter. He was the last one with any of the poison. We'll find the stuff and this thing will be wrapped up."

Jarvis was irritated. "Sure, sounds good. But I would have liked to have a chat with him. Maybe see if we're missing anything."

"Yeah, me too, but it wasn't worth the risk. Let's see if we can find his stash."

They didn't need to bother. Brin came down the stairs carrying a metal briefcase. "The house is clear. Look like two other rooms are used by different people, both guys, kind of messy. This was in a space under a couple loose planks, under the bed in the master." He pointed at the kid using the briefcase. "Nice shooting." It was complimentary and derisive in equal measure.

Timmons holstered his gun and took the case. He pulled out his cell phone and speed-dialed. "Clear. I've got the material. Need one clean-up." Before the phone was back in his pocket they heard a large engine coming up the street. The government SUV was moving quickly.

The three men stood near the bleeding body, ignoring it. Jarvis broke the silence.

"Well."

No one added anything. So Jarvis continued. "Brin and I were just getting geared up. Let me get this straight: you're saying you're covered now? The last guy with poison just stopped breathing, you've busted everyone on your list, and the ones I held back are covered?" He didn't sound as disappointed or surprised as he was. He just wanted clarification.

Timmons looked like a cop turning in his final report, ready to go home at the end of his shift and pick up a new case in the morning. "Yup, you've got it. Appreciate the help – couldn't have done it without you."

If Brin hadn't been so disappointed he'd have found that funny. Jarvis looked at him and raised an eyebrow. He turned back to Timmons. "No clean-up, no loose ends? You're saying you're all good. Mission accomplished."

"A lot of people are going to stay alive because of what you two did in Afghanistan. A lot more won't be afraid. And the Taliban gets another failure. I'd say that was pretty good work. And I'm heading back to DC." As he finished speaking, two men in suits and carrying duffel bags came in the front door. They didn't speak, just waited for Timmons, Jarvis, and Brin to move out of the way. Timmons walked past them and out the front door. Jarvis and Brin followed and the door closed behind them.

The three men stood in the front yard. There didn't seem much more to say. The SUV idled in the driveway behind Khalid's car. Timmons shook Jarvis' hand firmly, turned to Brin and smiled. "If you gentlemen need anything, any time, just give me a ring. And

I know you don't need me to tell you not to speak to anyone about any of this."

Brin's face filled with disdain. He held more secrets about government actions and black ops than a Tom Clancy novel. Timmons got in the rear seat of the SUV and didn't look over as the vehicle backed out and sped off. Jarvis assumed another would come by to pick up the cleaning crew. He shrugged his shoulders to let Brin know it was just the usual shit and headed to the rental. It smelled slightly of cigar smoke and vomit as they pulled into the street and wound their way back to the I95 North to New York. They were quiet for about ten miles.

"Shit." Brin drummed his fingers on the dashboard.

"Yup." Ten more miles passed under the car.

"I don't like him."

Jarvis couldn't stifle a grin. "Strike one, he's a government agent. Strike two, he interrupted a good hunt you were looking forward to." Jarvis let the Brin swing at the hanging slow ball down the middle.

"Strike three, he's a dick." Brin pulled out his gun and checked the clip. "Let me out in Hoboken."

Large green signs counted off the exits on the New Jersey Turnpike. Edison was coming up. Hoboken was twenty minutes away and a ten minute subway ride to Newark Airport. "You have some business there?" It was a rhetorical question. Jarvis was pretty sure Brin had business everywhere, and a rabbit hole to disappear down in any city they passed through.

"There's a pretty good ribs place there. Wanted to get a bite before getting back." If Jarvis were a novelist he could come up with some pretty good stories about what 'getting back' might mean.

"You know, you could stay with me any time you want to take a break from the Outlaw Josey Wales. Or Grizzly Adams." Jarvis looked over at Brin. Neither the movie nor the television reference registered. "Okay, think Neo from Matrix." Still nothing. "Geez, you've got to get out more. Rambo, then?"

That got a nod from Brin. "Yeah, I'll swing by some time. Meet some of your new g-man friends."

Jarvis liked poking Brin. It was fun, there was no down side, and he was pretty sure his pal liked it – since there probably wasn't anyone else in his off-the-grid world who talked about anything other than missions, conspiracies, and how much water to store in preparation for Armageddon.

Signs for Hoboken began to appear. Jarvis moved into the right lane as they got within a mile of the exit. Brin pointed at a quiet stretch of emergency lane a hundred yards ahead near a grove of trees – one of the last signs of nature before they reached the industrial part of central Jersey and into New York City. "Just pull over up there. I'll be good. Save you a few bucks on tolls."

Jarvis signaled and moved into the emergency lane. Gravel and a few pieces of trash kicked up into the air. He stopped at the spot closest to the trees and as near the guardrail as he could. "Hey, glad to see you up and around."

Brin showed appreciation for the deeply emotional moment and Jarvis' happiness that he was no longer in a coma by holstering the gun. He gave his friend a smile. "We're almost even." He pointed out the driver's window. "Isn't that Lady GaGa in that limo over there?"

Jarvis's shock at Brin's awareness of a hot pop star didn't interfere with his role in the game. He turned to look out the window and kept scanning the cars for the limo as he heard the passenger door softly open and click back shut. He gave it five more seconds and said to himself, "I don't see her. Are you sure it wasn't Madonna?" When he turned back to the empty passenger seat, Jarvis looked out the window toward the trees and fields beyond. They were empty. He signaled and pulled forward, getting up enough speed to merge into the traffic and pass by the Hoboken exit. JFK Airport was another forty minutes away. He'd turn in the rental and get back to LA and whatever case was waiting for him. He turned the air conditioning up to hide the stench in the rental.

CHAPTER FORTY-ONE

The gate agent looked at Jarvis' ticket and tore it up. He typed for a moment on his terminal and handed Jarvis the boarding pass the printer spit out. A smile accompanied it, neutral and pleasant. Not until boarding started for the 10:35 pm to LAX did he notice the line across the top saying First Class. He looked back over at the agent to catch his attention, but the man who looked like he'd been at the job for at least thirty years was helping a young, exhausted couple carrying two babies get seats together. Jarvis appreciated anyone whose job required them to assess the public and make split-second decisions. He wasn't sure what about his own demeanor had screamed the need for the quiet of the front cabin, but he was glad the man had picked up on it.

He settled in to 6A and was glad for the hushed atmosphere that accompanied not only first class but a night flight. Everyone just wanted to get settled and to sleep as quickly as possible. With headwinds, the flight was slated for an unusually long six hours and thirteen minutes. Jarvis also appreciated the stern purser who clearly intended to meet all the basic requirements of good service without lingering for an extended chat. She wouldn't have to fend off any advances from Jarvis, though twenty years earlier she might have. He accepted the offer of a glass of water, still feeling the dehydration of the desert whether it was real or imagined. The sense of his mission being not entirely accomplished was less imaginary, though he couldn't put his finger on why.

Jarvis had picked up a mystery novel at the Hudson News in Terminal 7, along with a pad of paper and pen. He was several hours from his sixty minutes of daily shut-eye. He cracked the spine of the Harlan Coben thriller and was quickly absorbed. Twenty minutes later the roar of the engines caught his attention. The force pushed him back in his seat and he looked up for the first time. The cabin was only half full, the seat next to him empty. All the travelers appeared to be road warriors, the rhythm of the overnight flight familiar and easy. The only exception was Row 1. The harried couple and their kids were safely ensconced and the previously severe purser smiled and awaited level flight so she could continue doting. Jarvis leaned over the seat next to him and craned his neck back. He could see almost the entire coach cabin. While he would have been fine with his original seating, from this position it looked crowded, cramped, and generally unpleasant. Perspective. He scanned the crowd, only a few of whom looked at him with envy or anger. Jarvis turned back to look out the window and watched Brooklyn and then a segment of Manhattan fall away. He closed his eyes for a moment and began to replay events of the last couple days.

One advantage he'd learned over the years was the opportunity for perspective associated with little sleep. Most people lived in phases. There was an active working part of their day, a lower-key couple blocks of time before and after work, and sleep. People behaved differently during those phases. It was true even for criminals or terrorists, whose notion of "work" was different from a fireman or store clerk or doctor. Jarvis had the chance to observe people during all three phases. The insight gained by spanning people's phases could be rich and revealing. Patterns were exposed. Mistakes easier to catch.

While everyone on the plane got ready to sleep or read or watch movies, Jarvis looked for patterns in the last week. The poisoners in LA, his visit to Racine and to Mohan in New York. Afghanistan and then Princeton. There wasn't anything to make him think he'd missed anything. It was just the loose ends – a dozen or more names on a few sheets of paper, all who wanted to kill Americans. All tied in some way to him and Brin. He was glad it was over, but he didn't like that he hadn't seen it to the end. It felt unresolved. He watched the lights on the ground grow dimmer and the view took on the look of a shot from space. He flipped on the overhead light and pulled out the legal pad.

He scribbled across the page. A map of the US, slightly better than a third-grader might produce. Asterisks for each of the cities he'd visited and a number indicating the names from the list. No real pattern, but a nice spread. Jarvis looked for something, a real loose end to pick at. He fabricated a wild tale of marauding Taliban racing across the Midwest; created images of a band of terrorists stepping off the Amtrak train in Boston; conjured a conspiracy of local mosques harboring poison and killers in the South. Nothing. Like a scab that had completely healed and no amount of scratching would make it ripe for picking. He was in equal parts frustrated and relieved. Back home he could put his focus on another case. There were half a dozen voicemails from former clients needing help and one new referral.

The cabin was mostly asleep, the kids settled in Row 1, and Jarvis closed his eyes. Fifty-four minutes later and two REM cycles filled with flashes of Afghanistan – both recent and old – he instantly and smoothly awoke. The most senior flight attendant was standing at her post by the galley, watching him like he was a reality tv show. He smiled and she smiled back. She reminded Jarvis of his mom. He'd call her the next day, wish her happy birthday, and not talk about anything earlier than a few years ago, when things had gotten better. The flight attendant worked her way down the aisle past sleeping passengers covered in blankets and in various states of mid-sleep disarray. Taking a drink order would break the monotony of the flight. He obliged.

CHAPTER FORTY-TWO

A week later Jarvis was sitting in a deli across from a very large, extremely angry man whose right hand held a soup spoon containing a chunk of matzo ball and bits of chicken. The spoon was suspended between bowl and mouth because his left hand, which had been reaching aggressively toward Jarvis's throat, was now twisted at a painful angle because of Jarvis' grip on the man's pinkie finger and the extreme rotation he had applied. It was a fascinating, silent tableau. Jarvis was being paid to deliver a message to this former bodyguard who had somehow confused his duties to protect a wealthy Brentwood housewife from an emotional relationship that only existed in the bodyguard's head. Their reasonable discussion had reached an unsatisfactory conclusion and the bodyguard decided to punch Jarvis. Now they were stuck. The bodyguard was embarrassed and even angrier, the soup was getting cold, and now Jarvis' phone was ringing.

The absurdity of the moment deserved escalation, so he used his left hand to fish out the phone from his front pocket. The number was all fives. He hadn't heard from Brin since letting him off on the freeway. Jarvis looked into the bodyguard's eyes and assessed the level of violence.

"I need to take this. Can we pick up again in a minute?"

Violent fury melted into confusion, which Jarvis took as assent. He released the man's hand and, not knowing what else to do, the bodyguard put the spoon to his mouth. It was a sufficiently good matzo ball that he continued to eat while Jarvis took the call.

"Hey, you wandering around New Jersey?"

"That reporter you made friends with in the desert? He's dead."

Jarvis wasn't expecting this news, but Afghanistan is a dangerous place. "Afghanistan is a dangerous place." That caught the bodyguard's attention but he was still unsure enough about what was happening with this overly calm and surprisingly quick guy across from him that he decided to stick with his soup.

"Yeah, real dangerous. Especially if there's a professional hit put out on you."

That distracted Jarvis. "How professional?"

Brin made a brutal guffaw. "Military training, one in the chest and two kill shots, neither one necessary. Place was ransacked. Pretty good work."

Jarvis watched a waitress deliver a pastrami sandwich and wait while the patron – a Doppelganger of Mel Brooks in *The 2000 Year Old Man* – inspected it by picking up the top piece of rye bread and critically examining it. "How'd you hear?"

"You don't want to know. It's the kind of job some people might want to talk to me about first." Brin was right; Jarvis didn't want to know.

"Could have been Taliban, or more likely Afghan army turncoats helping them out. I'm sure they didn't like the story he was working on after our visit."

Silence. "Yeah, that must be it." More silence. "Keep your eyes open, huh?" And Brin was gone.

Jarvis turned his attention back to the bodyguard. The rest of their conversation was civil, but he knew he'd have to visit the paramour again. He thought about Harding and wondered if the journalist died envisioning his Pulitzer.

CHAPTER FORTY-THREE

Another week passed and no one overtly tried to murder Jarvis. Harding's death might have been part of a larger, multi-national nefarious conspiracy, or he was killed for asking too many questions in a part of the world where looking directly at a woman could get your eyes gauged out. Jarvis leaned toward the latter. Two o'clock on a Tuesday morning he was thinking about catching his nap, watching CNN replay the news stories from hours earlier. They were the 24-hour news network, but that didn't mean twenty-four consecutive hours of new stories. He was about to flip off the set and grab a quick shower when the first fresh report of the day came on. It was 5:00 a.m. EDT and the anchors introducing their show looked fresh and ready to banter, enthrall, and inform. The lead story was about a Congressman denying he'd had an illicit affair with a supporter's daughter, but the talking head also teased a Breaking News bulletin about one death and six sick people in Denver. Jarvis stuck around through the lurid innuendo masked as reporting about the Congressman, then three minutes of commercials that were followed by another teaser about Denver. When the anchor reappeared, he described an e coli outbreak in downtown Denver. A local fast food restaurant was apparently the culprit and officials were looking for other patrons who might have been affected. The anchor promised to cut back in with additional Breaking News on this exciting Breaking Story, but needed to move on to a tale of a housecat that had ridden a jetliner's wheel well across country without turning into a feline popsicle.

Jarvis killed the television and stared at the blank screen as its glow faded to true black. He didn't need to pull out the papers with names, numbers, and addresses from a couple weeks ago. Denver had been one of the locations. No red ink, so they'd assumed no poison yet. And Timmons had said they'd cleaned up all the loose ends. And another thing…people got food poisoning all the time and Denver was not immune. He couldn't attribute every tummy ache or CDC report as evidence the Taliban had somehow evaded Homeland Security. Jarvis still had indigestion from the burrito he'd gotten at the truck on Wilshire earlier. He was pretty sure it wasn't a plot. No reason to see monsters in the shadows.

But still. He picked up his cell and found Timmons' number. The agent picked up before the first ring was done. "Timmons. Who's this?"

"You forget so quickly." He waited a moment. Timmons wouldn't have kept Jarvis' number in his contact list, but he didn't mind screwing a little with the agent. "E coli outbreak in Denver?"

Timmons let his breath out heavily. "Jarvis. Yeah, I saw that. My guys are looking into it. Probably just some moron leaving the meat out on the counter too long." Jarivs didn't respond. Timmons waited, then filled the silence. "It's a little suspicious, but we've got it covered."

"My confidence is oozing. You sure you got everyone on the list?"

Timmons sounded irritated for a moment. "Yeah, we got everyone. Everyone we knew about – but we don't know that the intel you got was comprehensive." He recognized the fallacy of the comment – it wasn't Jarvis and Brin's job to conduct an international investigation. Timmons' voice smoothed out. "You're right, we're checking carefully. We don't want to have missed any cells. You and your buddy saved a lot of lives – it's our job to make sure it stays that way and nothing is missed."

Jarvis murmured some encouraging sounds of agreement. He recognized bullshit when it was flung. "Okay, if you've got it under control, then I won't ride to the rescue."

"You did a real service for your country last month – again. By keeping it quiet, too. Your name's been mentioned a few times around here. If you ever need anything…"

Jarvis thanked him and hung up. Everything was cool. No reason to worry or take action. He should just let Timmons handle everything. He flipped open the laptop on the coffee table and booked a ticket to Denver for the next morning.

CHAPTER FORTY-FOUR

The two-hour flight was uneventful. Jarvis had booked a hotel in the Denver suburb containing the restaurant believed to be the source of the e coli outbreak. He walked past baggage claim to the car rental building. He climbed in to the SUV and as he backed out, the passenger door opened. Before his right elbow could complete the jaw-cracking swing he had instinctively sent it on, he stopped. Brin hadn't bothered to block the blow, knowing the same instinct that had initiated the attack would stop it in time.

"Yeah, I should've known. Did you walk here?"

Brin laughed and pulled the door shut. "I got in an hour before you. Sleeping in?" The humor left his voice. "You don't think this shit is food poisoning."

Jarvis sighed. "I don't know. Timmons seems like a pretty capable guy. Homeland Security's not all a bunch of Keystone Kops. But hard to believe they missed a cell out here."

He backed out of the space and headed to the exit. There was silence while he showed his license and rental agreement to the guard. They were on the long, flat Interstate 75 in minutes.

"Someone's been trying to find me." Brin didn't need to emphasis the word 'trying,' since the chances of anyone tracking him seemed slim. That said, someone had lured him in and almost killed him at a deli in Beverly Hills. No doubt he was being even more careful.

Jarvis took this information in and gave it the weight it deserved. "They must've missed someone, which is bad enough. It's worse that these guys have the ability to make more than a half-assed effort to track you."

"It was more than half-assed. These guys weren't total morons."

"Shit. Taliban can't do that without some help. The connection to the Afghan government must be deep. Intelligence service maybe? Timmons is going to be pissed – and maybe out of a job for missing it."

Brin barked, "Yeah, that'd be a damn shame."

They drove another five minutes, reaching similar conclusions via different paths. Jarvis said it for them. "We need to track it back. From this cell to wherever the origin is. At least figure out where it is."

That sounded very good to Brin. "I wouldn't mind a few more days in Kandahar."

"Nope, I don't think we'd get very far. We'll do our work here, let Timmons deal with the international stuff. I don't think our visas to Afghanistan will work for a while." They both appreciated the understatement – trying to get back in any way other than a military transport would land them both in a very ugly jail.

"Yeah, okay." Disappointment. "We'll work this angle."

Ten more minutes and they saw signs for Bartleton. The Coco's in the bustling megalopolis of fourteen Colorado residents was the believed epicenter of a lot of diarrhea. They pulled off the freeway and made their way a couple of miles to the surprisingly strip-mallish town; they'd been expecting bucolic and quaint. They found their hotel by looking up and seeing the blaring Four Points By Sheraton sign. It was slightly less dilapidated than the nudie bar they had to pass to get there.

"Sweet home, Colorado," Brin sang. Jarvis didn't correct his lyrics.

He'd only booked one room, not knowing he'd have company. Brin didn't mind taking the second bed. It was more luxurious than where he had spent the last few nights. Brin laid on the bedspread, dressed for both sleep and a quick escape into the night. Or battle. His clothes were always multipurpose. Jarvis sat in the one chair in the room sipping a beer and eating the surprisingly flavorful smoked turkey sandwich he'd gotten at the general store next door.

"I've got a name from the sheets Mohan translated, but hard to believe the guy would still be hanging around with the FBI on his ass. Maybe he's a suicide-bomber kind of dude, won't go underground until the mission is over." He took another bite. He screwed up his face but not from the sandwich. "Timmons said they're looking into it, but either they got the guy before or not. He made it sound like they did and we'd just be wasting our time. You think we're wasting our time?"

Brin was staring at the ceiling, counting water stains. "I think he's embarrassed they missed something. Thinks we'll make him look bad if we find out." He got to nine-teen and couldn't find any more so he started checking the wall. "I say we go make him feel bad."

Jarvis nodded around another bite of the sandwich. "Yeah, just in case." Brin looked over at him. They hadn't flown to Colorado to cover a 'just in case.' Both men trusted their instincts. "Let's swing by the Cocos early and poke around during breakfast – that's when the people got sick." He looked at the digital clock by his bed. It was 11:54 pm. "We'll wait an hour or so then go visit the name on the list. Just in case." Brin smiled as he resumed his count along the far wall.

"If we bump into Timmons' guys they won't be real happy." He closed his eyes and played some scene behind his lids that Jarvis didn't try to imagine. "That'd be too bad."

The hour passed quietly and quickly. They were in the car, headed to the address Jarvis had memorized, as the general store shut for the night and ushered out the last beer buyers of the evening.

CHAPTER FORTY-FIVE

Tired of carrying around incriminating paper, Jarvis had memorized the name and address. The SUV had, among dozens of useless fancy features, GPS. He punched it in and was surprised the destination was under two miles away. They passed out of the main garish part of town and along a darkened semi-highway. Expecting to head into a typical Colorado wooded area, they instead turned off into a well-lit planned neighborhood. The houses looked new, largely cookie-cutter, and exceedingly dull. What they did have, in addition to homeowners association fees, was a spectacular view of the mountains to the east. The address was in a cul-de-sac comprising of three homes, mirror images of one another. Despite the pitch dark of the mountain night, the smog less sky let the glint of thousands of stars illuminate the streets like an army of tiny flashlights. Fake gas lamps powered by electricity – which was probably generated by burning recycled water bottles or compost piles in the back yards of the homes in the eco-friendly state – gave more direct light. Jarvis passed by the turn into the cul-de-sac, continuing on for another fifty yards. Most cars were parked in driveways. A few remained on the street. He turned the car around so it was pointed back to where they'd entered and pulled in behind a large, powerful, spotless extended cab truck. He'd cut the lights before pulling the u-turn. With the engine off the only sounds were the cool night air settling in and the whining call of some animal he didn't want to know about, which was either three miles away and using the echo of the mountain or across the street and ready to pounce.

Both men looked at one another and Jarvis nodded. "Let's go see what's what." Brin gave him a thumbs-up and they softly, quietly opened their doors and slipped out. The doors closed just as gently and with barely a click.

They walked down the cement sidewalk. Anything more surreptitious would look suspicious. There were no guard dogs, no Taliban gunmen, no trip-wires. Either they were at the wrong place or the resident in the dark house on the right side of the cul-de-sac had gone to bed with a clear conscience and no worries. Or he'd skipped town. The Hyundai in the driveway suggested the former. Jarvis went to the front door, Brin slipped around the left side, cutting between the poisoner's house and the neighbor. Even from the outside, the house didn't feel empty. Jarvis waited thirty seconds for Brin to get in position and rang the doorbell. No lights went on upstairs, no sudden glare of a porch light where he stood. He pressed it again and listened to the double chime work its way around the foyer and echo upstairs. Jarvis turned and jogged over to the sedan in the drive. He put his hand on the hood. It was only slightly warmer than the night air but that was enough to tell him it hadn't been sitting more than a couple hours. He went back up to the door and edged past some bushes to his right and peered in the window. He could see past a darkened living room and a staircase leading to the second floor. To the right of the staircase a corridor led to what was probably the kitchen. A glimmer of light cut the darkness, as if the fridge were open or the microwave door left ajar. He craned his neck to see if there was an alarm panel near the front door. He couldn't see it clearly, but a faint red glow seemed to hover near the wall if he squinted. If it was an alarm, it wasn't armed. Fortunately, he was – Brin had been thoughtful enough to bring an extra Glock by whatever means of travel he'd used to get to Colorado. Or he'd used the extra hour before Jarvis's flight landed to obtain a small arsenal. Either way, Jarvis was more comfortable with the pistol in his hand now. He returned to the front door

and tried the handle. Locked, but no deadbolt. He pushed hard and there
was a little give. Not interested in bruising the hell out of his shoulder,
he took a step back and gave a hard flat-footed kick next to the handle.
It shook his spine but the door shot open. The noise was close enough
to a rifle shot that he was sure every light on the block would snap on.
Just silence. It was probably a neighborhood that was used to hearing rifle
fire from the surrounding woods as some non-vegan bagged a squirrel or
moose. Jarvis moved quickly into the foyer and swept the living room with
his gun in front. Brin would not have mistaken the sound for anything
other than what it was. He'd be coming in from the back. They'd just have
to be careful not to shoot each other.

Jarvis cleared the living room and looked at the stairs for movement
or a change in lighting. Nothing. He moved quickly toward the kitchen,
his hand relaxing in preparedness for pulling the trigger if needed. There
were no sounds in the house. He moved toward the glow that got slightly
less subtle as he approached. Jarvis took the last few steps quickly to throw
off anyone waiting around the corner who would have expected a slower
approach. He saw a small movement as he entered the kitchen but it was
sufficiently familiar that he did not almost shoot. Brin was hunched over
a body. A young man, similar to the others Jarvis had seen recently, olive
skinned and black haired. Maybe early twenties. It was hard to tell because
the hair was matted with blood and probably a smattering of brains. A
small caliber bullet hole was just off-center of this forehead, not much
blood around it. The disaster that had been the back of his head was
attributable to a large, marble rolling pin on the ground next to him. One
good blow from a strong arm would have cracked his skull like a melon, his
brain the ripe meat that was now exposed. The bullet was probably just an
exclamation point to the murder.

Jarvis could see the scene because the body was in front of the open
refrigerator. A carton of orange juice had drained next to the boy's body,
mixing with blood. He'd been caught off-guard, just grabbing something
to drink when he'd been killed. Brin looked up at Jarvis.

"Ya know, this isn't the strangest thing I've seen tonight."

Jarvis looked at the six-inch blade in his friend's left hand, held in an attack grip with the blade pointing down. Even with the modest light from the fridge he could see it was sticky with blood.

"I'm guessing you didn't stab the kid for good measure."

Brin was scanning the room, trying to detect any movement. "The back yard butts up against a forest. Kinda pretty. There was a guy with a scope halfway up a maple tree." Jarvis wouldn't know a maple tree from a bottle of syrup.

Jarvis looked at the body on the floor. "Yeah, that's not a rifle hole." He quickly moved from a casual position to a defensive crouch.

"Uh huh, the guy in the tree was waiting for someone."

Jarvis nodded with admiration and dry wit. "You just happened to check the tree line before coming in the back."

Brin ran the knife against his leg and it came away clean – the blood had not had time to congeal. "Hey, better safe than sorry. I'm pretty sure that guy's sorry now."

The blood covering where the young man's skull had been was thick but still oozing. Jarvis stayed crouched and went over to him, putting a hand on his throat then chest. "Warm enough, hasn't been more than an hour. Maybe a lot less." He looked back at the front of the house where the staircase was. Brin followed the look.

"The tree guy's partner might still be in the house."

Jarvis nodded. "I've got two questions. Who killed the kid? And who are they waiting for?"

"Yeah, I don't really care about the first one. The second is a problem."

Jarvis wasn't ready to give up the 'who' issue. It might relate to the more pressing second question. "Taliban handlers could be pissed if he went off on his own, ignored orders to chill out until the storm passed." By 'the storm' he meant all the shit they'd stirred up in Afghanistan. "Maybe they were waiting for the rest of his cell."

Brin sheathed the knife and pulled out a Heckler & Koch P7. Jarvis hadn't seen it before. "Nice piece."

Brin hefted it. "Thanks. Haven't tried it out yet. Maybe tonight." He low-walked past Jarvis toward the front of the house and stopped at the entry. "I don't think it was Taliban, unless they're recruiting Ivy Leaguers now."

The blood on Brin's camo pants was red - it didn't tell Jarvis anything about the sniper's nationality. "You know…I'm not doubting you of course, but what made you think the guy in the tree wasn't on our side – taking out the cell, maybe even Homeland Security?"

Brin raised his eyebrows as if he hadn't considered the question earlier. But he was screwing with Jarvis. "I was pretty sure when I noticed him flip on the infrared and target you as soon as you came into view. I could've asked to be sure but thought I'd just apologize later if I was wrong." He smiled broadly and Jarvis returned it.

"Okay, I don't like the way this is going. It's making me kind of paranoid. The healthy kind." He pointed two fingers forward toward the front of the house and then cut them left. He wanted Brin to go out and around the staircase; he'd follow and go up the stairs. They needed to clear the house of any hostiles – just bolting would make them targets. It didn't matter who the shooters were originally after; they were next.

Brin made his move without hesitation. He got past the door and Jarvis was hard on his heels when they both heard a click. They whirled in unison to the right, Brin even getting off a shot that thudded harmlessly into the wood of the front door before the concussion grenade went off directly in front of him. Jarvis missed almost the entire force because Brin's body absorbed it. Two shots followed but neither man heard them, the concussive force on their ears deafening for at least a full minute. But Brin felt both. The first tore into his left shoulder and spun him halfway around, the second followed instantly and would have pierced the ventricle of his heart if he hadn't made the partial spin. Instead it ripped into chest muscle, broke two ribs and came to a rest above the aorta. It wouldn't kill him immediately but the shard of rib broken off by its trajectory threatened to puncture the heart. He wasn't aware of the specifics but had a pretty good idea of the outcome as he fell on his back. He held onto his gun but the flash of pain followed by the sensation of floating and getting ready to die included a bit of paralysis.

Jarvis took three shots in the direction of the gunman, but there was no visible target. His goal was to keep another bullet from hitting Brin and maybe dissuade the shooter from finishing them both off. He rolled back into the main part of the kitchen, shaking his head to clear the ringing. He didn't know how many assassins were in the house and they had to be pretty good to have gotten past Brin's paranoia. He was crouching behind a cabinet to the left of the kitchen's exit. He could see Brin on the ground, bleeding out, moving one arm a few inches back and forth. His mouth was moving, probably mumbling a prayer – or more likely reliving some secret mission before he died on the kitchen floor. Jarvis tried to get his attention, signal that it would be okay even though it wouldn't. Brin finally looked in his direction but Jarvis couldn't tell if his friend was fully conscious. There was a hint of movement in the direction where the shots had come from. For an instant Jarvis caught Brin's eye but his lids fluttered, his body spasmed, and he exhaled one last time.

Jarvis fired off another shot, wanting to charge out of the kitchen and wring the bastard's neck with his hands, however many assassins awaited. A banging noise closer to the front door changed the direction of his attention, then a shot and a groan. A window broke and steps raced across the floor. Jarvis moved his gun side to side, not sure where the attack would come from or what was happening. For a moment it was calm, like the seconds before the grenade had gone off. Into the empty air a voice called out.

"Jarvis! Hold your fire! I nailed the guy pinning you down!"

It was Timmons. Jarvis wasn't surprised. "Careful! I don't know how many are in the house...Brin got a guy with a scope in a tree out back." He looked at his friend, lifeless, unmoving. The dead young man was still by the refrigerator. It was a mess.

"My intel had only two guys here. The house is clear." Timmons voice was closer and he stepped around the corner and into the kitchen, gun hanging by his side. He looked at Brin. "Jesus, I'll call an ambulance."

Jarvis stood. "Don't bother. He's dead." No emotion in his voice. It would come later. He looked at Brin. "Nice fucking job cleaning up all the names on the list." He pointed his gun at the kid on the floor. "Whoever took him out probably figured he was a weak link. Brin said the shooter out back was a pro, maybe someone on our side paid off by Taliban money. This is bigger than some pissed off Afghans trying to scare us off."

Timmons shook his head and said nothing, waiting for Jarvis to finish his rant. Jarvis wasn't done yet. "How the hell didn't you get this guy? I knew about him, how could your guys miss him? What morons did Homeland Security send? Huh? Jesus." He was more angry about Brin than governmental incompetence and Timmons was his only target. He looked at his friend on the ground, as quiet as if he were on a stakeout waiting to take a shot. Jarvis holstered his gun and put his hands over his face. "Goddammit. God Damn It." He rubbed his eyes and when he pulled them away he was looking at Timmons' gun pointing at his chest. He instinctively turned around to see who Timmons was aiming at, sure another gunman had sneaked up behind them. The space was empty.

Before he'd turned back to face Timmons, he'd figured it out. At least part of it. "Motherfucker." Jarvis instinctively reached for his piece and Timmons cocked the hammer on his government issued Glock, which was similar to Jarvis' favorite gun back home.

"Don't."

Jarvis paused. He didn't know why Timmons was pointing the gun at him, other than that it was related to Timmons being the one who had killed the kid on the floor. The gunman outside in the tree was as official as Brin had thought – either a mercenary or rogue Homeland Security doing dirty work for Timmons. He just didn't have the underlying why. One thing seemed fairly certain, though. Timmons had planned on killing Jarvis and Brin; one down and one to go. Jarvis felt a shoot-out in the air.

He wasn't going to just take a bullet without a fight. But no way he could draw his gun faster than Timmons could pull the trigger.

"You're a scumbag, you know that, right?" He looked over at Brin. He needed to buy a few seconds, distract Timmons enough to have at least a chance to get out of the direct line of fire and pull his gun. He figured he had about a one in seven chance of not dying today.

"I like you, Jarvis. You're a good soldier. You just don't understand." His eyes never left Jarvis. "You'll die a hero, I promise."

Jarvis recognized the finality. In a fight, the guy who does a lot of talking doesn't really want to throw a punch. Timmons was done talking. His finger started to tense on the trigger. Jarvis felt like a soccer goalie – pick left or right and just jump. Maybe he could take the bullet in a shoulder instead of the chest and survive. From five feet away it wasn't likely to work. His odds dropped to one in twenty of making it home.

His odds suddenly went up. There was a flash of movement on the ground at the same moment Jarvis picked the right side for his useless jump away from the bullet that was about to come out of the barrel of Timmons' gun. He heard three sounds almost simultaneously. A grunt of extreme pain, a shout of surprise and anger, and the firing of the Glock. He'd picked correctly on his jump. The bullet went to his left, though not entirely because he'd moved to the right. The shot was off its mark, a result of Timmons reacting to his Achilles tendon suddenly rolling up in his right calf. That was a result of the first sound Jarvis had heard, which was Brin exhaling in agony as he pulled the hunting knife from its sheath on his leg and rolled toward Timmons, slashing at the spot just above the ankle to slice through the tendons.

Jarvis didn't have a lot of time to wonder why his friend wasn't dead. Timmons still had the gun and Jarvis could see at a glance that the effort to intercede was Brin's last. He was face down, panting, knife in his hand but useless. Jarvis leapt at Timmons who was hunched over reaching for his calf but already turning the gun back toward Jarvis. Jarvis covered the few feet in a split second, arms wide like a linebacker. He hit Timmons full on, slamming him into the cabinet and breaking glasses inside. They slid to the ground, Jarvis on top. Timmons tried to turn and point the gun but Jarvis had his hand on Timmons' wrist and twisted hard. He heard a snap and the gun fell to the floor. Jarvis sat on his chest, legs pinning down any squirming and stared at him. Timmons' pain ran from wrist to ankle but his eyes locked on Jarvis and he quieted. Without breaking his gaze, Jarvis reached over and picked up the Glock. He put it against Timmons' forehead and was silent.

Timmons knew the school-yard bully rule.

"Talk." Jarvis cocked the gun. "Now." He could hear Brin moaning, no longer needing to play possum but desperately in need of medical attention. Jarvis wasn't going to screw around with Timmons. He'd put a bullet in his head now and get answers from someone else later. In case Timmons didn't get the message, he clarified: "I'll put a bullet in your head now and get answers from someone else later."

Despite the coolness of the air in the kitchen, Timmons was sweating. A few drops fell in his eye and he looked scared. Jarvis would pull the trigger sooner than later to get his friend an ambulance. Or not at all – Jarvis was a soldier, not a killer. Timmons' brain raced for a good lie that would save his life.

"I…thought you were part of it. Paid off by…Taliban money…look at evidence." He was out of breath from the fear and the pain. He'd spent too many years behind a desk to have the instincts of a field agent any more. He tried to slow down. "The reporter, he was killed. You let Said live…it was, I thought…"

Jarvis moved the gun to Timmons' shoulder and held it against the flesh. He pulled the trigger without breaking his stare into Timmons' eyes. The Homeland Security man convulsed and a shocked look came over his face. The bullet passed through flesh and muscle but no bone or arteries. Jarvis wanted him alive until he put a bullet in his forehead.

"Bullshit." The gun rested again on Timmons' sweating brow. Timmons' grimaced and tried to look side to side, searching for help or an answer that would get him out of this. He saw neither and looking back at Jarvis he knew his next words would decide it. The hesitation was too long and Jarvis jammed his thumb into the wound on Timmons' shoulder. The agony was excruciating and Timmons' back arched so hard it loosened Jarvis' perch for a moment.

"Talk."

Timmons was breathing rapidly now and could feel blood leaving the wound in his shoulder. "Okay, okay." His jaw tightened for a moment as he hesitated to take the final step. Jarvis deliberately cocked the gun again. Timmons made up his mind. "It was us. We set it all up."

Jarvis didn't understand. "You set up the hit? On the kid?"

Timmons shook his head under the barrel of the pistol. "The whole thing. The Taliban, the poison. Everything."

Jarvis leaned back, resting the bulk of his weight on Timmons' stomach. He put the gun under his chin. "How? How the hell did you make that work? The Afghans set up the attack on the school to look like we'd done it. What the fuck did…" And then he figured it out. He pressed the gun hard into Timmons' throat, cutting off air. He wanted to pull the trigger now. "You set up the whole thing. You worked with the Taliban so they'd RPG their own people and use it s an excuse to attack us here, in the States. And ambush my squad." His voice got lower and darker.

Timmons' knew now he was dead. It didn't matter what he said. All he wanted was a dying declaration, a moment of truth to clear his conscience before he went to heaven or hell.

He gasped through an almost closed throat. "We did it because it had to be done."

Jarvis looked at him like he was insane.

"People were going to forget, get lazy. This country always does that – wait until a crisis, make a big fuss, then forget…" He was speaking slowly, as if in a courtroom giving evidence, but it was hard with the pain, the bleeding, and Jarvis on top of him. "People would let their guard down, they'd forget…" He swallowed hard. "Funding was going to dry up. We…we wouldn't be able to do…"

Jarvis sat upright as if hit by a jolt of electricity. Funding. He pulled his arm away and swung the gun hard against Timmon's left temple. The agent felt nothing and was immediately unconscious. Jarvis stood up, shaky for the first time. Funding.

He went to the phone on the wall, and old-style landline. He dialed 911. "I need an ambulance. A man's been shot. Two men. One may make it." He hung up and pulled out his cell phone, dialing Rayford back in LA.

"It's Jarvis. I'm going to call you back in ten minutes, but you'll want to wake up your FBI buddy and have him ring the Denver branch right now." He clicked off before Rayford could ask any questions. Jarvis finally went over to his friend. He put his hand on Brin's shoulder. There wasn't as much blood as he'd expected. It was a bad sign.

"Just hang on, man. Help'll be here soon." He felt for a pulse. It was weak and thready. Brin was slipping in and out of consciousness. His breath was shallow and caught in his throat. He couldn't move but was whispering something into the floor, face down. Jarvis leaned in, his ear close to Brin's lips. He could just make out the words.

"Still...not...even..."

Jarvis smiled despite Brin's pain and held his hand on his friend's shoulder as a siren far in the distance slowly got louder.

CHAPTER FORTY-SIX

J arvis settled into the chair. It was only moderately uncomfortable. He put his feet up on the edge of the bed and leaned back. He counted water stains on the ceiling. It was 2:06 a.m. and there were too many sounds in the air for this time of the morning. But they were comforting and familiar. The most comforting was the steady sound of Brin breathing, deeply asleep. Jarvis shifted his feet a little further down the hospital bed in case his buddy shifted in the night. He pulled out the small notebook from his shirt pocket and flicked on the pen he'd taken from the Denver hotel room. Sleep was almost on him and an idea for a television series was brewing in his brain. He drew a couple of lines on the paper to start the ink flowing from the cheap pen.

A couple of buddies rent a house in LA while they figure out what they want to do with their lives. Regular guys, except they're crime-fighters when no one's looking. Modern-day superheroes. One apparently can't die no matter how many times he gets shot. The other seems to spend a lot of time cleaning up messes. Hijinks ensue.

He yawned and put the notebook away. Maybe Brad Pitt for the Jarvis character. Brin would want Schwarzenegger or Stallone. They'd figure it out later. Jarvis closed his eyes and counted the beeps of the pulse monitor for a minute or two. It began to match his own, low 40s, and he drifted off thinking about how he was going to have to take a gig that actually paid, since no one was going to reimburse him for his out-of-pocket expenses shutting down a conspiracy that killed dozens and could have wreaked havoc for years. He'd check his email and voicemail when he got home.

An hour later, when the nurse came to check on Brin, Jarvis was on the freeway.

If you enjoyed *Dead East*, then you may want to
read *Murder in Mind*, another thriller by Steve Winshel.
The work is available for sale where ever ebooks are sold

To find out more about Steve or his books,
please visit: **www.winshel.com**
or Like us on Facebook.

Please turn the page for the first two chapters from *Murder in Mind*.

The cell phone vibrated against the cup holder and McNair could faintly hear it beneath the blaring radio. He turned down the music and reached for the phone, stealing a quick glance at the number of the caller, then put eyes back on the darkened road curving ahead. It was a patient, ringing his emergency number at nine o'clock at night. They only did that if it was important. He closed the phone and tossed it onto the empty passenger seat. Hitting the accelerator, he made the back tires skid and thought about home, a beer, and a steak on the grill.

The phone went to voicemail and a woman began to plead. "Please, please, Dr. McNair...call me. Please call me back." Miles from where McNair drove through the night, she held the phone close to her face, the glowing dial pad playing with the dark closet interior. Shadows from her clothes slashed across her face. There was no lock on the closet but there was a flimsy one on the bedroom door and she prayed it was stronger than it looked. She pushed back further into the corner, the tips of a pair of shoes poking her, angering the bruise above her kidney where her husband had hit her with the base of the lamp.

She hung up and then hit the ON button to get another dial tone. She could hear it echo in the room and quickly covered the ear hole. She knew she should call 911, wanted to call the police, but her fingers hesitated just above the pad. She looked at her hand instead of the phone and saw the cracked, bleeding nail. Ten minutes earlier she'd clawed at the ground, then at her husband's arms, as his hands closed around her throat. He'd stopped – the, wild, distant look in his eyes fading for a moment, and the apologies had started to pour out. She'd run upstairs, banging into the wall as she made the turn on the first step going too fast. He'd called after her, wanting her to come back so he could make it right. His soothing voice started to change as she continued to hide. He started to sound irritated, then angry when she failed to come back and let him show her everything would be okay. And now he was on the stairs, demanding she come down, more strident with each step toward the bedroom.

Helen could feel the bile rising in her throat. Fear, pain, and guilt skewed her mind. She dialed, but it was McNair's number again. Her therapist would know what to do, tell her what to do. It went straight to voicemail. Before she could leave another message, the door handle in the bedroom jiggled, then violently shook. In a split second she heard it explode inward, wood splintering and the jamb slamming against the wall with the force of her husband's kick.

There was no hesitation in his footsteps. He came straight to the closet and pulled the door open.

"Oh, god, no, no…please, I'm sorry…no." She tried to press back into a space that wasn't there. The phone dropped between her legs. He grabbed her hair and wrenched her from the closet, half dragging her across the room as her legs kicked at the ground to keep from falling. He said nothing, only drawing in short, ragged breaths that rasped like nails on metal. He re-gathered a fist full of hair, his grip hard and rigid. Out the bedroom, and toward the stairs. She struggled to gain her balance, reached for the railing as they got to the first step. He pulled her down, his pace steady and uninterrupted by her flailing and grasping at the banister. Her knees banged sharply on the wooden edges of each step, her neck twisted and pain shot down her arms and back. The last few steps she gave up and he slid her like a rolled up carpet. At the bottom he changed his grip and locked onto her shoulder, fingers digging deep into the skin. Pulling her like a log at the end of a sharp hook, he dragged her onto the Persian rug in the living room. He stood fully, hands on his hips, and took a couple deep breaths. His eyes were far away. She laid limply, looking up at him, and when their eyes locked he gave her a sharp kick in the stomach that blew out what little breath she had.

On the glass coffee table, a pack of cigarettes sat next to a large picture book, Los *Angeles From Above.* He picked up the pack and fished out one of the last cigarettes. The lighter took only one try to catch, and Helen began to whimper.

Half an hour later, McNair tossed his keys onto the kitchen counter and pulled a beer from the refrigerator. Leaning back on the counter, he flipped open his phone. Two messages. He listened to the first and frowned. Helen Burrows having trouble with the husband again. He probably should have picked up and talked her down. He deleted the message and waited for the second as he drained the bottle, eyes looking around the kitchen for something to put on the steak. He stopped, half an inch of beer still remaining, and put the bottle on the counter. He stared at the fridge but his mind was elsewhere. Helen's voice was scared, terrified. He could hear the crash, then her sudden yelp and the phone hitting the ground. The rest was muffled, but angry and violent. His voicemail limited messages to one minute. He listened carefully, straining to hear, as the recording continued. There was a series of banging noises, sounds of terror. McNair hit "9" to save the message and in one quick motion picked up his keys and headed to the door, dialing 911. He identified himself as a doctor and gave the name and address of Helen Burrows and a one sentence summary of what had happened – or was happening. He was in the car and racing down the darkened Pacific Coast Highway before he'd hung up.

McNair arrived at the Burrows home as two paramedics brought Helen out on a gurney. The ambulance was parked in the driveway. A cop car with lights flashing was on one side. An unmarked detective's car was on the other at an angle, blocking one lane of the residential street. McNair pulled up behind it and watched the gurney. The sheet was not pulled over

Helen's face. She was alive, but even from 30 feet away McNair could see she was in bad shape. He hesitated for a moment, then got out of the car and walked toward the front door to find the cop in charge.

McNair watched the man on the couch squirm again. The patient still hadn't taken off his suit jacket or stiff shoes. Hands were clasped across his chest. He re-crossed his ankles for the tenth time in 45 minutes and once again halfheartedly tried to turn his head as he spoke, almost bringing the therapist into his field of vision. He didn't like talking without being able to see his audience. He fake coughed a couple of times to cover his discomfort, using it as an excuse to move his hands around before interlacing the fingers and resting them back on the buttoned jacket.

If the couch was at twelve o'clock, McNair sat in a stiff-backed chair at about ten. He didn't want patients looking to him for a reaction. Didn't want them interpreting each breath or blink. More important, he didn't want to engage with them too closely. He could do his job from here.

"I don't know why she's unhappy. It's no different from what I told you before. I tried that crap you said." The patient spat out "crap" but mid-word seemed to regret it. Not because he didn't mean it, but because he didn't want McNair to know how much he despised therapy. A dim-witted first-grader could have deduced it.

"She just mopes around the house all day, and when I get home she's all over me. Where was I? Why was I having an affair? All that crap." This time he let the word sit. "I told her I wasn't cheating, though god dammit if she doesn't get off my ass I'm going to." His fingers tightened and McNair could see the knuckles whiten.

The patient was a moderately successful lawyer. His wife was much richer. She'd kick him out if caught cheating. He had no interest in being forced to work hard for a living like everyone else so an affair would be a mistake. He insisted again that his wife was nuts. She should be the one in therapy.

McNair breathed in the air around the man. He could almost smell the lie. The patient was angry, but thought he was fooling the therapist, the secret of his infidelity safe and his future secure. He was wrong.

"You're having an affair. She's going to find out. Stop seeing the woman, or women, or man, or whatever. Or plan on a divorce." McNair sat quietly. The patient bolted upright and jumped off the couch.

"What the hell did you say, you goddamned sonofabitch! Who the hell are you to accuse..." He shook a finger at McNair, spittle forming at the corner of his mouth and McNair moved slightly to the left. The next explosion of fury included a few flecks that missed him by a couple inches.

"I'll sue you, you worthless prick. Who the hell do you think you are to call me a liar?"

McNair put his hands on his knees and leaned forward as if to stand.

"Our hour is up. I'll see you next week."

The man's eyes widened and McNair thought there was a real probability his head would explode. The patient, finger still pointing at McNair, couldn't think of a retort or action that would express clearly enough his desire to murder the therapist. By the time he turned and stalked through the inner door leading to the private exit, skirting the waiting room, the man's mind was already on how he could salvage the lie to his wife.

McNair stood and softly closed the inner door as the outer one slammed. He'd intentionally left it without a spring. Sometimes patients needed the release of whipping it into its frame, taking the edge off so they wouldn't get in their car and rear-end some unsuspecting old lady who wasn't driving fast enough for them. Occasionally McNair would use it for that purpose himself, when he felt like a caged animal stalking his office, hunting for a way out. The walls closing in after listening to a patient describe the ennui of life filled with marital loneliness. Sometimes it was after a court-ordered visit from a violent parolee who shared with the therapist dreams of smashing the face of a stranger on the bus for not looking away. McNair would slam the door hard, then open it and do it again. He never felt better afterward. This time he just leaned against the wall and rubbed his face with both hands. Two-day growth scratched his palms.

McNair went behind his desk and flipped off the recording device he used so he could avoid taking notes. He sat in the worn leather chair and reached for the lower right corner of the desk where there was a false front that looked like a drawer. He pulled it open and felt a cold breeze from the tiny refrigerator. The remaining bottle had water droplets from the neck to the base that puddled in his hand as he untwisted the cap. Leaning back, he swiveled around and looked out the tinted window. The view of the San Fernando Valley from ten floors up was both comforting and disturbing. Like a crazy Rube Goldberg device with some of the parts in constant motion and the other half waiting to kick into action, but with no real purpose. He was tired. A long drink felt good but didn't erase the exhaustion. He put the bottle to his forehead and could almost hear his pulse echo against the glass. Eyes closed, he summoned images of the night before and what little he could remember. He'd gone out after talking to the cops at Helen Burrows' home. Under the circumstances he was no longer bound by patient confidentiality and explained her husband had been abusing her. After leaving and heading to a bar on Wilshire, the most vivid memory was of the clock reading a little past three in the morning, a clock he didn't recognize. A woman lay on her back, hair obscuring a face he wouldn't have known anyway.

The phone rang and through slitted eyes he read the backwards display of the caller ID reflected in the window. A quarter of his practice came when the LAPD called. He reached around without turning his chair and hoped it would be something that gave him justification to cancel the afternoon's appointments.

To find out more about Steve or his books,
please visit: **www.winshel.com** or Like us on Facebook.

ABOUT THE AUTHOR

Shanghai. Phnom Penh. London. Vienna. New Dehli. That's a typical itinerary for Steve — but not on a single 'round-the-world trip. Instead, he goes overseas for one night then back home (to be with his kids) then off to another continent. In between are quick jaunts within the US to Chicago, New York, Boston, and DC. He claims it is all for business or recreation. But his novels of havoc, clandestine operations, and quiet unseen battles against forces causing mayhem suggest his travels may have another purpose. But he isn't talking.

What he will say is that the experience of launching new companies, fighting corporate battles, and periodically invading academia, are all fodder for his tales. So don't be surprised if one day, while you are on that vacation to Hawaii, business trip to Vancouver, or trek to Nepal, you look across the aisle of the plane and see a guy typing away, a slightly nefarious look on his face, and a picture of his kids on his laptop. You might even say hello, but be careful: you might end up a character in a novel.

Made in the USA
Charleston, SC
21 May 2014